Praise for the Merit Bridges

"Filled with great cha [...]earcned law, and suspenseful mysteries..." - Larry A. Winters, *Jessie Black Legal Thrillers*

"A legal thriller not to be missed, compelling and action-packed, with vivid characters and an authentic setting." - Mark Pryor, *Hugo Marston Novels*

"A high-speed storyline full of twists and turns upon a stark background of reality as lawyers might really experience it. Manning Wolfe is one of the up-and-coming legal thriller writers of this generation. Read her and enjoy her, but don't expect much sleep!" - John Ellsworth, *Michael Gresham Legal Thrillers*

"Dollar Signs is a fast-paced thriller pitting Austin attorney Merit Bridges against Boots King, a shadowy henchman. This no-nonsense lawyer knows her way around a wine list as well as around the legal system. Buckle up and enjoy this cinematic ride all the way to the end!" - Bill Rodgers, *Killer Set: Drop the Mic*

CHINESE WALL

Texas Lady Lawyer vs Archibald Duke

a novel by

MANNING WOLFE

STARPATH BOOKS, LLC

Starpath Books, LLC
Austin, TX
www.starpathbooks.com

Library of Congress Cataloging-in Publication Data: Paperback:
ISBN-13: 978-1-944225-50-6
Ebook: ISBN-13: 978-1-944225-51-3
LCN: 2021942833
Manufactured in the United States of America
10 9 8 7 6 5 4 3 2 1

Visit the author's website:
www.manningwolfe.com

Follow Manning Wolfe on Social Media:
www.facebook.com/manning.wolfe
www.twitter.com/ManningWolfe
www.instagram.com/manningwolfe/

Sign up for Manning Wolfe's FREE newsletter and get a FREE book.
www.manningwolfe.com/giveaway

ALSO FROM MANNING WOLFE

For Bill Rodgers, my partner in crime and in life. May we always keep each other's secrets.

Three may keep a secret, if two of them are dead.

— Benjamin Franklin

1

As a jet flew over Texas, its wings reflected the bright spring morning sunshine. Below, the colorful San Antonio streets were full of hustling and bustling workers and tourists celebrating Mexico's victory over French forces called Cinco de Mayo. None of the people below gave a second thought to the plane overhead, the busy street around them, or what harm might be coming next as they walked past the Alamo and scurried toward historic San Antonio Market Square. One end of the venue, the outdoor plaza making up El Mercado, was lined with shops and restaurants visited by locals and travelers since the 1820s. Mariachi music spilled out of many doors and Selena's voice singing "Bidi Bidi Bom Bom" blasted out of speakers mounted high on gaslight poles.

A pregnant woman and her sister, wearing breezy spring dresses, shopped for spices from the outdoor bins of Jalapeno's Hot Spot. The two pointed to the colorful trays full of chilis and ground powders indicating to the clerk their choices. A gaggle of middle-school children wearing identical yellow T-shirts were herded by two teachers toward Cocina's, a Mexican restaurant boasting a banner that advertised cooking classes. Three businessmen, wearing the latest style in sports jackets, talked on their cell phones about commercial properties available for lease in the downtown corridor as they wound their way toward Serrano's Restaurante.

A family of four pushed their way through the crowd toward the end of the long brick walkway making up the esplanade of the market. The father held a crying toddler, and the mother wrangled a stroller that was cradling a sleeping infant, oblivious to the activity around her. As the family exited the market and stepped onto the sidewalk, they were bumped and split apart by a man in military dress who didn't stop to apologize. The father looked at him in disbelief as the mother admonished her husband with her eyes to *let it go*.

The rude man in camouflage garb was Timothy Walsh, who wove his way through the crowds adjusting the strap of a multi-green camouflage duffel bag on his right shoulder. He wore military fatigues as part of his disguise as a young recruit from nearby Lackland Air Force Base. He kept his large brown eyes down and his focus inward. The edges of a dark-colored dragon tattoo peeked out from under a large bandage on the left side of his neck. His lips moved slightly as he listed a sequence of instructions known only to him and his brothers in arms.

Walsh moved into the line entering the southern entrance of the market, paused, and waited for the crowd to surge forward. As more shoppers and tourists moved in, he flowed with them, walking past the numerous shops and restaurants until he reached the end of the long mall and stood in an alleyway before a facilities door marked 'Maintenance.' He looked around for security guards, saw none, and tested the door handle. As promised, it was unlocked. He took one last look back down the walkway, then entered. He ducked under a large pipe, turned in the small space like a dog circling to lie down, and pulled the door closed behind him.

In the classroom at the rear of Cocina's, the middle-school children donned red aprons over their matching yellow T-shirts and chatted excitedly about the day's lesson. Their two chaperones sat at a nearby table and allowed the children freedom to fully experience the exotic smells and atmosphere of the restaurant.

The class started when the chef came out of the kitchen and shouted, "Hola!" The children looked at him in awe. He sported a colorful neckerchief in the pattern of the Mexican flag and pajama-looking chef pants covered in a chili pepper pattern. In his tall white hat and monogrammed white coat, he seemed like a character from one of the children's favorite books. His heavy Spanish accent lent another layer to the exotic fantasy.

"Today, we learn to make tortillas from masa," Chef said. "Masa is ground corn. We will mix our masa harina with water, then roll the dough into little balls. Then we will press it and cook it, and you can all have lunch. We may add a small vegetable to keep your parents happy. Si?"

One child stuck out his tongue and another groaned, "Vegetables."

Chef laughed and demonstrated. "First, we mix the masa with water and salt."

The children stirred the mixture in large metal bowls with wooden spoons as the chef moved about the room pointing and assisting the smaller children with the large utensils.

"Pour the dough onto the table and knead it until the gritty bits are incorporated. When it's all mixed up, form small balls and put them in a row before you."

The children followed his instructions, making all sizes of balls, and giggled when the dough stuck to their fingers. One boy wiped the sticky paste onto his friend's apron, and both said, "Ew."

Chef laughed at their play. "Now, place the tortilla maker before you, open the top, and place a ball of dough in the middle."

When the children picked up the metal press by the handle, the hinge opened and splayed the tortilla makers. Some were dropped on the floor and others were placed upside down. Chef went around the room, righted each press, and put the handle in front of the student. He demonstrated on a small redheaded boy's press.

"Next, push the handle down until the masa spreads flat inside the press. Open the handle, remove the tortilla, and place it on your plate. Repeat until you have a nice stack."

Little hands pressed and played with tortillas all the way around the table. The creations ranged in size from silver dollars to frisbees. The chef worked his way through the room again and again as he instructed each student on how to achieve a more uniform size.

"Muy bueno!"

Walsh set his bag on the concrete floor, turned on a small flash-light and held it in his mouth, pointing the rays downward into the duffel. He unpacked the materials and prepared the contents as he'd been taught, working swiftly as the room was tight and hot from the machinery running all around him. Fear beaded on his forehead, then dripped down his beard and onto his gloved hands as he twisted the last wires into place and adjusted the timer to allow fifteen minutes for his escape.

His focus was drawn from the task at hand as he thought of the process of his radicalization over the past months. Of course, that's not what he called the online facilitators and enablers of the process of indoctrination. He called them friends. He'd been searching for information when he'd happened upon an internet group that had welcomed him into a private chat room and shared his hatred of minorities and those who were different from him.

Walsh had made the lucky find the week after he was fired from his job in El Paso. "So sorry," his boss had said, "but we can get it done cheaper if we use labor from across the border. Nothing personal, it's just business—maximizing profits, staying competitive." His new internet friends had listened to his complaints and understood his anger. They provided a place for him to air his grievances, then invited him to train with them in the hill country outside of San Saba. While there, he'd felt like a frolicking child playing soldier with his new buddies, and at purpose for the first time.

Soon, the far-right homegrown terrorists told him he was valuable to their cause and promoted him to the accelerated training program, giving him the affirmation and admiration he sought. They provided funds, instruction, and friendship for four months, fast tracking his indoctrination and the development of his skills. They were his friends and his partners. He was loyal to them for life. His life, not theirs, but he didn't know that. He was a useful tool to them, but he wouldn't live to learn that. It wasn't in the cards.

Walsh awakened from his reverie, smiled at his good fortune, checked his watch, tucked the bomb behind the overhead pipe, balanced the device on a small strut, and secured it with duct tape. This was the last bomb of three that had been placed in strategic locations around the plaza. The two other members of his cell, known only to him as Trigger and Cobb, would be looking at their watches as well. Trigger was in a public men's room at the other end of the plaza, and Cobb was in a nearby office building that faced onto the plaza street. Walsh hoped his fellow militia brothers had also been successful in setting up their devices. The engineering of the detonations had been researched by their militia leaders in order to achieve maximum effect. Synchronization of all three bombs was the key to mass destruction. Two would do, but three would make an outstanding statement that the world would never forget. Walsh planned to celebrate the accomplishment of their goal when he rejoined them at a safe house on the other side of town.

As Walsh repacked his bag, he heard a noise behind him and felt air rush into the cramped space. He took the flashlight from his mouth and turned around, facing back toward the door. A security guard was standing in the open entrance with a pistol pointed at Walsh's midsection.

"Halt! Para, Cabron! I said stop!"

The guard gestured with the weapon as his navy-blue uniform stuck to his body when sweat broke through the fabric. The name embroidered on his chest was 'Jose.'

"What are you doing in there? Put your hands up." Jose's body shook.

Walsh held his hands at shoulder height, causing a round circle of light on the ceiling from the flashlight. "Don't shoot." He pleaded as he looked around, formulating a plan.

Jose Perez gestured again with the shaking gun. "Don't you move."

Walsh held Jose's gaze, then made one swift motion. He directed the beam of light into Jose's eyes, then swung the flashlight in an arc behind the pipe and hit the bomb hard as he said, "Not on our watch, Beaner." The bomb exploded as Jose shot Walsh in the chest.

Walsh never knew that his cohorts, Trigger and Cobb, were even more successful than he was. Trigger felt the blast from Walsh's bomb across the plaza and reset his timer for two minutes, packed his duffel bag, and sprinted from the men's room. He ran into the throng of people streaming out of the downtown area, away from the market bombing, and blended into the distraught and panicked mass.

Cobb had already set his bomb and the timer per the original plan and had left the office building. He was almost to the parking garage when Walsh's bomb went off, followed in a couple of minutes by Trigger's bomb. He threw his duffel into the cab of his truck, started it up and peeled out of his parking place, down a ramp, and out into the crowd. He honked and swerved, barely missing one startled person after another. He would just as soon have hit them with the vehicle if it would not have drawn unwanted attention to him and his cause.

2

M erit Bridges sat in Austin in the Law Office of Merit Bridges overlooking Lady Bird Lake and the distant Texas Hill Country. The National News Network showed on the television set on the credenza behind her. She often worked with the set on, and sound muted, catching a peek at the news crawl when she pleased. Her navy silk blouse, white pencil skirt, and sleek blond ponytail made her look more like a thirtysomething-year-old supermodel than a lawyer. Her black pumps were kicked off under her desk, and her jacket hung on a felted hanger on a hook on the back of the door. The wall opposite the television displayed a series of framed photographs she had taken of various bridges around Austin.

The aftermath of the explosion in San Antonio played onscreen as Merit, unknowingly, worked away on her computer. As she drafted a city tax reduction proposal for a new client's video game entertainment center and amusement park, San Antonio panicked onscreen.

Betty, Merit's office manager and right hand for many years, burst through the open door and came to a full stop before

Merit's desk. Her suit was neat, but one of her beige orthopedic shoes was untied. A strand of gray hair had popped loose and hung down from her Ann Richard's helmet head hairstyle.

Betty pointed at the television. "Merit, Merit. Look! There's been a bombing in San Antonio."

Merit spun around on the wheels of her chair, sending her ponytail and several sheets of paper flying. She groped around the desk until Betty reached over, found the remote, and handed it to her.

Merit turned up the volume and the two women joined the world and watched as television sets in every country on earth aired coverage of the disaster. Onscreen, first responders and press crowded around the perimeter of what was once the Historic Market Square of San Antonio. Yellow crime scene tape was being stretched by police teams to cordon off a steaming hole that covered three city blocks and part of Interstate 35. The pylons holding up the flyover were damaged, and mounds of concrete and debris were evident beside a cavernous hole. Cars had driven off the overpass and crashed into the hole, trapping travelers inside. Smoke and dust hung in the air, giving the scene a surreal and eerie cast. Overhead, news helicopters mixed with military choppers, like warring dragonflies, vying for air space.

Merit and Betty could not look away for over an hour as the National News Network aired coverage that filled in details. NNN's celebrity reporter, Ernest Anguish, featured various aspects of the story as they became available. Anguish squared his handsome jaw and bore his blue eyes directly into the camera as he lamented the victims and speculated about who might be to blame for the 'savage crime.' Video showed the crowd and emergency vehicles circling a pile of steaming rubble. On-the-scene reporters yelled into microphones, in order to be heard over sirens and the general mayhem as

Anguish, from news headquarters in New York, teased every detail from their lips.

The military helicopters overhead won the battle and news copters were vanquished several miles away under Homeland Security orders. The network birds skirted the perimeter, filming with the most powerful lenses in their arsenal.

Below, NNN reporter, Jana Williams, moved amongst the crowd, holding a microphone as the camera images jumped from one talking head to the next. At six feet tall plus heels, she towered over most people in the crowd, including the other reporters, who moved their microphones close to their mouths in order to be heard.

"This is a major event."

"The president will visit tomorrow. He says this will not change our way of life."

"There is no word on whether anyone has taken responsibility."

Jana's focus settled on a short Hispanic man in the crowd, and she addressed him. "May I ask you a question?"

The man appeared to be in shock. His eyes were glazed and cast downward. "I guess so."

Jana put a comforting hand on his shoulder. "Were you here when the bomb went off?"

"I was over by the Alamo walking this way. A few more minutes and I might have been killed. I was meeting my wife for lunch and I'm trying to find her. There's no cell service."

Jana moved the microphone back to her mouth. "Yes, sir. The system is so overloaded no one can get through right now. Public officials will probably setup a check-in desk and a website soon."

"I'll find her then. I know I will."

"I hope so." She saw the doubt in his eyes. "I'm sure you will."

Anguish re-summarized up to the minute news and showed the same scene of the bombing rubble and chaos over and over, checking in with Jana from time to time as she approached another member of the crowd.

Betty leaned on the edge of Merit's desk, tucked in the loose strand of hair, and bumped the bob at the nape of her neck as she let out a long breath. "What a waste. What a damn ridiculous act of violence. Makes me madder than a wet hen."

Merit turned away from the screen. "Betty, please check on Valentine. His law school isn't near the market, but let's be sure he's okay."

Betty turned toward the door. "Right. I'll call Ag and the rest of the staff as well. This is too close to home."

Merit picked up her mobile and went to the first name on her list of favorites, her teenage son who was away at boarding school in Houston. "I'll call Ace."

3

Simultaneously to the bombers setting their timers and executing their tasks, and unbeknownst to Walsh, Trigger, or Cobb, an entirely different crew, in a panel van, entered an upscale residential area on the northwest side of San Antonio. This all-male team had been selected for their military intelligence backgrounds and had been trained at a site outside Waco, hidden in thick woods off unpaved roads. The team consisted of four masked men in the back, a driver, named Cupcake, and the team leader, known as Six-pack, who was sitting in the front passenger seat. At the appointed time, Cupcake pulled the van up to the security entrance of Dominion Estates, slowed to a crawl, and saluted a middle-aged uniformed security guard sitting on a stool in the guard house. The attendant returned the salute and raised the gate by pressing a button.

As simple as that, the van entered one of the wealthiest neighborhoods in town. The trespassing crew passed the homes of San Antonio Spurs basketball players, PGA pro golfers, actors and actresses, and a myriad of lawyers, doctors, and tech moguls. They wove through the fifteen hundred acres of the planned community until they reached a sprawling Spanish Hacienda style house, slowed, and crept by. It was the home of the mayor of San Antonio, Javier Raoul Sincero.

The four masked kidnappers chuckled out loud when they saw how simple the job would be. The mayor was on the lawn in front of his home, tossing a football back and forth with his teenage son, Javier Jr. The kidnappers nodded at each other knowingly. The home's perimeter would not need to be breached, and they would not have to deal with the mayor's wife or daughter. Their intelligence from the guard at the gate was that Mrs. Sincero was at home, as were both children of the couple and their live-in housekeeper.

Six-pack adjusted his package between his legs and cracked his neck, first left, then right. "Could he have made this any easier?"

Cupcake laughed. "Only if he climbs in the van without resistance."

Three of the kidnappers in back adjusted their masks and put their handguns in the holsters on their hips. Six-pack, up front, and the fourth masked kidnapper in back, adjusted their weapons, long black assault rifles.

Cupcake drove the van around the block. Six-pack saw nothing in the nearby homes that they couldn't handle if necessary, and the vehicle pulled once again onto the mayor's street. Cupcake slowed the vehicle beside a house two doors down, then crept along the street and stopped by the mayor's yard. Sincero saw the van moving toward him and seemed to recognize the Primo Cable Company logo on the side of the vehicle. He tossed the football, then shouted over to Javier Jr. "Just a minute, Mijo. They must be lost."

As Sincero approached the van, the rear door slid open and two strong males jumped out and grabbed at him. Sincero, a six-foot-two star quarterback in his younger years, spun away from the outstretched arms at the last minute, tripped on a sprinkler head, and fell in the grass facing his son. "Correr! Run!"

Javier Jr. froze for several seconds as his mind processed the danger his father was attempting to thwart. Instead of running into the house, he ran toward his father and plowed into the closest kidnapper, who grabbed him around the waist and lifted him while his legs kicked the air. Mayor Sincero jumped up and tackled the third kidnapper as he exited the van behind his buddies. As the two Sincero men struggled against the masked attackers, Javier Jr. yelled as loudly as he could and pulled on his father's arm. The first kidnapper recovered from the initial avoidance moves and grabbed Sincero by the shoulder. Both Javiers, father and son, kicked, yelled, and cursed at the masked crew who were unable to get a decisive grip on the two victims. The front door of the home flew open, and two women and a young girl ran out calling, "Padre, Javier, para." Neighbors on the right came out of their door upon hearing the noise and ran toward the melee, punching numbers in cell phones as they moved.

The kidnapper in the back of the van watched the scene and raised his weapon. Six-pack opened the passenger door and jumped out. He took a military stance and raised his rifle, aiming at the four fighting men.

He yelled at his colleague in back. "Time for Plan B."

Cupcake adjusted his mask and stayed behind the wheel, ready to depart. "Agreed."

The team leader-turned-gunman took aim, waited for an opening between his co-conspirators, and shot the mayor in the head. The gunman in the back of the van shot a second later, hitting Javier Jr. in the thigh, causing him to drop in pain. As the three females and neighbors realized what had happened, the kidnappers jumped back into the van and sped away as they slid the van door closed. Javier Jr. crawled on his knees over to his father's dead body and wept. "Papa!"

In Austin, Betty returned to Merit's office after making several phone calls.

"I reached everyone. They're all shocked, but safe."

Merit nodded. "Good. Ace's roommate said he was in class. He'll call me when he gets back to the dorm."

Both turned back to the television set as BREAKING NEWS filled the screen and Ernest Anguish reappeared.

Merit patted the papers on her desk looking for the remote.

Betty found it under a manila file folder. "If it was a snake, it would have bit you." She unmuted the sound.

Anguish seemed energized. "We've just received word that Mayor Javier Raoul Sincero of San Antonio has been shot and killed at his home in Dominion Estates, a gated community where he and his family reside. We have been able to confirm that his son, Javier Jr., is suffering from a non-fatal wound and is on his way to St. Mary's Hospital. We turn to our reporter at San Antonio, Milli O'Flaherty at City Hall, who's waiting on a press conference with the city manager. Milli, what do you know?"

Milli appeared with microphone in hand and the San Antonio press room as a backdrop. Other reporters were bustling around, within camera view, as city officials prepared to begin.

"Ernest, it hasn't been confirmed that the assassination was connected to the market bombing, but we assume, based on the timing, that the same group is responsible. We'll listen to the press briefing and talk about it on the other side." As the camera focused on the lectern, a small box appeared in the bottom right corner of the screen showing the bombing site and streaming the continuing tragedy a short distance away.

The city manager, a handsome Latino man who appeared too young to hold such a position, stepped onto the stage and up to the podium. He adjusted his tie and then the mic and read from a written statement. "We can confirm that Mayor Javier Sincero was shot and killed about one hour ago in what appeared to be an attempted kidnapping. His wife and children are alive and safe and being questioned about the facts surrounding the assassination. It's our understanding that the mayor's son was shot in the leg and is being treated at St. Mary's. Our thoughts and prayers are with them as they grieve this terrible loss."

Betty sucked in a strong breath at the news. Merit stared without blinking at the screen.

The city manager continued. "Police are currently searching for six men and the security guard who may have allowed the assassins into the gated community. It has been reported that he disappeared or was taken from his post before SAPD arrived. We haven't ascertained if he was complicit or abducted by the kidnappers. We do not have much more information at this time, but will take a few questions."

The manager looked up from the statement and several reporters shot hands into the air. The manager pointed to Milli. "Thank you. Is there any evidence that the assassination of the mayor is connected to the bombing?"

"Officials are looking into it. In my opinion, it's a pretty good bet that the two are related. Our community is hurting right now and our focus will be on administering to their needs while at the same time seeking revenge against these unlawful actors. We will not stop until every evil-doer is brought to justice."

Betty and Merit looked at each other, showing their mutual despair.

A few moments before the mayor of San Antonio was shot by his thwarted kidnappers, Clover Thibodeaux was being surveilled leaving City Hall in downtown Austin. She was followed as she was driven by her security team, under Mopac, less than three miles to her home in Tarrytown. As the mayor of Austin, a blue city in the middle of a red state, the mayor had been assigned security from her first day in office. There were unsubstantiated rumors that militants could be going after her as one of a few powerful Democrats in a mostly Republican state.

Clover was the lovely and exotic wife of Merit's long-time friend and business associate, Kim Wan Thibodeaux. Clover was of Ashkenazi Jewish decent, from Poland on her mother's side, and Indian and British heritage on her father's side. Her maternal grandparents had immigrated to the United States before World War II, passing through Ellis Island. In most of Texas, that wasn't enough to be considered a true American. Her dark skin and accent further placed a large target on her back—hence the security detail.

The surveillance team tracking the mayor in Austin was unknown to the San Antonio bomber teams and the San Antonio mayoral kidnap-turned-assassination team. All were in the dark about the other cells operating at the same time on the same day. All were unaware that their handlers were simultaneously operating the other active teams.

The van kept a safe distance behind the mayor's detail to avoid detection. It was easy to blend into the heavy Austin traffic. The team leader, called Tank, adjusted the chunky black automatic rifle strapped across his chest and checked his watch. He looked around at the other four team members. "Thirty minutes and counting. One good to go."

One by one, the all-male team members, dressed in identical military garb, and holding the same model of deadly rifle, responded:

"Two good to go."

"Three good to go."

"Four good to go."

"Five good to go."

Four, who was driving, pulled over and parked a few blocks down the street and watched the security detail escort Mayor Clover into her home. The escort consisted of one policeman and one policewoman in APD uniforms with pistols on their hips.

Two watched from the van's safe distance through military-style binoculars and briefed Tank. "They took her in the house. Looks like the lawyer husband and two kids are at home."

The APD escorts came back out the front door and returned to their SUV to stand post. Two watched them through his binoculars. Both were sipping coffee through holes in white plastic lids on paper cups.

Four gripped the steering wheel. "Looks like they're settled in for the night." He drove the van, with a Super Man Plumbing logo on the side, away from the curb, held the 35 mile-per-hour speed limit, and drove past the security SUV. The dark windows on the van provided plenty of privacy for the team, but it didn't matter, as the coffee-drinking-cops were facing the other direction with their eyes on the mayor's house.

The stolen plumber's van stopped at a corner two blocks down, made two rights, and found its destination, a home on a parallel street that backed up to the Thibodeaux' property. The team could not see the mayor's back yard from their parking spot, but prior research had shown them that the houses shared a common privacy fence that separated the two neighbor's homes.

The Drake family living in the back house were not at home, as planned by the advance team when they flooded their house with a manufactured plumbing issue. The Super Man van pulled into the driveway, knowing that not much suspicion would be raised in light of the Drakes' bad luck with their leaky pipes.

Two scanned the street and adjacent houses with his binoculars as Tank checked the same areas with bare sharp eyes, then checked his watch. "Time to go."

Four stayed behind the wheel with the engine running as Tank and the other three armed men quickly got out and went around the right side of the house through a wooden gate and into the Drakes' back yard. Tank closed the gate behind them and looked at his watch again. He held up his hand with five fingers indicating seconds, then one by one lowered his digits until only his thumb was up.

At the same time as the bombs went off in the San Antonio Market and San Antonio Mayor Sincero was murdered, Three made quick work on the slats of the Austin mayor's back fence with a roundhouse kick, opening a hole for the team to push through. Five stood guard at the fence providing a security link between the van, the Drakes' house, and the Thibodeaux' back yard.

Synchronicity with the other terrorist cells was key, as one event would have triggered increased security at the other two events, making them more difficult if not impossible to pull off.

Two, Three, and Tank moved quickly through the fence in coordinated fashion and rushed the back door of the Thibodeaux home, breaking the patio door glass as the lock gave way with another kick by Three. The mayor's son and daughter sat at the kitchen island doing homework, and Mayor Clover stirred a large pot of matzo ball soup at the stove with a wooden spoon. She dropped the spoon into the pot as she heard the glass break and turned toward the intruders. All three residents screamed, alerting Kim Wan, who was in a bedroom upstairs. Before her husband could reach the first floor, Tank grabbed Mayor Clover around the waist, lifting her off her feet, and propelled her toward the broken back door slider. Two and Three knocked the children off the barstools and onto the floor, pointing their rifles at the children's innocent heads. Kim Wan ran into the room and stopped short at the sight of his son and daughter being threatened and his wife being carried through the broken glass door and across the back yard.

"Halt! Don't be a hero." Two and Three backed out the broken door, while aiming the weapons at the children until they heard Four honk the horn of the van, indicating that Tank was secure with their captive. Both men opened fire. Kim Wan threw his body onto his children as Two and Three sprayed bullets across the kitchen cabinets and into the ceiling. Both stopped shooting, turned, and ran through the back yard and the hole in the fence. Kim Wan, gasping for breath, thought he heard Three say, "That was fun."

In her office, Merit and Betty continued to glean details, via news media reports, of the assassination of Javier Sincero, when Merit's mobile rang with her son's robot ringtone.

"Ace."

As Merit spoke with Ace, at school in Houston, the office phone rang.

Betty picked up on Merit's line. "Law Office of Merit Bridges. This is Betty."

Betty paused to listen, then pulled the phone away from her ear and covered the mouthpiece with her hand. "It's Red Thallon."

Merit looked up. "I'll take it." She turned back to the mobile. "Hey, Peaches Boy, I'll call you tonight. Everything's okay. Don't worry. I need to run for now. Glad you're safe."

She and Betty juggled the landline, prompting Betty to say, "It's as busy as a one-legged man in an ass-kicking contest around here."

Merit nodded her agreement, then spoke. "Hey, Red, are you watching this?"

"Yes. I'm in the thick of it. Merit, something has happened to Mayor Thibodeaux."

"Clover? No. What?"

"I'm not sure, but there's going to be a press conference at City Hall. I'm headed over there now."

"I'll meet you there."

Merit hung up and looked at Betty.

"It's Clover Thibodeaux. They must have gone after her, too. I'll call you from City Hall. I'm going to rush over and meet Red. See if you can reach Kim Wan."

"Will do." Betty slumped into the office chair in front of Merit's desk and put her head in her hands. She closed her eyes in prayer as Merit grabbed her jacket and left the office.

4

Archibald Duke, a man who was bigger than most, dressed in jeans, polo shirt, and windbreaker, walked into the safe house of the patriot group known as the American Freedom Militia or AFM. The house was actually a mobile home that looked more like a clubhouse or mancave with guns. When Duke opened the door, the aroma of stinking trash filled his nostrils. Two men looked up from a small dining table where they were cleaning a variety of pistols. They were sitting in a nasty kitchen full of pizza boxes, greasy pots, and dog food cans. A mangy mutt weighing about thirty pounds, who looked like he hadn't had a bath since birth, perked up for a moment, recognized Duke, then laid back down under the table. In the living area, two military uniforms of green camouflage and tactical gear were piled on an old brown sofa, the color of dog shit. A dusty boombox played a Toby Macintosh song about proud Americans fighting for their rights.

Duke stumbled on a pair of dirty combat boots, righted himself, and looked at the men. "Damn! You two alright?"

Jason Trigger, a robust man about thirty-five years old,

wearing an NRA cap and dark mismatched socks with holes in them, looked up. "Fine. What are you doing here?"

Duke moved into the living room area where a hall went down to two bedrooms. "Where's McDonald?"

"He went to meet you."

Duke nodded. "I'm headed there next."

The younger man, Harvey Joe Cobb, also seated at the table, was muscular, shirtless, and unshaven, except for his head, which was shaved to his white skin. Tattooed on his chest and shoulder was an American eagle with a Confederate flag between its talons. When he moved, the muscles of his chest caused the rebel flag to move around as if waving. "Too bad about Walsh."

Duke nodded. "Bad luck, but he went out a hero."

Trigger and Cobb looked reverential but said nothing.

"Good job getting those bombs off in time."

Cobb smiled. "Thanks."

Trigger saluted with two fingers.

Duke looked back toward the bedrooms. "Anyone else here?"

"Ain't nobody here, just me and Cobb."

"Well, I've got to go meet McDonald. Just checking on you. Need to make a quick call first." Duke hit a speed dial number on his phone and said, "I found them. Get over here." He hung up the phone and dropped it in his pants pocket.

As Trigger and Cobb looked up to see who Duke had found, he pulled his Glock 17 from inside his vest and shot Trigger in the head. When Cobb stood, bringing one of the reloaded weapons from the table up with him, Duke shot him in the wing of the eagle on his chest. Blood poured out of the tattoo as the mutt shot out from under the table and ran down the hall, barking and mewling. Duke put a bullet in the dog's back, silencing him along with his two buddies.

Duke looked around the scene, assessed the angle of the bullets, put one of the guns from the table into Trigger's hand, and fired a single shot into the wall by the door. When he was satisfied that the scene looked authentic, he quickly checked the trailer for any indications of his prior presence, finding nothing.

When he heard the alerted FBI members arriving, he reversed his jacket so the FBI logo was showing, moved to the door, opened it, and held his badge out before him.

FBI from the nearby San Antonio field office swarmed the trailer in response to Duke's call. The team leader, a scruffy Latino male who looked like he'd been undercover too long, addressed Duke. "You alright?"

"Yeah."

Duke was the special agent in charge and technically the team's boss, but he went along with protocol and answered their questions.

"How'd you find them so fast?"

"Got a tip from San Antonio PD," Duke lied. "Drove up from Austin to check it out."

The interviewer made a note. "You here alone?"

Duke pointed to the dead men. "Well, except for those two. I didn't really expect to find anything. I'd have called for backup if I'd realized what I was walking into." Duke observed the team leader and decided that he was believing his story.

The leader gave directions to a few of the team members then turned to Duke again. "Since you're in charge of the case, I assume you'll file a full debrief when you return to Austin."

Duke nodded. "Of course. I'll send you a copy."

Leaving the secondary FBI team to mop up the mess, Duke got into his vehicle and opened the glovebox, locating a burner phone with numbers programmed in. As he pulled away from the trailer park, he pushed the first number that connected him to Six-pack, the team leader on the Sincero attempt, and got an immediate answer.

"What happened?" Duke asked.

"It went bad, we had to go to Plan B. We nailed him and got out of there. Hitting the kid was a happy accident."

"Okay. We'll debrief later. Get your crew back to Waco and lay low until you hear from me. Share no info and don't see anyone. Understand?"

"Roger that."

Duke rang off and hit the next phone number that went to Tank, the lead on the Clover Thibodeaux kidnapping, who also answered immediately.

"You have Four Leaf?" Duke used the code name for the Austin mayor. He knew scanners would be checking all calls for key words by now.

"Yes, sir."

"Condition?"

"Undamaged."

"Head to Waco. Give me a couple of hours and I'll check in again."

"Roger that."

5

Merit quickly walked the few short blocks from her office to City Hall in downtown Austin. When she approached, the crowd was already forming around the mayor's chief of staff and second in command, Peter Jones. He stepped up on the podium as Red Thallon approached from the other direction. She wore a short denim skirt and a bright green blouse that set off her flaming red hair.

Red authored an online news blog for KNEW Austin News and often consulted with Merit when she had legal questions related to a story. Red, Clover, and Merit regularly met for lunch or drinks and supported each other's careers in the Austin community.

Merit saw Red and waved her over. The two women shared a hug of concern for their missing friend, then joined the throng of press and officials.

Red let go first. "Poor Clover. She must be totally traumatized."

Merit nodded. "If she's still alive."

Both women fought tears and turned toward the podium.

Chief of Staff Jones briefed the crowd. "We know that Mayor Clover Thibodeaux was kidnapped at approximately the same time as Mayor Sincero was assassinated and the San Antonio Market was bombed. This was obviously an orchestrated attack on Texas officials, citizens, and government. Austin Police Chief Chaplain will give us an update."

Chaplain maneuvered his way around the chief of staff and to the microphone at the same time that Merit's primary investigator, Albert "Ag" Malone, emerged from the crowd and joined Merit and Red.

Ag was the freelance investigator for several attorneys around Austin, but Merit was his favorite client, and he considered her a friend. Merit considered him the same, but also admired his tall, graceful movements and his abs under the Aggie maroon shirts that were a part of his uniform from his days at Texas ATM University. He didn't have a clue about the effect he had on women. Merit admired that about him as well.

Merit whispered to Ag. "What do you know about Clover?"

Ag leaned down toward her ear. "Didn't get a chance to talk to Chaplain yet. I'm learning as you are."

Chaplain cleared his throat and began. "A few hours ago, Mayor Clover Thibodeaux was taken from her home in Tarrytown by masked gunmen. Her security detail was unable to apprehend the perpetrators. The mayor's husband, Kim Wan Thibodeaux, and her two children were terrorized but physically unhurt during the execution of the crime. It was clearly an organized maneuver that we believe was designed to coordinate in time with the attack on the mayor of San Antonio and the bombing at the San Antonio Market."

Red held her phone up to record the statement as Chaplain continued.

"We have stepped up security around Austin's public venues and entertainment events. All APD officers have been called in, and the city is on high alert. If you do not have a reason to leave your home, please shelter in place and avoid public venues until further notice. All public events that have been permitted by the city are canceled until further notice."

Chief of Staff Jones took over again. "We will have hourly updates via Facebook, Twitter, and posted on the city's website."

The reporters in the crowd shouted questions at the chief and Chaplain.

Chief of Staff Jones held up his hand. "We have nothing further. Please check the updates. Thank you."

Red turned to Merit. "I need to get to my desk and post this online. Talk later?"

Merit hugged her friend. "Yes. Be careful."

"You, too."

Ag fell into step beside Merit as she made her way down the street toward her office. "I'll get more from Chaplain when he comes up for air."

Merit nodded. "I'm so glad Clover's children are safe. Betty was trying to reach Kim Wan when I left."

Ag's expression was grave. He took Merit's arm when she stepped up from the sidewalk onto the landing outside her building.

Ag squeezed Merit's arm. "Kim Wan is a strong man, but I can imagine what he's going through."

"And I, her."

They traded a look that said they were both remembering when Merit had been kidnapped by Browno Zars's right hand and fellow assassin the year before.

6

M erit and Betty monitored the news shows and social media outlets, waiting for someone to take responsibility or for police to find the perpetrators. No one in the office got much work done. Occasionally, they popped online to check Red Thallon's web news, but found that her reports added little as her blog followed the national news. They knew she was working the story as it was her job, but also because Clover was special to them all and would garner supreme effort from Red.

Betty whispered, "I pray Clover's okay."

Merit whispered back, "Me too. But why are we whispering?"

"I don't know, it just seems like the right thing to do."

Finally, that afternoon, Ernest Anguish broke the story when he looked directly into the camera and said, "We have breaking news in the San Antonio bombing. Two men have been located and shot by a member of the FBI domestic terrorist team during attempted apprehension at a mobile home park in Blanco County, just west of San Antonio. The suspects, Jason Trigger and Harvey Joe Cobb, were identified by CCTV cameras as the militia members who planted two of the three bombs around the San Antonio Market during Cinco de Mayo."

The screen showed the run-down mobile home park with crime scene tape wrapped around the trailer. News crews, cameras, and tech vans were held at bay about ten yards from the property by FBI agents and what appeared to be local sheriffs from Blanco County.

Anguish continued. "We have been advised that the perpetrators were traced to this trailer park, via an anonymous tip, received by the SAPD which was passed on to the FBI."

In the driveway and street outside the mobile home, reporters attempted to obtain sound bites from any law enforcement agent who walked by, but gave up after every response was, "No comment."

Jana Williams reported from the scene. "As we know, two bodies are inside that mobile home as crime scene investigators examine the evidence. A third member of the terrorist team, Timothy Walsh, was killed during the bombing." Jana spotted a vehicle coming into the mobile home park and rushed over with the other reporters. It was a neighbor in a rusty pickup truck driving by toward his trailer.

Jana stuck her microphone in the driver's window along with six other mics. "Did you know the people who lived in this trailer? We're told their names were Trigger and Cobb."

The driver spit a large splat of tobacco out the window barely missing Jana's shoes and said, "No, not really. They kept mostly to themselves. Saw them with a mangy mutt they called Cartridge. They seemed like good folks to me."

The bombing terrorist plan was wrapped up in a tidy bow when Anguish broke the final news of the day. "It is reported that a man, Bobby Ray McDonald, a United States citizen, was stopped at a roadblock on Interstate 10 between San Antonio and Houston. Law enforcement reports confirm that the thirty-seven-year-old has been taken into custody."

McDonald's outdated and expired driver's license photo appeared on the screen.

"The suspect has been associated with the American Freedom Militia, also known as the AFM, and is possibly the ringleader. The militia is allegedly responsible for the bombing. McDonald has been tied to the three men who actually planted the bombs, all killed earlier today. We do not have footage of the McDonald arrest. Nor do we have evidentiary links to the assassination of Mayor Sincero and the kidnapping of Mayor Thibodeaux at this time. It is presumed that those crimes were part and parcel of a master plan orchestrated by McDonald. We now go live to Mary Ellen Garza."

The screen video changed to a ranch style brick home in an urban neighborhood where Mary Ellen, a petite lovely Latino woman wearing a dark green business suit, was reporting. "McDonald's wife and daughter were located at this eastside San Antonio home and taken into custody pending an investigation as to their participation in the bombing. Both have been sequestered at an undisclosed location by the FBI, as the result of the raid on their home. Authorities are currently conducting a search of the house under a warrant."

Ernest Anguish filled in the story. "The connection between McDonald and Walsh, the man who detonated the first bomb, has not yet been revealed by authorities. They are, however, presumed to be co-conspirators."

Mary Ellen's voice was broadcast over video footage of a slim woman and young girl, both in jeans, being taken from the

South San Antonio home in handcuffs. "It is not known if McDonald's family was involved with planning or execution of the crime or is in the dark as was the rest of the world."

The two McDonald women's shocked faces were shown onscreen as they were loaded into the back of a white transport van with blue San Antonio Police Department seals on the sides.

Betty looked away from the television and made a questioning face at Merit. "Seems very tidy, doesn't it?"

"Just what I was thinking."

Merit stretched her arms over her head and spun around in her office chair. "So, McDonald sends Walsh, Cobb, and Trigger to blow up half of San Antonio, kill Mayor Sincero, kidnap Clover. Then, within forty-eight hours, all but McDonald are dead and we have no idea where Clover might be, if she's still alive. McDonald has been arrested and his wife and daughter are in custody and hidden away somewhere by the FBI."

Betty made a face as if she smelled something stinky. "Seems like a lot of moving parts and dead participants boiled down to one freedom fighter in a very short period of time."

"I agree. What's going on here?"

7

At FBI headquarters in Quantico, Virginia, Agent Edward Johnson sat behind a huge wooden desk with an American flag behind it, along with a picture of the current president of the United States. He wore a dark suit and adjusted a striped tie as he spoke into his phone's speaker. "I'll get down there as soon as I can. For now, get extra agents in Austin and San Antonio to help with the investigations. Who's the special agent in charge?"

Someone on the other end of the phone responded while Agent Johnson waited, then said, "I'll be wheels up in thirty minutes. When I land, I want a full report with the local agents and the special agent in charge, and they better have some answers."

Agent Johnson hung up the phone, scratched his head, and spoke to the FBI seal on his wall. "How did this happen on my watch?"

Johnson had been hired twenty years before by his mentor and hero, Darius VanDyke, who'd gone on to head the FBI until his death last year. Johnson had moved up the ranks quickly, in part because VanDyke watched out for him and in part because he was honest, worked hard, and kept his nose clean. No hookers in hotel rooms, no looking the other way when the law required an arrest, and no taking bribes although they'd been offered more than once.

He picked up the phone again and hit the intercom for his assistant. "Gas up the plane. I need to get to Texas."

8

SIX MONTHS LATER

Ag joined Merit and Betty for a pause in the day's work to watch the television in Merit's office. Merit sat behind her desk, turned around to face the TV on the credenza. Betty sat in one of the guest chairs and saw Ag come in.

"Take a load off."

Ag sat in the other guest chair. "Don't mind if I do."

Ernest Anguish from NNN, New York headquarters, broadcast the story along with the rest of the world's news organizations. The picture on the television screen showed a partially bombed-out shell of an office building next to a hole that was formerly the market. "We see here what remains of the buildings around the San Antonio Market."

A group of over one hundred dignitaries, survivors, family of the deceased, and press were gathered behind barriers. Juan Ruiz, the Bexar County commissioner at large, gave a brief speech about the lawlessness that had been experienced at the hands of domestic terrorists and expressed condolences to the families present.

Sirens began to scream. Followed by an abrupt roar that shocked the spectators into silence with the detonation of two hundred pounds of strategically placed dynamite. Although the spectators knew what was coming, the warning sirens didn't seem to prepare the crowd for what happened next. In just fifteen seconds, the collapse was complete, reducing the building to a compact pile of rubble.

Merit let out a long breath she hadn't realized she was holding. Betty didn't blink for a full minute.

After the dust settled, Anguish continued. "The San Antonio Market was just imploded, in order to clear the debris from downtown San Antonio, Texas. Some attendees must have felt a similar shock to what they experienced at the time of the market bombing just six months ago. Officials warned those who planned to be at the implosion that PTSD symptoms were anticipated. We go to Mary Ellen Garza on the scene in San Antonio."

Mary Ellen spoke into her microphone in a low respectful voice from the edge of the crowd. "No one applauded or cheered today when the Bexar County Office Building tumbled down in a thunderous bang followed by billows of gray smoke. For over six months, the bomb-damaged remnants have served to remind downtown workers and visitors of the awful events of the market bombing where five hundred and eighty-three lives were lost, and countless others wounded. The demolition today, attended by family and observers, was met with almost church-like reverence."

Mary Ellen turned toward an observer, George Martinez, as the screen widened to include him in the shot. "Mr. Martinez, you lost your son in the bombing. Lo siento. You drove over three hundred miles to be here today. What does this mean to you?"

"Even though it's only been six months, I'm sure San Antonio residents couldn't stand to look at the remains of the bombing any longer. We want to move forward, but our hearts are broken. We hope this will give us closure, like the funeral we had, with ashes, not a body. Still, it seems impossible to reconcile." Mr. Martinez teared up and moved away from the camera.

Mary Ellen turned to Juan Ruiz. "Commissioner Ruiz, what would you like for your constituents to know?"

"Our prayers go out to the families and all San Antonio residents. At least two souls were entombed in the building and released today. We need some type of closure, but there is no closure on something like this. It's like going to the cemetery long after a funeral. It allows for some comfort, but also serves as a reminder of traumatic events. We hope that this will help families to move on as much as they can." Commissioner Ruiz began quietly shaking hands with people in the crowd.

Mary Ellen looked directly into the camera. "Ernest, many spectators began to cry as they stared at the scene. Some reported they didn't know why they came here today or what they expected, but they were compelled to attend, all with broken hearts and aching souls. Maybe the events of today will allow them to heal. Back to you, Ernest."

Anguish in New York appeared. "Thanks, Mary Ellen. We're told that the crews from Texas Demolition Company placed explosive charges in three hundred locations in the wrecked building, strategically inserting them into small holes drilled into the remaining support columns and walls. The firm has razed earthquake-damaged buildings in California, Scud missile launchers in Hungary, and the Starlight Hotel and

Casino in Las Vegas. The company issued a statement asserting that it was a sad job for them to have to perform."

The screen cut back to San Antonio as a policeman, inside the fenced area containing the rubble, picked up a small piece of debris and handed it through the fence to a crying woman, obviously in mourning. She took the memento and held it to her heart, thanking him through her tears.

Back to Anguish as he seemed to compose himself. "No decision has been reached as to what to do at the site. Some want the market to return, and others are pushing for a memorial or a park. Regardless of what they choose, nobody in San Antonio or the entire country is ever going to forget what happened there."

Betty popped a tissue from the round box on Merit's desk and dabbed at the corners of her eyes.

The screen changed to a close-up of Anguish. "This takes me back to a story reported by my father, Ernest Anguish, Sr. As you all know, he was with BCS news for over thirty years prior to his death. He once showed me footage of his report of the Hindenburg explosion of 1937, which was caused by an electrostatic discharge, or spark, that ignited leaking hydrogen. The tail of the balloon fell over New Jersey sending the nose into the air like a toppled whale."

Anguish adjusted the knot on his tie and composed himself.

"There was no foul play then, as we have in the San Antonio bombings. However, the Hindenburg disaster came during the Great Depression and the tragedy was compounded by the aftermath of the war against Hitler. My father told me that anytime people are killed in an explosion, and there were thirteen souls on the Hindenburg that day, the shock reverberates around the world. I see how right he was as we look back over the San Antonio bombing and the aftermath."

"What a thing," Merit said.

Betty looked at Merit and nodded.

Merit looked at Ag. "No word on Clover? Last I read, she was presumed dead."

Ag nodded. "Chaplain says that's a strong possibility, but why would they kidnap her if they just wanted to kill her?"

Merit looked pained. "Kim Wan is homeschooling the kids. They're not adjusting well at all. He has them in therapy. He's going too."

Betty straightened in her chair. "Only thing they have is hope, but is that good for the children?"

Merit swiveled toward Betty in her chair. "They can't have a real funeral and there's no closure."

Then to Ag. "Anything else from Chaplain?"

"Nothing. The trail has gone cold. No ransom note, and no one's taken credit for the kidnapping. APD is working closely with the FBI. They expect to either find her body or eventually learn what the kidnappers want with her."

Betty appeared chagrined. "What she must have gone through."

Ag looked at Merit. "Or is still going through."

9

Betty arrived at the office early, as usual, and woke up the office by turning on lights and machines. It was the day of the grand jury hearing to consider probable cause to indict Bobby Ray McDonald and other unnamed co-conspirators for the murders of the San Antonio residents in the market bombing. Merit and Betty had been tracking the story, wondering if there was enough evidence to indict McDonald and what that might be. He was allegedly the mastermind behind the three bombings, but law enforcement had not been able to tie him to the killings or the kidnapping of the two mayors.

Valentine Lewis, law clerk extraordinaire and clothes horse, known around the office as Val, came in the door whistling "Mama Mia." He joined Betty in the breakroom as she brewed a pot of dark coffee. Val had been the office paralegal for years and had been promoted to research clerk when he started law school, part-time, at St. Mary's in San Antonio.

"Smells wonderful."

Betty smiled. "Almost ready. This mud is so strong it will climb into your cup."

"I need it. I don't see how Merit gets her motor running on that breakfast tea she drinks."

Betty laughed. "To each her own."

Merit arrived, walked into the breakroom, and pulled a bag of breakfast tacos out of her Tumi briefcase. "I heard that."

Val peeked inside the brown bag and sniffed. "Oh goodie. Designer tacos. What else do you have in that bag?"

Merit laughed. "Nothing for you."

Betty poured filtered water from the large upside-down jug in the water dispenser into an electric tea kettle. "I'll bring your tea to your office. Go get settled in."

"Thanks. Looks like we'll find out about the McDonald case today." Merit went down the hall to her office, yelling over her shoulder, "I'll let you know when the news about the indictment comes on."

Betty poured two mugs of steaming coffee and handed one to Val and chided, "There. Now get to work."

Val straightened his Versace tie with his perfectly manicured hand and took the cup and a taco wrapped in foil. "Yes, ma'am."

Merit unpacked the files from her briefcase onto her desk and hit the remote on the television set on her credenza. The news came up as she muted the sound and set to work on a stack of files Betty had left for her the night before. Most documentation was stored on the law firm's private server, but there was a summary file for each client containing case notes with a reference to the electronic documents. It didn't save all the trees, but it did cut down on the devastation. Recycling did the rest.

Betty slipped in and placed a tray with tea and a breakfast taco on Merit's desk. The law firm settled into its daily routine of quiet work in individual offices until around noon when Merit noticed the 'Breaking News' banner light up on the screen.

She unmuted the sound, hit the intercom button, and told Betty, "It's time."

Betty and Val joined Merit and moved the guest chairs in order to see the TV screen. A celebrity onscreen held up a jar of mayonnaise and licked his lips.

Merit turned to Val. "It will start after the commercial break. Have you studied federal grand juries yet?"

"Yes, but the only thing I can remember from that class is that some judge named Wachtler said that a prosecutor can get a grand jury to indict a ham sandwich."

Merit laughed. "That's mostly true because prosecutors don't usually go to the grand jury unless they have their case nailed down solid."

Betty nodded.

"Doesn't have to be unanimous either. Just a majority of the group to return a true bill. They're determining probable cause, not guilt, so the standard of proof is far lower than in a criminal trial."

"How many citizens serve?" Val asked.

Merit turned up the volume as they waited for the commercials to finish the cycle. "Sixteen to twenty-three are required, but San Antonio had twenty on this case."

Val looked confused. "Why don't they just charge McDonald without the indictment?"

"Prosecutors don't like to go to the judge with it. Too iffy. This way, the charges are more likely to stand, especially in circumstantial evidence cases. All three bombers are dead and there are no other identified militia members, so there aren't any witnesses so far. This is a conspiracy case. Very difficult to prove."

Betty looked at a hemorrhoid commercial on the screen and shook her head. "Well, if he did it, I hope he fries in hell."

When NNN returned, Ernest Anguish's handsome face showed on one side of the screen and a shot of the federal courthouse in San Antonio on the other side. "Grand jury hearings are closed to the public, but we have just been given a copy of the indictment. We have Mary Ellen Garza standing by."

The screen changed to Mary Ellen in front of large white columns of justice. "That's right, Ernest, today the grand jury indicted Bobby Ray McDonald, and other possible unnamed co-conspirators, for plotting and executing terrorist attacks on American soil. The eight-count indictment includes murder in the first degree and conspiracy to commit murder. Other lesser charges include conspiring to provide material support and resources to the cause, including weapons, explosives, and personnel. The indictment asserts that McDonald knew and intended that such support be used in preparation for, and in carrying out, the use of explosives to maliciously damage or destroy property and take lives."

On Anguish. "McDonald is currently being held in federal custody without bond."

On Mary Ellen. "That's right. The Assistant Attorney General for National Security, Robert Bowser, reported that the charges are the next step in holding Mr. McDonald accountable. He also thanked law enforcement members and federal prosecutors for their involvement in the ongoing investigation."

On Anguish. "Of course, a jury of McDonald's peers will evaluate the evidence against him at trial."

On Mary Ellen. "Correct, Ernest. Every defendant is presumed innocent until and unless proven guilty in a court of law."

On Anguish. "There is no judge or defense counsel in a

grand jury hearing, so we do not know what actually went on behind those closed doors."

On Mary Ellen. "That's right. Our sources tell us that McDonald has not made any statements as to his terrorist affiliations, and his attorneys have yet to issue a statement in response to the indictment. Back to you, Ernest."

Merit muted the screen again. "Well, looks like we have our answer."

Betty nodded. "Wouldn't you like to be a fly on the wall in that grand jury room."

Val stood. "I better brush up on my criminal procedure before the bar exam. I'd forgotten almost all of that from my Fed courts class."

Betty stood as well. "You better believe it. No failing the bar exam."

Val blanched white as the blood drained from his face.

Betty announced Red Thallon on Merit's office line. She picked up and greeted her dear friend.

"Hey, Red. I've been reading your online reporting. Nice work."

"Thanks, Merit. I was wondering if you had any legal tips for me to include in my story on the grand jury indictment."

"I doubt the Feds would have brought charges if they didn't have a very strong case."

Red grunted. "There've been some rumors that the prosecutor didn't present all the evidence and swayed the jury to indict without the full picture of what happened."

Merit answered. "That wouldn't be so unusual, but a regular courtroom jury will hear the full story at trial. Any good defense attorney, especially one for McDonald, will dig out the series of events that led up to the arrest."

"I guess it will be a long time before we find out."

"Correct. This will probably not go to a speedy trial."

"Drinks later?"

"Yep. It won't be the same without Clover."

"No. I wonder if she's still alive. It's always on my mind."

"Mine too."

10

Merit Bridges sat in the darkly paneled office of Judge Harold Ginsberg. The judge was a tall man with a small, round belly that looked like a beach ball had been cut in half and placed on his abdomen under his shirt. His black robe hung on a coat tree in the corner. Ginsberg was somehow related to the supreme court justice of the same name. Merit had read they were distant cousins. The judge was known to be tough but fair, and Merit respected and admired him.

"It's good to see you, Judge. What can I do for you?"

"Have a seat. I called because we need you to act as special counsel to enable the use of a Chinese Wall around information in the McDonald case." The judge spoke with a sophisticated voice, hiding hints of a Texas drawl. He pronounced all of his 'ing' words without shortcut, but when he said get, it sounded more like git.

Merit blanched. "I'm flattered to be asked, but why not get someone in San Antonio?"

"The case has been transferred to Austin due to a change of venue hearing. The judge there was convinced that the high

Hispanic population of San Antonio would not allow for a fair trial. Most of those who were killed were Latinos."

"I've kept up with the news about McDonald being arrested and charged, but I didn't know the case was coming to Austin. Why me? As you know, litigation is not my speciality."

"That's why you. I want a strategist who can manage a lot of detail, legal parties, and points of law, all while having some perspective. That's my experience of you. Besides, you'll only present in court if there's a challenge to the information you let through. You'll mostly be a glorified editor-in-chief."

Merit half smiled. "Thank you, Your Honor, I appreciate your confidence in me. What do you mean about my letting information through?"

"It's a sequestered case. The Chinese Wall, or ethics wall, will allow the FBI to funnel evidence through you to the defense counsel for McDonald. You'll decide what to redact as a matter of national security and what is necessary for the defense to know."

"I'll be responsible for unmasking the information?"

"Yes, you'll also separate out anything to do with Mayor Sincero's assassination and Mayor Thibodeaux's kidnapping. There's been no evidence connecting McDonald to those crimes."

Merit blanched. "Isn't law enforcement fairly certain it was the same group?"

"Yes. I'm sorry. I know you were friends, but her kidnapping will not be part of the trial. There's no definitive evidence that McDonald was involved with the mayoral issues, and prosecutors have decided to go with the indictment on the bombing alone. They feel they have a stronger position without muddying the water."

"I understand. Who will handle the case as defense counsel?"

The judge handed Merit a sheaf of papers with the names of all the participants in the trial. "Jerry Webb will be attorney for McDonald. His firm has offices here and in San Antonio. The firm has been involved since the beginning, but Webb will be the new lead at the trial as one of the former partners at his firm, Robert Riley, is now deceased."

Merit's eyes flew to Judge Ginsberg's face. "Deceased? I hadn't heard."

"Yes. He killed himself yesterday. Jumped off a chair in his garage with a rope around his neck. Apparently, he had a history of depression, and this case may have pushed him over the edge."

Merit flinched visibly thinking of her deceased husband, Tony, Ace's father, who had put a bullet through his brain in their back yard a few years back.

Judge Ginsberg seemed to notice her reaction. "Sorry to open up old wounds. I seem to be the bearer of bad news today. Let's move on to the task at hand."

Merit steadied herself. "Right. How do you want me to handle the information from the government?"

"The FBI has a strong set of rules about their documents, how they're handled and where they're kept. I'm going along with their wishes for now, but if they challenge your authority as special liaison in any way, I want you to file an application for a hearing and let's get it on the record in open court. You'll basically act as go-between for the defense counsel."

"Jerry Webb would not be my first choice of an attorney to work with."

"Why not? Jerry's is one of the few federal criminal defense attorney firms in Austin large enough to handle a case of this size. The fact that they also have a San Antonio office is a bonus."

Merit began wringing her hands in her lap. "Your Honor, I need your advice."

The judge stared at Merit intently. "If I can help."

"I'm wondering if I should sign on for this task. I feel my experience may fall a little short of what's needed here."

"Why's that?"

Merit dropped her eyes and didn't respond.

"You're not thinking this through. I went out on a limb to have you, a woman of your young age, assigned to this case. Attorneys ten and twenty years your senior lobbied for this appointment. You will be the only one to see the files and decide what to allow into court and out into the public. It's a big responsibility, but it's also a career maker. Headlines every day, lots of notoriety."

"That's what I'm concerned about."

Judge Ginsberg looked Merit squarely in the eye as if to say, *The answer to my next question will change your life forever.*

Merit gulped, but held his gaze, waiting for the question.

"Do you have any doubt that the judicial process will remain fair, transparent, and unbiased?"

"Of course not."

"Well, there's your answer. Unless you'd still like for me to find someone to replace you?"

"No. Don't do that, please. Sorry. It will be fine."

"See that it is. This will be our last ex parte meeting until the trial is over. I'll see you only in court and in chambers with all attorneys present. You can't tell me what's redacted from the files. No one will know except you. I'm counting on you to pave the way to a fair and impartial verdict in this case."

"Yes, Your Honor."

The judge nodded in approval. "The world will be watching."

Defense Attorney Gerald 'Jerry' Webb ran around Lady Bird Lake on his usual five-mile jog. He was tall and lean with a strong jaw. His shaggy Robert Redford style hair was longer than it should have been for a courtroom lawyer, but he got away with it in Austin. The Live Music Capital of the World, with remnants of a hippie vibe, barely survived next to the newly transplanted hipsters taking over the town. Progressive Austin was always more liberal than the rest of the state and Republican haircuts were all but outlawed.

Jerry's Bluetooth headphones provided privacy and a driving beat from Bob Wills' version of "Miles and Miles of Texas" that kept his thirty-five-year-old body moving. It was a lovely and peaceful day, and he could smell the food from the restaurants downtown wafting over. His Zen was interrupted when his phone buzzed in the pocket of his sweatpants. He pushed the button on his earpiece and the speaker engaged as he slowed to a trot to catch his breath.

"Hello."

Jerry listened as several joggers passed him on the trail. His peaceful demeanor changed when he received the news.

"Robert Riley?"

Jerry came to a full stop and strained to hear.

"Suicide?"

Jerry looked stunned.

"Does this mean I have the bombing case?"

.

11

Merit and Betty returned to their television watching vigil in Merit's office as Ernest Anguish in New York, and all the major news networks around the United States, covered the one-year anniversary of the San Antonio Market bombing. A memorial, an angel with upswept wings, made of Texas limestone and metal had been erected in downtown San Antonio on the site of the north end of the former market. A wall of names commemorated each soul lost that day. A few small businesses had started moving back into the area, but most buildings had not yet been repaired and retrofitted.

At the scene was reporter Jana Williams, holding a microphone, but quiet as were the hundreds of other spectators and reporters around the bomb site. There was a period of silence for almost ten minutes. At the end of the remembrance period, the crowd was subdued. No one seemed to know what to do next.

Anguish's voice-over broke through. "The final death toll in the San Antonio bombing totaled five hundred and eighty-three men, women, and children. In addition to those lost, over two hundred additional people were injured, most of them hospitalized for some period of time. Out of those, forty-eight were permanently maimed or handicapped in some way. We now go to San Antonio NNN correspondent, Jana Williams."

The camera panned over the bomb site to Jana. "Yes, Ernest, the five hundred and eighty-three lost souls were mourned with five hundred and eighty-three seconds of silence. One second for each of the dead. To put it into perspective, a Boeing 777 holds four hundred and fifty passengers. The size of the loss is definitely felt here today."

Anguish asked the traditional question. "What is the mood, Jana?"

"The mood is somber and subdued. As you can see, as we pan down the line of visitors, most are common working men and women still in their uniforms and business attire. We've been waiting for local authorities and the governor of Texas to address the crowd. It looks like they're getting ready to begin, Ernest."

The governor and various other speakers stepped onto a podium at the edge of the site and began to sort themselves out. The newly elected mayor, Manuel Sanchez, acted as emcee. He had lost his wife in the bombing and had run on a platform of law and order which had handed him a landslide win. He introduced the governor, who spoke, then introduced the next speaker and so forth until all except the new mayor had said their piece. Their words were not inspiring and seemed like platitudes, but what could they say or do that would make a difference? Bobby Ray McDonald, Timothy Walsh, Trigger, Cobb, and the American Freedom Militia were not mentioned, only the lost souls that meant so much to the citizens in attendance.

Finally, Mayor Sanchez thanked the officials, all attendees

who'd joined the ceremony, and began to speak to the crowd in Spanish. The crowd took a collective sigh upon hearing the melodic sound of his voice. What he said didn't really matter, it was the tone, the soothing lilt, the feel of a lullaby comforting those in pain. The attendees could tell that he was in pain, too.

12

J erry Webb sat in downtown Austin at the law offices of Alistair, Riley, and Webb. He was settled behind his desk and deeply absorbed in the information on his computer screen when the firm's head partner entered his office. Alistair was a distinguished man of about seventy with gray hair and intimidating height. He handed Jerry a sheaf of papers.

Jerry grabbed the documents. "Is this the application for judicial reassignment?"

"Yes. There will be a hearing to make it official, but you'll be substituted as lead counsel. The judge has given it the nod. McDonald will be prosecuted in the Federal Criminal Trial Court here in Austin."

Jerry almost licked his lips but refrained before the partner.

If Alistair noticed, he didn't comment. "Merit Bridges will serve as special counsel to the defense and supervise the release of the sequestered materials. She is young, like you, but has a track record and the stamina to hold up to the grueling schedule that will surely be part of the process."

Jerry kept a poker face. "We don't get access to the FBI and Homeland Security files?"

"No, and the press will have a field day with this. Part of the case will only be shown to Bridges with FBI attorneys and agents monitoring and supervising her redacting of the materials."

Jerry groaned.

"You and the rest of the defense will not see the entire contents of the FBI files, although you will be defending McDonald. They're calling him a terrorist mastermind. You can see him later today."

Jerry showed his displeasure. "A Chinese Wall? Redacting. I hate that shit. It's all so subjective."

"May no longer be politically correct to use that terminology, but in essence, yes, a Chinese Wall."

"How can there be a fair trial if the defense is not allowed to see the entire FBI materials?"

"I'm sure Ms. Bridges, as special counsel, can fairly evaluate what is and is not necessary for the defense and the public to see and hear. The FBI counsel, Richard Dell, says the files are full of names, secrets, and information that would put agents and the nation at risk."

Jerry lowered his eyes. *Merit Bridges, of all people.*

Alistair didn't seem to notice. "Your father would be proud of you. Keeping his name on the firm's masthead when he died was my idea. I always knew you'd be a partner some day. You could be the next Webb in Alistair, Riley, and & Webb."

Jerry blinked. "Does that mean?"

Alistair laughed. "Not yet, Grasshopper. Let's see if you can earn your stripes on this case, then we'll talk about you becoming a partner when you get a few more gray hairs."

13

_____

Merit went back to her office after her visit with Judge Ginsberg and found Betty waiting with a cup of tea and a question mark on her face. "Well, what did he want?"

Merit went to her desk as Betty followed her.

"The McDonald terrorist case is moving to Austin under a change of venue. Judge Ginsberg wants me to play middleman between the FBI and Jerry Webb, editing and redacting documents that the defense is entitled to have to prepare a defense."

"A Chinese Wall? Are you going to do it?"

"It's the case of a lifetime, and I can't say no to the judge. I'm going to talk to Woody for advice, but I think I have to."

"Can you do the work from here?"

"No, I'll have to spend most of my days on the FBI campus."

"You've got a lot coming up on your schedule."

"We'll need some help. Maybe Val can work extra hours for a while. Also, would you ask Ag to come in? I'm going to need his advice and assistance."

Betty clucked, "Lordy, Lordy."

"I was thinking of stronger words."

14

In downtown Austin, St. David's Episcopal Church was filled with mostly suit and tie mourners. It appeared that those in attendance had left their offices and walked over for the service. A few wore boots with their jeans and blazers, a nod to Texas style.

Robert Riley, the attorney who'd committed suicide and made way for Jerry Webb to take over the case, lay quietly in his casket. Jerry sat four rows from the back with head partner, Alistair. A respectful distance from the body, Jerry thought. *For someone whose demise has given me the case of my lifetime.*

Jerry and Alistair huddled closely and whispered about those in attendance.

Jerry cleared his throat. "Is that Senator Daniel over there?"

Alistair looked around to see who might be eavesdropping on them. "Yes. Good turnout for a suicide."

"As opposed to what?"

Jerry caught movement from the corner of his eye and spotted Merit Bridges walking up the center aisle of the church and seating herself in a pew, about four rows ahead of them and across the aisle. She turned and looked back at them.

Alistair nodded to Merit. Jerry avoided eye contact and did not engage her.

Merit turned back to face the casket.

Alistair elbowed Jerry's side. "You might want to get on her good side."

Jerry frowned. "Right."

In his mind, Jerry flashed back to the first time they were together. *I've been on all her sides.*

Alistair looked straight ahead. "I know you're being thrown into this. Sorry for it having to be under these circumstances, but next man up, as we say."

"You can count on me." Jerry nodded toward the casket. "My mental health is just fine."

"I'm betting on it."

The robed and adorned reverend stepped up to the casket to begin the service. "Let us pray."

The grievers bowed their heads. Jerry kept one eye open and looked at Merit's blond hair.

After the funeral service, and a few moments of shaking hands and expressing condolences, Jerry walked to his car. He opened the door, then closed it, turned back toward the parking lot, and shielded his eyes from the sun. He spotted his target and walked over to Merit who was walking toward a cherry red BMW SUV. The vehicle seemed inappropriate amidst all the black and gray limos and cars.

"Hello, Merit."

"Jerry." Merit's face masked all expression, although heat shot through her at his closeness.

Jerry smiled in a way that looked tight and inauthentic. "I understand we'll be working together. I'd like to talk to you."

Before Jerry could finish, a young pup of a reporter, Lyle Ryder, who looked like he'd just learned to shave, called to them.

"Ms. Bridges, Mr. Webb. May I have a brief moment to ask a few questions?"

Jerry scowled. "Not now."

Lyle ran over and passed both attorneys his card. Jerry tucked his into his pocket without looking at it while Merit read the name. "Lyle Ryder."

"I know I don't look like much, but I am with the *Washington Times*. I'll be here in Texas for the duration of the trial. How about an appointment at a better time for you?"

Merit looked at Jerry. "I think he means you. I need to run." She got into her SUV and closed the door with a bit more force than was necessary.

Jerry turned to walk back toward his car. "No comment."

"You do believe in freedom of the press, don't you? I can meet with you anytime."

Jerry shrugged. "I don't know when that might be."

"You don't believe Riley's death was really suicide, do you?"

"Of course I do."

"Are you sure?"

Jerry looked stunned. "The evidence satisfied the police."

"It was meant to."

"Who would want to kill Robert Riley?"

"Who has the most to lose? Or win?"

"What do you mean?"

"How did the FBI arrest your client and his family within hours of the bombing?"

"He was stopped at a traffic stop on his way out of town."

"Check the files. Maybe he wasn't."

Jerry looked at him and blinked. "That's ridiculous."

15

Merit entered the Law Office of Merit Bridges and proceeded down the hall to her office. She passed Betty's desk on the way.

"Morning, Betty."

"Mornin', Merit. Want some tea?"

"I'll get it."

"I'll get it for you. I'm going to the breakroom anyway."

Merit laughed. "No, you're not. You just can't stand for me to serve myself. I am a big girl."

"What a cockamamie thing to say. I've been bringing you tea for years. Do you really want to argue about it again?"

Merit smiled at Betty's lovely, crinkled face. It reminded her of some Georgia O'Keefe photographs she'd seen in Santa Fe. "No, ma'am. I'd appreciate a cup."

Betty started down the hall. "Fast as greased lightning. That box from the San Antonio PD came in. Since it's not prohibited, I have Val sorting through it for you. He'll give you a report in a few minutes."

"Thanks."

"The Sandersons, new clients, will be here in half an hour. Better get a move on."

"Yes, ma'am."

Betty smiled as she walked on toward the breakroom, leaving Merit to settle in behind her desk.

Valentine tapped on the door frame and walked into her office with an iPad and a cup of strong black coffee. He waited without speaking for her to look up from her computer.

"Hi, Val. What do you have for me?"

"At Betty's request, I've organized the files from the SAPD into folders to make it faster for you to review and find things. It's in the conference room."

"What's in the files?"

"Bombing details including witnesses, damage reports, body counts, etc."

"Sad. What else?"

"Arrest details on McDonald's family."

"Not on McDonald?"

"No, just documentation of the referral to the FBI. They took over before McDonald was arrested."

"Okay, I'll check it out when I can get into it. I'll have some research assignments after that."

"We had a short seminar on domestic terrorism and the law at school right after the bombing, but nothing that's not fairly common knowledge. I can do some research on any topic you'd like."

Merit looked at her watch. "Okay, I'll make a list of what I need."

"Should I bring it all in here so you can use the conference room for the Sandersons?"

"You read my mind. Thanks, Val."

Half an hour later, Betty escorted John Sanderson and his wife, Ariana Sanderson, into the conference room, offered coffee, and went to fetch Merit for the meeting.

John was an inch shorter than his wife, but they made a handsome couple. It was evident to anyone who knew them that Ariana was a beautiful and sophisticated woman of action while John was quiet and intelligent, still waters running deep. Together, they made a powerhouse team on the Austin business, philanthropic, and social scene.

Merit entered the room and observed the couple for a moment.

Ariana, wearing a simple Tom Ford dress and a string of pearls around her neck, stood at the expansive conference room window, looking at downtown Austin. There was a diamond on her platinum engagement ring that Merit estimated at about ten carats. She guessed there were another ten carats embedded around the wedding band next to it.

I'm surprised she can lift her hand.

John sat at the conference room table, sorting a file of documents he'd brought for the meeting, wearing a simple platinum wedding band.

Merit extended her hand to both in turn, and John stood. "Hello Mr. and Mrs. Sanderson. I'm Merit Bridges."

The Sandersons returned pleasantries, and they all sat at the conference table. Merit liked them immediately. She began the meeting. "I assume you know all you need to know about me and my firm. If you have any questions, just ask. I understand you have a real estate matter you'd like to discuss."

Ariana smiled. "Yes, we own a large warehouse on St. Elmo that is being unused at the moment."

John handed her a document. "It was rented to FunMart as a distribution center for their toys, calendars, and novelties. They bought their own building and moved to Kyle. We've been approached by AmFlix to put in a studio for local filming of a new sci-fi Western television series starring Rocky Gordon."

"Star power. Impressive. What is it that you need on the project?"

Ariana reached over to the file in her husband's hands and pulled out a page with a list. "We have a firm on retainer for the construction contracts and corporate-type documents. They've referred us to you for the lease and the entertainment law aspects of the deal. We understand you have some experience in that area of the law."

Merit took the list. "Yes, on the real estate, some on the entertainment law. There are a lot of moving parts to something like this. I see you have a pretty good grasp of that from your list."

Ariana smiled. "We'll need a contract with the studio, including the length of time they'd like to use the space, and fair market rent."

"I'll be happy to help with this, but I should warn you, I've just been assigned a case that will eat a lot of my time. I also have my regular clients to maintain."

"No problem, we gave them a three-month lease for equipment only so they can start moving wardrobe and sets into the space. That should give you time to draw up the longer lease."

"When do you need the full lease?"

"We saw in the paper about your appointment to the McDonald trial. We've got plenty of time. Just get the ball rolling, and you can dive down into the details as time opens up. AmFlix won't begin shooting for several months."

Merit looked relieved. "Excellent."

John handed Merit another sheet of paper. "One more thing of special note. We need to amortize the construction and fixture improvements that they want us to make over the term of the contract. That sort of thing."

Merit took the paper. "That's pretty standard in this type of arrangement."

John nodded. "They'll need showers, offices, wardrobe rooms with at least four washers and four dryers, and a very expansive open warehouse area for set design and shooting. Part of that is there now. Some of it needs upgrading. We'll build out the rest."

Merit continued to look at the list. "Right. You'll want to be able to recoup that initial investment in the event they should vacate the lease early."

John nodded. "Yes, they'd like a pre-set penalty figure to be paid if they break the lease. Just in case the show is canceled or something catastrophic happens after the first season."

Merit made a note on a legal pad. "Makes sense. Or, we could have the first six months' rent cover the build out and then have the rent start after that. Maybe some upfront larger payments dropping after the build out is repaid. Of course, you'll want all fixtures to remain on the premises when the lease ends. I can draft some language both ways and run it by their attorneys. Who's representing them?"

John handed Merit another page from the file. "Eastwood & Newman out of Los Angeles. Here's the attorney's name, email, and phone number."

Merit took the page. "I've worked with them before. Very fair and knowledgeable group. They represented Fairway golf shoes in a public relations deal for one of my pro golf clients a while back."

John smiled. "Yes, we heard."

Merit laughed. "You do your homework."

Ariana smiled. "Always."

16

J erry and Alistair walked down the hall of the law firm of Alistair, Riley & Webb. They entered the elevator, and the partner pushed the button for the third floor and turned to Jerry. The firm was filled with well-appointed rooms and fancy decor by the elevator banks.

"There's a war room that Robert Riley setup, prior to his death, with all the evidence and documents laid out. You can work there if you like. Security is better than your office, and there's more room."

The elevator door opened, and they both walked down the third-floor hallway and into a room filled with file boxes, corkboards holding photos with push pins, and temporary work tables covered with files and papers.

Jerry walked around the room getting an overview of the overwhelming amount of documentation. A team of four young lawyers was hard at work around a large conference table.

Jerry looked at a thin, bony young woman with short black hair. "Tell me about our client."

She stood up. "I'm Helen Sharp. I supervise the other junior attorneys compiling research. We think Bobby Ray McDonald was born in Louisville, Kentucky, about forty years ago. There's no confirmed record of his birth except for a family Bible. Probably born at home.

"He married at twenty-one and moved his wife to San Saba, Texas, when he was twenty-five. Her name is Faye McDonald. Not much on her background. They met when they were both in high school in Louisville. He was a pretty good football player, and she was a twirler in the band."

"Got it. What else?"

"They had a son in Louisville who died in the hospital a couple days after he was born. Probably why they got married. Shotgun wedding. Faye almost died, too. Surprisingly, the couple stayed together. The next year, they had a second child, their daughter, Lucy. She was born before McDonald was arrested by local police."

Jerry seemed to be evaluating her ability to be useful through the Socratic method of questions and answers. "Why was he arrested? Terrorist activities?"

"No, we think it involved drug or gun sales or both. We're nailing that down."

Alistair joined in and pointed to a stack of documents. "More reports are from Riley's investigator. I recommend you continue with him, or you can hire your own."

Jerry flipped through a few pages from a stack on the table. "Right. Continue, Helen."

"McDonald and the family wound up in Houston about five years ago. They stayed with his aunt and uncle and worked in their butcher shop for about six months until the relatives kicked them to the curb, according to them."

Jerry sat, pulled over a legal pad, and started taking notes. "Where did they go next?"

"Back to Louisville for about three years, then back to Houston."

"With a felony arrest he's able to move between states undetected? Was he on parole? What was he doing for the three years in Louisville?"

Alistair answered for her. "Becoming radicalized, we guess. Influenced by someone or some group. The prosecution will contend that McDonald is the leader of the cell that planned the bombing."

Jerry nodded. "Of course, they will. How will they prove it?"

Helen sat back down. "Through the top-secret documents that only Merit Bridges will see, I guess."

"Except for the secret documents, is this all of the discovery?"

Helen pointed to a file on top of the stack. "Yes, that file includes the witness list to date. The prosecutors say they've sent everything they have or plan to use in court, except for what needs to be redacted."

Jerry scratched his chin. "Well, the man who set the bomb, named Walsh, died on the scene. According to this, two more alleged co-conspirators were killed during their attempted arrests at a mobile home. Is that the entire cell?"

Helen nodded. "That's what we've been told, but there may be more information in the FBI documents."

"What about the killing of the San Antonio mayor and kidnapping of the Austin mayor? Any evidence that connects those incidents to our client?"

"No, and we've been told they won't be amending the indictment to include those charges, so we don't have to worry about that, at least for now."

"That leaves our client as the last man standing to take the blame."

Alistair nodded. "That's about the size of it."

17

Most Saturday mornings, for years, Merit had donated her time to the homeless and indigent by giving free advice to walk ups at a picnic table on Lady Bird Lake near Austin High School. There was a removable sign hanging on the splintery wooden table that said Austin Legal Clinic. A stack of brochures with the same name were stacked on each end of the table. The jogging path went right by the makeshift desk and Merit always got in a jog either before or after her shift, as did most of the other volunteers.

This Saturday, as she approached the table, she greeted a male family lawyer who was counseling a woman with an infant on her hip, and a female attorney who specialized in elder law who wasn't busy at the moment.

Merit sat. All three were lined up on the bench on one side of the table with briefcases and legal pads in direct contrast to their jogging attire. All three wore shorts, T-shirts, and running shoes. Merit's hair was bound up in a ponytail that stuck out the hole in the back of her Texas Exes ballcap. It sported the classic Longhorn logo from her alma mater, the University of

Texas School of Law. Her T-shirt had no wording, just a big-eyed owl, the logo from her undergrad days at Rice University. The other two wore similar law school identifying garb, a pony from SMU and a bear from Baylor.

After the mother with the infant moved on, seemingly happy with the advice she'd received, an older gentleman, who appeared to be homeless, approached the group. He walked toward the table, then stalled out mid-step as if he didn't know who to talk to.

Merit smiled at him. "How may we help you?"

The man blurted out. "My daughter wants me to go into a nursing home. I'm homeless. I live about three streets down under the bridge. Can she make me do that?"

"That's an elder law issue, and you're in luck. We have an expert who specializes in that area of the law right here."

Merit pointed to the woman in the SMU T-shirt and the worried client stepped sidewise and continued his explanation to her.

Next, an Hispanic woman in an embroidered dress came up to Merit and the guy in the Baylor T-shirt.

"Do either of you sue people? My brother was killed in the bombing in San Antonio, and I need to find a lawyer to collect the insurance money for his kids."

Merit smiled at her. "Sure, we can help you. Neither of us is a torts expert, but I know a good one who'll be happy to meet with you."

The woman looked apprehensive. "Do I have to be homeless to get help? I have a home."

Merit smiled and pointed to the picnic table. "Nope, we help anyone who walks up to this lovely desk. Rich or poor, happy or sad, skinny or fat."

The woman laughed and seemed to relax.

"If we take your case, we either do it pro bono or we work

out a fee arrangement to be paid out of any money we recover for you. Here's a brochure with the rules of the legal clinic."

The woman took the pamphlet. "Thanks."

Merit picked up her pen and wrote the date on her legal pad. "Why don't you tell me a little more. Let's start with your name and the name of your nieces and nephews."

After Merit had teased out the pertinent facts from the children's aunt, partly in English and partly in Spanish, she took a business card from her briefcase and handed it to the woman.

"I have a conflict of interest with your case because I'm handling a matter for another client involved in the bombing. This card has the office number of Kim Wan Thibodeaux. He specializes in litigation and handles a lot of tort cases."

"Was he the mayor's husband?"

Merit frowned at the use of past tense. "Yes, and he's a very good lawyer."

The woman looked worried. "My brother wasn't here legally. Does that mean my nieces and nephews can't get help? They are Americans, and I have a green card."

"If they were born here, that's not an issue. Kim Wan is a good friend of mine. I'll let him know you'll be calling next week. Give me Monday to bring him up to speed and then get in touch with his office on Tuesday. He'll be a great fit for your case."

After the woman left, Merit looked at her watch and then at the people on the jogging path. Today, she had a second task in mind when her shift was over and it came time for her run. About half an hour later, her obligation at the picnic table ended when her replacement arrived. She put her briefcase in her SUV, hooked the key inside her shorts pocket on a snazzy loop sewn in for that purpose, and took off down the trail at a steady pace.

Merit made a loop around the hike and bike trail, then paused near the Mopac Pedestrian Bridge, watching and waiting. Several lovers stole kisses and took selfies nearby with the lovely view of the lake as a backdrop. She looked down the path and spotted her target.

Jerry Webb ran his usual route around Lady Bird Lake, dodging tourists, bikers, and other joggers along the path near Austin High School. When Jerry turned the corner and started over the bridge, Merit jogged behind, then up beside him.

"Jerry, what are we going to do about this?"

"What are you doing here, Merit? Stalking me? You know we can't talk about the case."

"I haven't seen any protected documents yet. Besides, I'm not here to discuss the case. I'm here to discuss us."

"We're supposed to avoid even the appearance of impropriety. And there is no us. Was. Past tense. If our affair is revealed, this case will be jeopardized."

"As you said, there is no us. Besides, we are two consenting adults."

Jerry grimaced. "Were. And I was married at the time."

Merit kept pace with him as he continued to run. "Technically correct but separated and now divorced."

Jerry settled into a nice pace. "Regardless, there can be no conflict of interest, or even the appearance of a conflict."

"We are not adversaries. There is no misalignment of our interests. We both seek truth and justice for McDonald, even if I am in charge." Merit grinned.

Jerry grinned back. "I don't think so. It's my case."

"Our case. My job is to make sure you get what you need from the FBI files."

"As before, we are both alphas. Not a good recipe. Maybe

you should resign. There has to be another attorney in this town who wants to redact documents all day."

Merit kept pace beside him. "Why don't you resign. I'm the big dog here. Two alphas make for alphabet soup."

Jerry looked at his Fitbit for the time and his pulse rate which was going up even though he'd slowed down. "Or alpha pit bulls."

Merit smiled. "I like soup."

Jerry didn't smile. "Then that settles it. We both stay on the case. I won't see you again except in court, so don't track me down again."

Merit nodded. "Right, court only. You will only see the FBI documentation that I deem relevant and nothing more. You'll have to trust my judgment on that."

Jerry started to pick up speed.

Merit didn't try to keep up. "It would still be better if you resign."

Jerry called over his shoulder as he sprinted ahead. "After you."

Merit laughed, "See you in jail!"

18

Merit entered the southwest regional office of the FBI on the Live Oak Federal Campus on East 11th Street in Austin, Texas. The reception area was government standard, nice enough but with little decor or color to liven it up. No plants or any living things. She checked in with the receptionist who was young but seemed pleasantly mature.

"I'll let them know you're here. Please have a seat."

Merit deposited her briefcase in one of the many beige chairs and sat in another. After she waited for about twenty minutes, she looked at her watch, stood, and returned to the desk.

"Excuse me. I do have an appointment. Did you tell them I'm waiting?"

"Yes, ma'am. I'm sorry. A previous meeting went over. It won't be much longer."

Merit didn't sit this time, she paced the room and looked at the door to the inner offices, waiting for someone to emerge. She looked at her watch again and then at the receptionist. "I've been here for over half an hour. I'll give him five more minutes, then we'll have to reschedule."

The receptionist looked embarrassed. "I'll let him know."

"Please remind him that this is a court-directed meeting and he chose the time. Judge Ginsberg will not be pleased."

The receptionist picked up the phone, but before she could connect, the inner door opened and out stepped Archibald Duke. He looked to Merit like a cross between Arnold Schwarzenegger and a white Lance Riddick. Robust, fit, about forty-five years old, and sporting a haircut so short it was almost a buzz cut. His suit was dark, and his tie was red, white, and blue striped. He had an American flag stick pin in the buttonhole of his lapel. He walked over to Merit and extended his meaty hand. "I'm Archibald Duke. Archie is fine. Sorry to keep you waiting Ms. Bridges. May I call you Merit?" His voice was deep and gravelly.

First name basis, Merit thought as her tiny hand disappeared in his when she returned the shake. Her armpits prickled so robustly, she shivered.

"Are you cold?"

"No. Merit is fine. Let's get started."

"Straight to business. I like that. Let's go into the conference room. I don't have much of an office here in Austin."

Merit followed him through the door and down the hall. "Where are you from?"

"I work between here in Texas and the Washington D.C. area."

"Quantico?"

He laughed as if she was making a joke. "Classified."

Merit wasn't amused. "Hmm."

Duke escorted Merit down a long hallway toward a small conference room. As they entered, a group of dark-suited men and one woman, who were walking away, turned the corner at the end of the hallway. Duke directed Merit through an open door then closed it after they entered. The room was totally bare except for a rectangular table with eight swivel chairs and the FBI seal on the biggest wall. No phone, no windows. Duke indicated a seat on the long side of the table for Merit. He sat at the head of the table and folded his hands.

Power play already, Merit thought.

Duke began. "I understand you will meet with the defendant."

Merit blinked. "How do you know that?"

Duke smiled. "Just keeping up with the case. It's a logical assumption."

Merit grimaced. "Let's get started."

"Fine. As you know, McDonald's legal defense team is entitled to the evidence we have on the physical bombing. A portion of it came to us via the San Antonio Police Department. We've sent copies over to Jerry Webb's office and messengered a duplicate to your office."

"I received them from you and from SAPD. So, if that's the crux of it, why am I here?"

"What we haven't sent to anyone yet is the intelligence on the bombing. We also have the information on the assassination of the mayor of San Antonio and the kidnapping of the mayor of Austin. Since there is nothing to connect McDonald to those other events, they have to be removed from what's shown to the defense team."

"Judge Ginsberg filled me in. I'll cull that out of the documents if I deem them irrelevant. I'm ready to get started."

"Not so fast, Merit."

He said her name in such a way it made her wish she'd insisted on using Ms. Bridges.

"Well, Archie, I think I've wasted enough of the court's money today at my billable rate. Why don't we get to the point or the documents or whatever it is you're not telling me."

Duke frowned. "I have a series of documents comprising eight file boxes that must be reviewed here in our offices. You can work in this room and only here. An agent will bring in one box and you will be allowed as much time as you'd like to work through it. When you complete that box, it will be removed and the next box brought in."

"What about copies of what I need?"

"All of the documents are copies. You will be provided special redacting markers that completely blot out the wording you choose to strike. You'll be given a list of code names for all of the agents involved. Their names have been redacted already, and their code names written in above the redacted names."

"Why can't I do that redacting as well? If I'm to see secrets, what's the difference?"

"We will not allow the names of our NOC agents to be exposed. The code names will allow you to inform the defense team without confusion. When you send them reports, you'll use the code names we've provided."

"Am I allowed to take notes or make copies after the redacting is complete?"

"You may make notes that stay in this room, on a laptop or legal pad. You will have a tray where you can leave any documents you'd like to have sent to defense counsel after you've completed the redacting. You must strike everything that is not necessary to the defense's case. We'll make the copies for you and send them over."

Merit grimaced. "That sounds like a lot of redacting."

Duke nodded. "We've narrowed down the files as much as possible under the judge's orders. The rest is up to you. If you place a document in the tray for copying that we think reveals too much, we'll kick it back to you for further redacting."

"And if I disagree?"

"It won't be copied."

"And if I still disagree, we'll let Judge Ginsberg decide."

Duke narrowed his eyes and bore into her. "I hope it doesn't come to that. And remember, you may not speak ex parte with defense counsel or the judge about the case. The defense team will receive only the documents we send over from the tray."

"I understand the rules. I'm to support the defense team only via the documents. I may not offer my legal opinion or confer with them in any way outside of court or while seeing the defendant."

Duke stood and tapped on the door. A woman, who Merit had seen earlier in the hallway group, entered. She wore the stereotypical dark suit and carried a manila file folder.

"This is Agent Rachel Ward. She'll be assisting me with the rotation and protection of the documents. You may refer to her as Rachel. We're very informal around here."

Yeah, right, Merit thought.

Merit did not stand and Rachel, a plain vanilla white woman with brunette hair, did not offer her hand to shake. Next to Duke, Rachel looked child-sized, although, in reality, she was fairly normal height and weight for a fortysomething-year-old woman. Merit and Rachel nodded a perfunctory greeting at one another.

"I'll be shuttling documents for you while you're working here." Rachel had an accent, from the East Coast by Merit's guess.

Rachel placed the manila folder before Duke, took a last look at Merit, and left the room.

"This is our confidentiality agreement as approved by Judge Ginsberg. It sets out the rules of use of information, your specific assignment as special counsel to the defense team, and also defines treason under the U.S. Constitution. We take it very seriously. I'll give you a few minutes to look it over. Please sign it before you leave. We'll be ready with your first box of documents tomorrow morning. We can start with the initial arrest and the bomb-making evidence."

"I've wondered how you found the bombers so quickly. How did you know about the storage unit?"

"We'll get to all that. Let's take it one day at a time."

Duke stood and extended his hand. Reluctantly, Merit stood and shook it but did not meet his gaze. She sat back down and reviewed the agreement as Duke left the room. When she was satisfied that she understood clearly what the requirements were, she signed the document, closed the file, placed the pen on top, and let out a long breath.

What have I gotten myself into now?

19

Merit entered the Bastrop Federal Correctional Institution, about twenty minutes east of Austin. She tried to remain calm and remember to breathe. Although she was free to leave at any time, she always felt claustrophobic when she had to visit incarcerated clients and was thankful it didn't happen often. She approached a tired-looking desk attendant, showed her ID, and signed in.

Jerry Webb walked in behind her, showed his ID, and signed his name directly beneath hers on the sheet. Merit nodded and Jerry returned the nod.

The attendant took back the clipboard. "Any weapons?"

"No." Jerry was allowed to carry a concealed weapon on his person, under Texas statute, because of his job but had never taken his pistol out of his car or home.

Merit echoed, "No." She had a concealed handgun license and had left her Ruger in the BMW outside.

They were directed to a small room at the end of a long hall marked with a large, red '4' painted on the door. McDonald had been relocated to the facility in order to be accessible to legal counsel and assist with the preparation of his case. Didn't matter much, all prisons looked alike.

Merit and Jerry prepared to meet the monster who allegedly killed and maimed over five hundred people. When they were settled on one side of a metal table, their client was brought into the room by two uniformed guards. The escorts unlocked the inmate's handcuffs from a chain around his waist and relocked them to a bar across the metal table, the length forced him to lean over at the waist or sit. He sat.

Bobby Ray McDonald was lean and gaunt. His orange prison jumpsuit swallowed him, and his facial bones seemed to show through his paper-thin skin, creating a skeletal effect that resembled a corpse. Merit was taken aback, as she had expected a husky football player physique.

Jerry extended his hand across the table. "I'm Jerry Webb, your attorney, as I'm sure you know. I've been appointed to replace Robert Riley and represent you on the charges in the federal trial. This is Merit Bridges."

Merit extended her hand. "I'm special counsel appointed by Judge Ginsberg to evaluate the FBI documents in your case. I'll be sending the necessary information to Mr. Webb."

McDonald stared at them with sunken eyes. "I know who you are. There's nothing you can do for me."

Jerry cleared his throat. "That's open for debate, but be careful what you say here. I'm assuming this room isn't monitored, but answer only the questions I ask you."

Merit glared at Jerry. "And, the ones I ask you."

McDonald showed no emotion. He answered in a deadpan monotone. "I know the drill. I'm not a total redneck."

Jerry grimaced. "I didn't mean to imply anything like that. Just being careful. I'll do my best for you."

McDonald glared at Jerry. "I said there's nothing you can do."

The attorneys assessed their client, then Jerry spoke. "I'm going to see your wife and daughter tomorrow. Is there anything you'd like for me to tell them?"

McDonald's eyes sparked for a moment, then returned to their emotionless state. He shook his head.

Jerry opened a yellow legal pad and took a pen from his breast pocket. "Okay. Let me know if you change your mind. We'll be here for a while. Let's begin."

Jerry ran through a set of background questions confirming what Helen Sharp had told him about McDonald's geography and family background.

McDonald answered without hesitation, leading them to believe he was being candid until Jerry's next question. "How did you get out on the street after your criminal conviction? Were you paroled?"

"Yes. Good behavior."

"How did you make money?"

McDonald faltered. "I don't know."

Jerry looked at McDonald in disbelief. "Drugs? Gun running? I know you didn't work at Burger King."

The prisoner was sarcastic. "Not with a name like fuckin' McDonald."

"Funny. What allowed you to hook up with domestic terrorists without the FBI tracking you? Did you use false names? Fake ID?"

McDonald clammed up and shifted his eyes to the corner of the ceiling.

Merit tried her luck. "Did you have a reason for bombing the market? Are you a member of a militia, white supremacist, or boogaloo movement?"

No response.

Jerry resumed the questioning. "The FBI and SAPD say you were connected to Timothy Walsh and the other two co-

conspirators who died during attempted arrests. Did you know them?"

"Of course, that's easy to confirm. I don't have anything further to add."

"I can't help you if you don't work with me. You have to give us something."

McDonald looked at Jerry, started to say something, then stopped.

A lightbulb went off in Merit's head. "Did your wife and daughter know that you were planning to bomb the market?"

"No, no, no, no. They knew nothing about it." McDonald tried to stand and was jerked back down by the handcuffs.

His only vulnerability is his family. Merit felt a cold chill sweep through the institutional space. *Something's not normal here. What's going on?*

20

Duke walked outside and strolled around the FBI campus to avoid any eavesdroppers who might be listening. He called Tank on the burner phone designated for that purpose and asked for an update. Tank had been at the encampment between Waco and Dallas since the initial kidnapping of Mayor Clover Thibodeaux. He was Duke's eyes and ears, and one of the few people left alive who knew Duke's identity and involvement in the domestic terrorism movement.

Duke and Tank had met years ago when Duke arrested Tank at a militant rally for spraying a policeman in the face with pepper spray. Duke had Tank in the back seat of his vehicle in handcuffs.

Tank had spewed a litany of extremist rhetoric, mixed with an impressive amount of profanity, then clammed up.

Duke turned around and asked, "How would you like to work for me?"

Tank responded, "No fuckin' way, I'm no snitch."

Duke had winked at Tank in the rearview mirror and said,

"That's good to know. I know all about your military background. I've been watching you for a while. I think we can figure something out."

What followed was a long relationship between the two based on hate and violence. Both embraced it fully.

Today, Tank informed Duke of the state of affairs surrounding Mayor Thibodeaux. "We're keeping these militant yahoos busy with this faux trial of Four Leaf. After they convict her, they will want to kill her. They want to punish her for her sins."

Duke grunted. "That's a good one."

"Yeah. They're talking about a lynching. After they have the militia ceremony, they want to leave her body in the middle of the River Walk hanging from one of the bridges over the river. They think the tourist boats will go under it and find her. Making a big statement is their primary goal at this point."

"Good. Play that up all you can with the militia without taking charge. Let the yahoos think they're in control."

"Roger that."

"We don't want her harmed before we're ready to use her."

"She's in a makeshift jail in the old barn behind the big house. We brought her in drugged and with a hood on, so she has no idea where she is or if she's even in Texas. She hasn't seen me, Six-pack, or Cupcake without a mask, but she's seen most of the militia at the play trial."

"Has anyone figured out our real goal?"

"Just my team of two, Six-pack and Cupcake. The rest still think I'm all in with the trial and punishment. They have no idea I'm just keeping them busy for now. And, of course, neither my team nor the militia have any idea who you are."

"Right, let's keep it that way. I'll keep you posted about any movement by the FBI that might cause problems up there.

Homeland Security has been sniffing around as well. I'll see what I can find out about their agency."

"Roger that."

"Out."

"Out."

21

Merit returned to her office to find Betty, Valentine, and the rest of the staff gone for the day. She locked the front door and took her briefcase to her office. She wrote a note on the back side of a Post-it and returned to the front door where she left the note on the inside of the glass so it could be read from the hallway. She went into the breakroom, flipped on the light, and found a wineglass. Clean, and right where the glasses were supposed to be.

Thank you, Betty.

Merit pulled a nice Malbec from the wine cooler, opened it, poured a generous amount in her glass, and sipped.

"Yum."

She took the glass to the conference room, flipped on all the lights, and sat down next to the box of documents that had been organized by Val. When she took off the lid, there was an inventory on top of the files with multiple references to the San Antonio Police Department.

Next to the box was the list Val had compiled with a summary of what was in each of the red accordion files and folders he had organized. She scanned the list and made checkmarks by what she thought were the most important documents. She put an 'S' beside the ones she wanted Betty to scan into her computer. Then, she took both the inventory and the list to the copy machine, made a duplicate and wrote Ag on the top of the first page of the copy, along with the date.

She went back to the conference room, snagged a yellow highlighter from the cup holder on the credenza, and highlighted the documents on Ag's copy that she wanted him to read and possibly follow up on with the SAPD.

Her iPhone played a guitar riff, Ag's ringtone, and she pushed the green button to talk on speaker.

"Pizza delivery."

She laughed. "Hey, Ag. About time you got here. I'll be right there."

She went to the front door, turned the key she'd left in the lock at the bottom of the glass, and let him in. She could smell yeast, sauce, and pepperoni coming from a box in his hands.

"Hi. I opened a bottle of wine, but I bet you'd rather have a beer."

"What have you got?"

"Not sure. The usual that Betty stocks, I think. Want to check the refrigerator in the breakroom and meet me in the conference room?"

"Sure." Ag handed Merit the pizza box marked Home Slice.

"Will you grab some paper plates and napkins while you're in there?"

"Yep."

When Ag joined her with a frosty bottle of Lone Star beer, they both sat down at the conference table. They ate and sipped for a while, then looked at the inventory, the list, and at each other. Over the years, they'd developed an unspoken communication, like an old married couple, without the benefits. It wasn't for lack of trying on Ag's part, but Merit kept it business between them. Not that she didn't admire his long, tall, lanky walk and his beautiful curly eyelashes. She knew that crossing that line would not allow her to come back and after her husband, Tony's suicide, she wasn't in any hurry to go there. Superficial sex was the only thing on the menu in the relationship department for now, and Ag didn't fit that category.

Ag took a pull on his longneck and took another slice of pizza from the box. "I've seen the news for the basics. Want to fill me in on the rest?"

"Yep. Technically, our client is Bobby Ray McDonald, with a limited scope of participation by us. Jerry Webb is defense counsel. I go to the Federal Live Oak campus, go through the records there, and redact anything that isn't applicable to the case in the FBI files. I send the pertinent docs to Jerry's office. I do go to interview the defendant, just to provide context for the review."

"Judge Ginsberg appoint you?"

"Yes."

"Nice."

"I guess. It's complicated. My loyalties are split four ways. Keeping myself from committing treason by revealing government secrets, doing a good job for the judge as special advocate, and making sure McDonald has a shot at a fair trial, while assuring defense counsel that I have his back and can provide all the documents that pertain to the case."

Ag took a sip of beer and laughed. "I'd say the treason part might be the highest priority."

Merit chuckled. "Agreed. This FBI Agent Archibald Duke, Archie he says he's called, gives me the creeps. He's a patronizing son of a bitch on a power trip from what I can tell. Maybe worse. Bad vibe all around."

"I'll ask around about him."

"Thanks. I was hoping you could do that."

Ag nodded.

Merit continued the summary. "As you probably saw on the news, a terrorist named Walsh blew up the San Antonio Market, but he obviously had help. The maintenance door was either left unlocked or Walsh had a key. The SAPD found out quickly that Walsh was connected to McDonald, our client. I hope we can tell from these documents how they did that so expediently and how the FBI made an arrest within hours of the bombing."

"Does it matter to your review of the FBI documents?"

"I think it would help me get through the FBI files faster if I knew the basic story of what happened outside the intelligence arena. And Duke dodged my questions about it. Made me curious."

Ag scratched his chin. "Odd."

"Yes. My thoughts exactly. There are eight boxes at the FBI office, that's a lot of reading. And we're going to trial soon."

"I get it. Time's limited."

Merit stood, walked behind Ag, and pointed over his shoulder. "See this document I've highlighted on your copy? It's a report on an anonymous tip that came into the SAPD right after the bombing. Let's start there, number 14."

Ag pulled the file labeled number 14 from the box and flipped it open so they could both read it.

Merit pointed to the top. "The story broke the news at around 2:00 p.m. Looks like the call came in at 3:00 p.m. So, within one hour, someone realized they had information linking McDonald to the bomber, let the police know, and didn't leave their name."

Ag took a sip of beer and looked up into Merit's blue eyes

over his shoulder. "The timeline just doesn't fit. Lucky or what?"

Merit looked down at the document, ignoring the familiar heat between them. "My thoughts exactly. Then go to document number 18."

Ag diverted his attention from Merit to the work at hand. His Adam's apple bobbled as he pulled the folder labeled number 18, opened it, and they both read aloud. "FBI will handle from here. Cease all attempts to locate or apprehend any known associates of Walsh."

Merit contemplated the facts. "So, the FBI claimed jurisdiction within hours, had someone from their offices in play, arrested McDonald, and had him in custody before nightfall."

Ag nodded. "That's fast."

"Really fast."

"You think McDonald's associates could have ratted him out?"

"Or maybe he was already being watched by the FBI?"

"Or some quiet citizen saw something, said something, and didn't want any further involvement."

"True. I don't know what the theory of the case will be by the defense team. Jerry and I are not allowed to confer outside of court or jail during our visits with McDonald."

Ag nodded. "What's the prosecution's case?"

"As best I can tell, it's very tidy. There was a terrorist cell, including McDonald, Walsh, and two other men."

"Do they know who he was connected to? If there were any other cells?"

"I don't know much about that yet and, if I did, I couldn't tell you. I'll be working my way through the documents at the FBI for a while. One box at a time."

"Ugh!"

"My thoughts exactly."

They both took a long pull on their drinks and stared at the rest of the cold pizza.

After Ag left, Merit wanted another glass of wine, but forced herself go to into her office and work on the John and Ariana Sanderson file. She reasoned that Betty could do a lot to keep the file moving while she worked on the McDonald case, but only if she got the file setup and the work started.

She reviewed a rather lengthy email from Ariana Sanderson, the notes and lists that the couple had given her in their initial meeting, and a Google map she had requested from Val showing the location of the property on St. Elmo. When she clicked on the map attached to Val's email, it opened to a satellite view of a large tract of land about the same size as the new car dealership which was right next door to the studio. She looked around the satellite map. There were two large warehouses, three parking lots, a covered metal storage area, and an open field that looked like it had rusted metal, rebar, tin, and broken-down equipment piled all around.

Merit made a list of questions for the Sandersons, bullet points in a list, and notes to herself for possible negotiation later. She then drafted a memo, attached it to an email, and sent it to the L.A. firm representing AmFlix, the lessee. Putting the ball in the L.A. law firm's court would allow her to work on the McDonald case while they took their turn on the lease. She hoped they could go back and forth for a while before she was required to have meetings or dig into documents further, requiring more time than she had at the moment.

After taking a potty break, Merit sorted through her IN box. She knew that Betty would check it in the morning and did not want to slow the office's workflow, not to mention suffering Betty's joking admonishments. She found the usual daily mail and a few letters that she quickly signed and put into the OUT box. At the bottom of the stack was a bridal magazine, *Love Knot*, with a Post-it note sticking out the side, bearing a question mark in red ink. On the cover was a sixty something-year-old woman with lovely gray hair in a vintage white brocade suit sporting a matching pillbox hat with veil. Merit flipped to the marked page and found a photoshoot of the cover model in various wedding attire, all focused on the mature bride.

Guilt swept over Merit as she realized it had been months since Betty had asked her to be her matron of honor and she had done nothing to assist with the wedding. Merit had introduced Betty and her fiancé, Bob Tom Jakes, at the Austin Country Club, during a golf outing, when the firm was representing a young golfer working toward the PGA Tour. Betty and Bob Tom had become inseparable since that day, sharing their quirky sense of humor and swapping unlimited Texana quotes.

Merit was happy for the couple, but with all the sadness in San Antonio and Mayor Clover still missing, Merit had completely dropped the ball. She took out a fat red Sharpie and circled two of the outfits. One was a periwinkle-colored suit with lace appliqué around the collar and wrists, and the other was an off-white tea-length dress with a full skirt and fifties vibe. Both would look flattering on Betty. Next, Merit drew a heart around the question mark on the Post-it note and put the magazine in the OUT box along with the correspondence.

It was the first time she had felt lighthearted in months. "Time to go home. Who knows what will happen tomorrow."

22

The next night, Ag and Merit met again. This time at Ag's request, at Opa on South Lamar, for a nightcap and to recap the day's events. The writer's hangout was furnished indoors with grandma furniture and outdoors with eclectic picnic tables and patio sets. Merit waited in a corner at the back of the main room, seated on an upholstered settee beside a wooden trunk turned into a coffee table, and sipped a glass of red wine. She'd placed a frosty mug of draft beer for Ag on the coffee table beside a stack of books and puzzles provided for customers' enjoyment. Ag entered through the back door and joined Merit by sitting in an overstuffed chair, his long legs stretched out across from her. He looked at the beer and smiled. "Hey, thanks."

"Hey yourself. Couldn't stay away from me for a single day?"

Ag grinned and batted his curly lashes at her, totally unaware that women around the room were admiring him. "Guess not. But seriously, I called because I've got a complication with the case."

Merit took a sip. "This entire case is going to be complicated, might as well start now."

Ag nodded. "There are so many moving parts and participants, I hope I can keep them all straight."

Merit smiled at him. "I'm sure you won't have any trouble. Your role will be minimal. You'll do the great job you always do."

Ag set down the mug on a coaster that said: *Get your facts first, then you can distort them as you please. Mark Twain.*

"Well."

Merit looked fully into his face. "Well, what?"

"I need a little help with the minimal role stuff."

"What do you mean? My job is going through the documents, and I can't share them with you."

Ag shifted in his seat. "I know. That's what I want to talk to you about. The only private thing you've asked me to do so far is to unofficially snoop around about Duke. The SAPD files have been distributed to everyone and are part of the court record and that's all I've seen in your office, so no conflict there."

Merit sipped her wine. "You're making me nervous, Ag. What are you getting at?"

"Jerry Webb has asked me to be his investigator on the McDonald case. I worked for him a few years ago, thanks to your referral, and he's asked me to start right away."

"Well, as you know, I can't share unredacted information with him, so if you work for him, I can't share it with you. It's a sticky situation. We need to avoid any appearance of impropriety. Judge Ginsberg may not approve."

"Jerry's sent his team selections to the judge and included me as investigator. I haven't billed you for any time yet. I'd have to go through the SAPD documents for him as well, so that's not a conflict. I can switch over to his team without any issues, but the discussions between you and me would have to end tonight."

Merit took a sip. "No more wine and beer together for a while?"

"That's about the size of it."

"I really don't have a lot left for you to do. I think it would be great to have you on the full case. I don't blame him for asking you. Did you tell him you'd already talked to me about the file?"

"Yes. I fully described the scope of work to date, except for the skinny on Duke. He informed the judge, and it appears we're good to go. This way, I'll know everything by the end of the trial. If I work for you, I'm limited."

Merit looked pensive and thought of Jerry. *You won't know everything.*

Ag started to speak. Merit interrupted him, "Yes, great. Let's give this no-good terrorist bastard a full and fair trial with the best people on the case. Correction. Alleged no-good terrorist bastard. You have my blessings."

They clinked glasses, then slumped back into the puffy furniture and went quiet.

23

J erry Webb climbed out of his car at the site of the former market in San Antonio. He stood beside a chain link fence on the end farthest from the memorial site. Bulldozers, cranes, and other noisy dirt movers worked around a large pile of rubble, making the old disappear and the new come to life. Months of cleanup and sanitation had rendered the site similar to any other construction zone, but it wasn't the same at all. The lost souls spoke to him as he looked at the excavation being performed on the land. He wondered how the victims would feel about the man he was defending who was accused of their loved one's tragic deaths.

Jerry walked down the fence line on the south side of the site. It was covered with photographs of those lost. Flowers and notes were pushed through the fence. A young girl and her mother removed a spray of dead flowers beneath the picture of a middle-aged man and replaced them with a fresh bouquet. Even now. No one had forgotten. No one had moved on.

Jerry felt a presence behind him that was not in the normal flow of pedestrians on the sidewalk. He turned to see Lyle

Ryder of the *Washington Times*. Lyle had on a pair of designer jeans and a T-shirt that said: *Tell the truth—You'll feel better.*

Jerry didn't smile. "Are you following me?"

"Yes, and no. I'm down here at least once a week. Keeps me moving on the story."

"I got your messages. Couldn't call you back. Attorney/client privilege and all that jazz."

"Right, but there are a few things not protected. Let me buy you a couple of tacos and a beer."

Jerry shook his head. "Why don't you just publish your story? There's plenty out there in the public domain."

"I need corroboration on a few key things, and, as you said, you never called me back."

"That's refreshing, Lyle. Lack of factual data hasn't stopped many reporters lately."

Lyle smiled. "Reward me for my ethics with something I can use?"

Jerry didn't smile back. "What are you sure of?"

"The bombing occurred on a happy Texas spring day in May. Innocents were walking around. No one saw the duffel bag. So many tourists in San Antonio with luggage for Cinco de Mayo, so forth and so on."

Jerry nodded. "Right. But, if someone had seen the bag and called it in, it would probably have been too late anyway."

Lyle nodded. "True. The security guard was missing from his post and a door was accessible. It was unlocked or the bomber had a key. He probably wouldn't have taken time to break in. He would have been seen."

Jerry turned. "Then boom!"

Lyle jumped. "Very funny. Later that day, while everyone was looking for terrorists, an anonymous tip gets called in to the SAPD. The caller says there is suspicious behavior around a self-storage facility in Helotes, a suburb on the west side of San

Antonio. Turns out the unit is rented to your client, Bobby Ray McDonald."

Jerry nodded. "As you probably know, there's no video to show who actually rented the unit."

"I do know that. But, it's very convenient that SAPD also gets a tip that McDonald is on I-10 and notifies the FBI, who takes McDonald away. SAPD happily hands the case off to the FBI as they're out of their league with bombings and terrorists."

Jerry nodded. "Happy to wipe their hands of the matter."

Lyle looked incredulous. "According to my police sources, McDonald said he knows nothing of the unit and no idea what was stored there. As you said, no video to show who actually rented the unit."

Jerry's head swiveled on his neck. "What sources? You have police sources?"

Lyle didn't take the bait. "My guess, the prosecution will say that's because the storage facility rented the place for cash to the bomber, Walsh, on behalf of McDonald. Convenient because he, being a bomber, blew himself up at the market and can't confirm or deny that he rented the storage building for his own use or anyone else's."

"Sounds good." Jerry watched a large piece of machinery move around the site, scooping and dumping debris.

Lyle nodded. "There's no evidence of bomb-making materials in that storage unit according to the police who investigated on the day of the tip."

Jerry blinked in the sun. "So, that moves the ball even further from my client."

Lyle nodded. "If the bomb wasn't constructed there. Doesn't change anything, he could have assembled it elsewhere. But why do your client's cell phone LUDs show repeated calls to Walsh leading up to and on the day of the bombing?"

Jerry looked at him with suspicion. "Do they now? How did you get those?"

Lyle seemed to mentally strategize a bit before he responded. "Give me a little credit and answer the question."

Jerry grimaced. "No comment."

Lyle grew agitated. "You think Merit Bridges is going to be able to get what you need from the FBI? They think she's naïve and ineffective."

Jerry became equally agitated. "I know her to be otherwise. I have nothing on the record for you, and it's not my intention to answer any of your questions. But thanks for the information."

A large dirt mover started loading a dump truck and the noise overwhelmed their voices.

Jerry walked back to his car, leaving Lyle in the cacophony behind him holding his notebook.

24

Agent Duke was in the conference room at the Live Oak Federal campus the first morning of Merit's scheduled review of the secret FBI documents. The receptionist closed the door behind her and left them alone in the windowless sterile environment.

Duke looked up from a stack of papers on the desk. "Good morning, Merit."

Merit sat at the other end of the table as far from him as possible. "Morning, Agent Duke. I'll have more room to spread out down here."

Duke's lips curled up in an almost smile. "Call me Archie, please. I'm not staying. Sit where you like."

Merit nodded, grabbed a file box sitting in the middle of the table and pulled it toward her.

Duke remained seated. "Just a quick reminder, we've filed a copy of the confidentiality agreement with the court. There's a cafeteria across campus that closes at two. They serve a nice lunch."

Merit looked up. "Do I have a key to this room?"

Duke handed her a piece of paper with two phone numbers on it. "The receptionist will let you in and out any time between eight and five. You can stay here after five, as late as you'd like, but once you leave the building, the door will lock and you can't return. There are security guards who roam the campus all night. Here's a number if you'd like to be escorted to your car after dark."

Merit looked at the page. "What's the second number?"

"That's my mobile. Call at any hour if the documents should be in jeopardy or if anyone tries to get information from you or interfere with the case."

Merit pondered who might try to interfere. "I've been thinking, why doesn't the FBI redact the agents' names and identifying information and give the documents directly to defense counsel?"

"The judge wants an independent third party to decide what is and is not necessary to the defense. He thinks a lawyer's eye might find things to help McDonald. You'll see when you get into the documents. We are counting on your discretion, and may I remind you, you've taken an oath to protect this information from being revealed."

"As you've repeatedly said. Don't worry about it. You have your rules, but the law is my master."

"Regardless, if you need any help, or have any questions, let me know."

"Yeah, thanks. I'm sure I can manage."

"If you should feel threatened or pushed to reveal these secrets, I can protect you."

Merit's head jerked up. "Pushed or threatened by whom?"

Duke grinned just a bit. "Just keep it in mind."

25

Duke met Tank in the woods outside of Waco on Highway 84 near Gatesville. They pulled into an old picnic area with a couple of decaying wooden tables nestled between a grove of live oak and cedar trees. The men backed their SUVs together, jumped out, and opened both hatches. Duke pulled a green camo-colored footlocker over to the back edge of his SUV and opened it.

Tank peeked in. "Ooh wee!"

Duke smiled. "Nice, right?"

Tank lifted a Glock 17 handgun from a stack in the footlocker. There were about two dozen in the box, with packing straw providing a nest for transport.

"Where in the hell did you get these?"

"From a Federal Bureau of Alcohol, Tobacco, Firearms, and Explosives' sting operation. But, you can get the convertors online from China. Really cheap. Less than a hundred bucks each. All of these have been altered to become fully automatic. The gadget turns any ordinary pistol into a machine gun. Continuous fire with a single pull of the trigger."

"God almighty!"

"Just don't get caught with it. Possession is a federal offense. ATF thinks thousands have been imported. They're trying to crack down, but good luck with that!"

Tank held the pistol, gingerly moving it from hand to hand. "Same as a bump stock for a rifle?"

Duke pointed. "Exactly. That's a high-capacity magazine with twenty-two rounds."

Tank admired the weapon in his hand, then pointed it at a gnarly cedar and pretended to site it in. He put his finger on a switch on the rear of the pistol. "What's this?"

"Convertor switch. Makes it a machine gun with one flip of the thumb."

"Sweet. These for me?"

"Yep. No serial numbers. Take them out to the militia. Do some training. Should keep the crew busy and happy for a few more weeks. Toys for boys."

Tank smiled and moved the footlocker from Duke's SUV into his hatch. "Playtime."

26

Ag arrived at the Austin Police Department downtown and asked to see Chaplain. After a short wait, Ag checked his gun in a locker provided for such purpose and lumbered down the long hall to Chaplain's desk.

After a fist bump between the two and a quick catch up on personal things, Chaplain changed his tone. "What are you working on now?"

"I'm assisting in the McDonald defense. I was wondering if you could help me out with a couple of things."

"I don't envy you that. Very unpopular case. What do you need?"

Ag adjusted his posture. "First thing, have you had any word on Mayor Thibodeaux? You know Merit Bridges and Clover are good friends."

Chaplain trusted Ag completely and often shared information with him that he might not reveal to just anyone. They'd been in many situations where their lives were in the other's hands. It had cemented a bond that allowed for confidential sharing.

"Nothing directly on point with Mayor Thibodeaux, but we did get some information about the security guard who let the van into Mayor Sincero's gated community. He disappeared the day of the assassination, but his body was found a few days ago near Waco. We're sharing intel with SAPD about the two kidnappings. We assume they're connected, and we assume they have something to do with somebody's domestic terrorist agenda."

"Aren't there a lot of encampments and militant sites in the woods around Waco?"

"Right, but that's a big area. It could be attached to some militia or just a good place to dump a body. Homeland Security is looking into it, but the FBI has lead on the investigations and they're sharing nada, nothing, big zero."

"There's an FBI agent that Merit Bridges is working with on the case, Archibald Duke, Archie Duke. Have any background on him?"

"I know he's special agent in charge of the federal part of the investigation, but I haven't met with him. Word around the agencies is that he's a real hard ass, but a patriot and very committed to his work."

Ag scratched his chin. "Any funny business?"

"I heard one off-the-record thing. He was cited at Quantico for supposedly roughing up a Muslim prisoner. Seems the guy got loose of his cuffs and attacked Duke. Prisoner said Duke unsecured him and attacked him. It was one of those he said/he said, so it stopped there. No charges were filed, and of course, I wouldn't know if there was a reprimand in his file or not."

"Well, if he's in charge of the biggest bombing ever to occur in Texas, he must be in someone's good graces."

"You'd think."

✶

Ag and Merit met at the Saxon Pub on South Lamar. It was dark inside, even though the sun hadn't yet set. The live music stage was empty except for a roadie setting up for the night by bringing in a drum set through the doggie door behind the performing area. The jukebox was playing Hayes Carll singing "Sake of the Song."

Merit was tucked into a booth at the back drinking a Tito's Margarita on the rocks. Ag picked up a bottle of 512 beer at the bar, looked around, strolled over, and sat.

Merit smiled, then said, "This has to be our last meeting. You're not supposed to know what I know, and I don't want anyone assuming you're taking information from me to Jerry that isn't FBI approved."

"I know. This is my last task for you for a while. You asked me to check around about Duke and Mayor Clover. I met with Chaplain and he gave me an earful, as Betty would say."

"Oh yeah?"

"Seems there may be militant activity around Waco and south of Dallas. Homeland Security is looking into it. Clover could have been taken by them."

"Why do they think that?"

"The man from the guard shack at Mayor Sincero's gated community was found dead in the woods up there. No sign of any encampment, at least not so far."

Merit took a gulp of wine to steady her nerves. "And Clover?"

"No sign of Clover, but Chaplain hasn't given up hope and you shouldn't either. Why would they take her instead of just shooting her like Mayor Sincero if they didn't need her for something?"

Merit took a sip of her drink. "I don't know which is worse."

Ag patted her hand. "Stay calm. I'll keep you posted."

Merit sat back against the upholstery and let out a big breath of air. "Okay, what about Duke?"

"Duke was involved in an incident of violence against a minority. Duke wasn't cleared of wrongdoing, but he was moved from international terrorism to domestic terrorism. Sort of a demotion, but he's worked his way back up. He spends a lot more time here in Texas than in Virginia these days."

"So nothing definitive."

"Seems so. Chaplain says he'll let me know if anything else comes to light."

Merit nodded. "There's something about him that's just not right."

"Trust your gut."

27

In response to Lyle Ryder's admonition, Jerry went to the Travis County medical examiner's office. It was not an official act on behalf of the firm, but Jerry hoped no one asked that question directly. He had in his briefcase a power-of-attorney from Robert Riley's wife, in the event that the information he needed wasn't forthcoming. After a brief wait, he was escorted down a long white hallway lined with metal doors to a small office.

A friendly-looking man of about fifty in a white lab coat, carrying a file and a plastic bag, pointed to a chair. "I'm Lawrence Addison, the medical examiner. What can I do for you?"

"I'm Jerry Webb of Alistair, Riley & Webb. I'm here about a deceased member of our firm, Robert Riley. The family has authorized me to take possession of his belongings and to obtain information about his death."

The M.E. handed Jerry the plastic bag. "His wife called and said you'd be coming in. There wasn't much. Here are his wedding ring and watch. He was found at home, so there was no wallet or car key on his person."

"Thank you. I'll see that the family gets these. Can you tell me anything about the cause of death?"

"We deemed it a probable suicide."

"Probable? What determines if it was a suicide?"

"The evaluation was inconclusive. Since we weren't sure from the condition of the body, we looked at his history of depression and medication and ruled it a probable suicide. I notified the police and the FBI."

Jerry nodded. "I was told by the family that he hadn't had any issues in sometime. I saw him frequently at the firm and he seemed very excited about a new case he'd been assigned in federal court."

"Sometimes suicide victims hide things from their friends and family, but, as I said, inconclusive."

Jerry scratched his chin and thought, *Sounds like guessing.*

The M.E. closed the file he'd been consulting.

Jerry nodded. "I understand. He didn't leave a note?"

"None that was turned over to us or the crime lab. As you probably know, he was found hanging in his garage with a belly full of Mexican food and margaritas. A chair was tipped over near the body, and the crime lab found no fingerprints."

Jerry recoiled.

"Sorry, forgot myself. I'm sorry for your loss."

"It's okay. No fingerprints? Not even the deceased's or the family's prints?"

The M.E. flipped open the folder again. "None near the body. It was unusual, but not impossible as crime scenes go. I suggest you speak with the FBI if you have further questions."

"Why would they have information that you don't?"

"No reason. They've taken a special interest in the case. I guess because of the link to the bombing."

Jerry was a good judge of character. He looked long and hard at Dr. Addison. His instincts told him the good doctor was telling the truth as he knew it to be.

28

Ag kicked back on his sofa at his home in Briarcliff, about thirty miles west of Austin. His place was a masculine combination of a house and a cabin, with his carpentry handiwork displayed in most rooms. Ag looked out over the cactus out the window at Lake Travis, happy that the rain had brought up the lake level. He sipped a SOCO Home Brew craft beer while checking the game on the television while muted. Between plays, he leaned forward and worked on his laptop set up on his coffee table.

Several YouTube videos, as well as NNN coverage, rewarded Ag's search for 'San Antonio bombing security guard.' Most of the videos consisted of viewpoints of conspiracy theorists who accused Jose Perez of being absent from his post in order to facilitate access for Walsh, the bomber.

Ernest Anguish and several other NNN reporters, as well as those on MSNNN and NBS, listed interviews with Jose Perez's family members who pointed out that forensic evidence indicated Jose's innocence. He had been blown up in the blast and his gun was found out of its holster. Because of this, it was assumed that Jose came upon the bomber and tried to stop him. Nothing was certain, however, as there was little evidence left to investigate.

Jose Perez's family and friends described him as a hard-working ex-cop, who'd give the shirt off his back for a friend and would never violate the trust of his fellow officers. Ag made a note to go to SAPD and get their take on Jose's possible participation.

Ag picked up his iPhone and called Chaplain, at the Austin Police Department.

"Hey, Chaplain. How's it hangin'? Could I bother you for a quick favor?"

The deep voice on the other end of the line answered. "Another one? How many does that make?"

Ag laughed. He knew they were even on the number of favors each had done for the other, if they could even be counted, from years of cooperation and friendship. "I'm calling as chief investigator for Jerry Webb on the McDonald trial."

"So, we're on the record. What can I do to help?"

"I'd like to swing by and talk with you again soon, now that my role is official. But, tomorrow I need to go over to SAPD and get the skinny on Jose Perez and their take on the bombing. He was the security guard at the market. He died at the scene, but there was some question about why he was away from his post. He was a cop so it was probably a coincidence, or the bomber waited for him to leave."

Chaplain cleared his throat. "There are bad cops, but since he's dead, he probably wasn't one of them."

"Probably, but I'd like to talk to someone over there, without being labeled the enemy, since I work for the defense counsel. Do you know anyone who might give me some insight?"

"I'll make some calls and text you a name."

"Thanks, Chaplain."

"You owe me."

"Always."

Ag arrived at the SAPD downtown station and went to the desk sergeant. "I'm here to see Detective Merrill Haas."

"He's expecting you, but you'll have to check your weapon before I can allow you through to his office." The officer pointed to a door marked 'Lockers.'

"No problem. Thanks."

Ag put his weapon, keys, and other metal into a small basket and went through the metal detector. He grabbed the basket with his belongings, then entered the locker area for visiting officers. He restocked his pockets with his personal items and placed his weapon in a small cubicle that looked more like a safety deposit box than a locker. He then proceeded through an inside door marked 'SAPD PERSONNEL ONLY'.

Ag found himself in a bull pen of cubicles with police men and women working diligently. Each partition contained a desk with computer and rolling chair. Most had sticky notes and wanted pictures tacked all over the walls of the dividers. Ag followed the directions he'd been given to the workspace of Detective Merrill Haas.

Ag extended his hand. "Hello, Detective. I'm Ag Malone. Chaplain at APD is a friend. He said you might be able to help me out."

Detectives in other cubicles looked up at Ag, saw that he was with Haas, and put their eyes back on their work. Haas pointed to a chair at the nearest empty cubicle. "I've been expecting you. Bring that chair over and have a seat."

Ag rolled the chair over, sat down, and tried to appear

friendly. He saw a picture of Haas with several musicians, including Gary Clark Jr. "You a music fan? You know he lives in Austin."

"Yeah. I've seen him perform a couple of times. Once with Eric Clapton. Unbelievable. Best guitarist in the biz in my opinion."

"I'm a big Stevie Ray Vaughan fan, but Gary Clark is close. You play?"

"A bit. Not very good."

Ag smiled.

"Did Chaplain tell you what I'm doing over here?"

Haas sized him up. "He said you had some questions about the bombing and Jose Perez."

"Right. I'm not trying to disparage him in any way, but I just need to tie up this loose end. I want to find out if he was connected to our client and, if not, mark him off the list. Everyone who knew him seemed to think the world of him."

Haas leaned back in his creaky chair. "I'm one of them. He was one of the finest cops I've ever known. Retired about two years ago with a full pension."

"Did anyone look into his finances? Any possible point of contact with the terrorist cell? Sorry. You know I have to ask."

"No offense taken. I'd do the same. He was pulling in hours as a guard at the market to help put his grandson through college. We checked every contact and bank account for the last three years. Found nothing. FBI did their own review and reported the same."

"Thanks, good to know."

Haas nodded. "I'd bet he wasn't involved."

Haas looked at Ag with an 'anything else' expression on his face.

"One more thing. When the two co-conspirators were

found and killed in the trailer park, who was trying to arrest them? How did all that go down?"

"Bad scene. Even shot the dog. SAPD wasn't involved in that. After we picked up the family at their home and alerted the FBI, they took over. I was told they'd found the bombers through McDonald or his family. When the agents went to pick them up at the trailer park, they were met with lethal force and returned fire."

"What happened then?"

"We got calls from the neighbors around Eastgate. Dicey area. We sent officers in, but FBI had the trailer and half the street cordoned off. Said they didn't need any help. We were glad not to have the headache."

Ag rubbed his chin. "Do you have any type of report or written information on that?"

Haas clicked around on his computer. "FBI is required to file an incident report since it happened in Bexar County. It's not much, but I'll print it out for you."

"Thanks. Do you have any reason to suspect anything hinky about it?"

"Other than the fact that a bucket load of FBI agents couldn't arrest two men without shooting them and a dog? No."

While Ag was in San Antonio, he decided to tick off another task on his list and check out the self-storage facility where McDonald had allegedly rented a unit. He drove out I-10 to Helotes, a nice suburb west of San Antonio proper, and located the small facility on the edge of the business district. It consisted of about seventy-five storage units surrounded by a chain link fence that was partially rusted.

As Ag opened the door to the office at the front of the property, a small Border Collie ran out and onto a small patch of grass near the gates. Ag tried to catch the door, but it swung open and banged the wall. "Sorry, didn't mean to let him out."

A handsome young man with shoulder length dreadlocks stood up behind the Formica topped counter. "No worries, mon. Marley, he knows where to go."

"I'm here about the storage unit rented to Bobby Ray McDonald."

"Oh no, mon. I been so tired of that dude and all the trouble he cause."

Ag frowned. "I just need to know if you remember renting the unit to him."

"No, mon. He rent it online. I'm only here part-time. This place is a shithole. Mostly the body shop down the road store they parts here."

"I'm trying to find out about ID for renting the unit."

"We don't ask for ID, just credit card number. You pay, you rent."

"How do they get the codes and unit number?"

"All that go out in email. They bring they own lock."

"No driver's license or anything?"

"No, mon. We figure they put stuff in and pay for the space, they not trying to run away."

"What about security?"

The manager huffed at Ag's questions. "Do you realize how many people asks me these same things?"

Ag smiled. "Sorry, man, but it's my job."

The manager grabbed a ring of keys. "Okay, mon. Best if I show you." The manager rounded the counter, escorted Ag outside, locked the office door and pointed around the side.

The manager drove and Ag rode shotgun, in a six-seater golf cart, from the office to a metal ground-level building at the rear of the facility. Marley rode in the back seat, with his tongue hanging out to catch the air.

As they left the office area, Ag pointed to a CCTV camera on the side of the office building. "Anything on that camera?"

"No, mon. We add it the month after the bombing. We had camera on the front gate at the time, but it won't identify nobody if a person want to hide they face. Probably why most people rent here. New CCTV system cost us a fortune. For what? The owners think another terrorist will be by soon?"

Ag laughed. "Got it."

The manager parked and pointed to an orange and white metal building with a long row of roll-up doors. "That's the unit in the middle over there. The one with crime scene tape on it. It's empty and it's been a year, but we still can't get clear to rent it out."

Ag climbed from the cart and walked over. "Is it locked?"

"No, mon, but you can't go in there. See the sticker and tape. It's a crime scene, or so they say. It just as empty as it was on the day of the bombing."

Ag took out a court order and showed it to the manager. "Since I'm on the defense team, I have the authority to investigate all of the elements of the case. You can keep that for your records. I have lots of copies."

The manager looked impressed. "Well, okay, mon. Knock yourself out."

Ag rolled up the metal door and looked inside. The unit appeared to be about ten by twenty feet and, as promised, was totally empty except for a few dust bunnies in the back corners.

"As you said, nothing here."

"Irie."

29

B ack in Austin, Ag met with Jerry at Coopers Old Time Pit Bar-B-Cue on Congress near Jerry's downtown office. Both men ordered brisket with all the fixins and big ass iced teas. After they settled at the end of a long table and took a few bites, Ag opened a file folder marked LUDs.

"Per your request, I've organized all the calls to and from McDonald's smartphone. I went back two years, just to make sure I didn't miss any patterns or hot spots of activity."

Jerry took a bite of pickle spear and nodded.

"Last year, nothing unusual with regard to the other three members of the terrorist cell."

Jerry stopped him. "Alleged terrorist cell."

"Right. I assume the prosecution is going to use these same phone records to connect all four co-conspirators. I also assume the FBI used them to see if there were any other members of the group that they may have missed."

Jerry washed down a big bite of beef with iced tea. "I assume the same. Continue, please."

"So, year before last, activity between McDonald, Walsh,

and the other two began slowly around late summer. By January, before the bombing, McDonald and Walsh were talking almost every day. The other two dead terrorists were contacted occasionally up until the month before the bombing, then the calls heated up there too."

Jerry swallowed. "Anything else of interest?"

"Yes. There is a burner phone number, that we obviously can't trace, showing calls for the entire two years I researched. It's no longer in service. The calls were every Wednesday night and Sunday morning, just like church, for eighteen months. Then, around the time of the bombing, they increased to every day, sometimes several times a day."

"No ideas about who that might be?"

"None. Might be the head of the militia or other extremist organization or might be another co-conspirator. Might be his mama."

Jerry looked at a few of the pages. "So, if you're a terrorist and you're going to bomb a market, why wouldn't you buy all burner phones and try to keep down the evidence of the co-conspirators' interaction?"

Ag took a bite of brisket wrapped in white bread and washed it down with a big gulp of tea. "I was wondering the same thing. Three possibles come to mind. First, it's easy for the FBI to get a warrant for information about cells through which calls are routed. So, the information could be cobbled together that way even with burner phones since all four of them had houses where they lived under their names. In other words, they weren't hiding out in safe houses."

"More difficult, but still doable. And the other reasons?"

"The terrorists aren't terrorists and they were just talking about soccer."

Jerry snorted. "I think we can take that one off the list. The third idea?"

"They didn't care if someone knew they were talking because either they didn't plan to survive it, or the Feds were already watching them and they knew it."

"I've been thinking the same thing."

Ag wiped his mouth with a paper towel he'd ripped off a spool in the middle of the table.

Jerry snacked on a pickle. "Time to visit the client again."

"Sounds about right."

Merit and Jerry sat in the usual interview room across from McDonald and eyeballed their client. As usual, McDonald said little. He did not greet them or shake hands, just slumped in his chair and looked at the table before him.

Jerry opened his briefcase and took out several printed pages showing the usage details from McDonald's phone as provided by Ag. He placed the documents on the metal table and flipped to the pages he wanted to discuss. "These are your cell phone records for the months preceding, and the day of, the bombing."

McDonald didn't flinch.

Merit pointed to the pages. "It's clear that you spoke to the two dead co-conspirators over five times a day toward the end, right before the bombing. These are their phone numbers."

Jerry picked up the thread. "Is there an explanation I can use in court for that? Did you work with them? Were you sharing a hobby together, like sports or boating?"

Merit almost scoffed, but held it in.

McDonald looked at the pages. "We were just friends. We talked every day because that's what we did."

Merit looked incredulous. "Men don't talk to their friends half a dozen times a day without a reason."

McDonald stared at her. "We did. That's my reason."

Jerry drilled down on his client with his gaze, obviously waiting for further details.

McDonald blinked first. "Okay, you need a reason? We were hunting buddies."

Merit jumped in. "Do you have any evidence of hunting trips? Receipts? Photos?"

"I might be able to stir something up."

Jerry then pointed to the burner phone number on the list with calls on church days. "Who does this number belong to?"

"I can't remember." McDonald was obviously lying.

Merit pressed. "You spoke to someone every Wednesday and Sunday for almost two years, and you can't remember who that was?"

"Oh, that. It must have been my cousin."

Jerry chimed in. "Where does your cousin live?"

"Outside Little Rock. He has a burner phone."

Jerry didn't seem to buy it. "What's your cousin's name? The number is disconnected. The last call was on the day of the bombing. Any reason your cousin would suddenly stop using the phone that day?"

"Well, maybe it was someone else."

Merit sounded exasperated. "Maybe?"

McDonald didn't respond.

Jerry tried another tact. "We're your lawyers. Anything you say to us stays with us. I can't represent you if you don't tell me what happened. What are you hiding and why?"

"I never asked for a lawyer. The court gave you to me without my permission when that other lawyer died. I don't owe you an explanation or anything else. And her," McDonald pointed to Merit, "she's just a tool for the FBI. They won't give her anything they don't want her to see."

"How do you know that?" Merit asked.

McDonald slumped further.

Jerry frowned. "You'll fry if you don't help yourself."

McDonald stood up but gave away his composure when he wobbled on weak knees. "I'll fry anyway. Guard!"

"Wait. Sit down. We can discuss this."

"No. Guard. Guard!"

30

Ag arrived at the police vehicle impound in San Antonio. He checked in with the uniformed guard through a small window beside the double-wide automatic gates that secured the property.

"I'm Albert "Ag" Malone with the law firm of Alistair, Riley & Webb in Austin. I believe you're expecting me. The firm is attorney of record for Bobby Ray McDonald. I'm their investigator."

The policeman grimaced at Ag, when he identified his client, and pushed a clipboard through the window. "Got ID? Sign here."

Ag showed his investigator's license, gave the guard a copy of the court order, signed the paper on the clipboard as instructed, and waited for directions.

"Drive through the gates, then back to the far left end of the lot. Spot F17. Says here a Hummer." The gates began to swing open.

"Got it." Ag got back in his truck and drove through the gates, followed the directions past dozens of cars in various conditions to the far left, and found a faint painted marker on the concrete, F17.

To Ag's surprise, the car was a Hummer H3. *Not new, but pretty nifty for a butcher.*

Jerry had indicated that McDonald's only skill was what he had learned at his uncle's butcher shop. General Motors had stopped production on the Hummer in 2010, but they were still considered collectable. Ag had heard Jerry Seinfeld took some comedian out for coffee in one. Or was that Jay Leno?

How the hell did McDonald afford that?

Ag looked at the impound report from the SAPD files and confirmed that there was no evidence found in or on the vehicle. He looked in the glove box, but found nothing except for some tissues, a Starbuck's coffee card, and ChapStick. He looked under the seats. Nothing. On the back seat were a couple of books published for teenage girls with ordinary American themes. He examined the area behind the back seat and found the usual emergency road kit and a folded green blanket. Under the blanket was a stack of extremist pamphlets.

Looks like recruiting info. How did SAPD miss that?

He checked the pockets in the rear hatch and found a Glock 17 with an extra clip in a brown paper bag. Ag rechecked the evidence list on the SAPD report. No mention of anything related to extremists or terrorism.

He took out his phone and snapped pictures of all surfaces inside and out, the parking spot number, and the VIN on the windshield. He made extensive notes in his notebook for use in writing up his report for Jerry.

Might as well be thorough.

Ag got in his truck and went back to the front, drove out when the gate opened, parked, and walked back to the window where the uniformed policeman was eating a burger and fries. He had a thirty-two-ounce drink beside him on the window ledge and a bag with an orange and white striped W on it. He held up a finger for Ag to wait while he swallowed.

Ag nodded. "Take your time."

"What else do you need?"

"My SAPD report doesn't show where the car was found. Where did they tow it from?"

The guard stonewalled.

Ag smiled. "Come on, man. It's public record. Don't make me go all the way down to the police station to get what you can tell me here."

The guard looked at his food getting cold, pulled another clipboard hanging from a peg on the wall, and flipped a few pages back over the clip.

"Looks like it was found on Bowie Street, 300 block."

Ag wrote the information down in his notebook and pointed to the burger bag. "Thanks. You know they sold out to a company in Chicago, don't you?"

The guard grunted. "Still good."

"Yep."

Ag got in his truck and headed north on I-35 back to Austin. As he drove, he called Officer Haas at SAPD and put him on speaker.

"Hey, sorry to bother you again. I had something come to light that generated another question."

Haas's voice came through the speaker. "No problem. Shoot."

"The impound report shows that McDonald's car was towed from Bowie Street. I was told that SAPD had taken it at the traffic stop when they arrested McDonald."

Haas grunted. "Some kind of rumor maybe or the press taking a guess. If there was a traffic stop, it wasn't SAPD."

"Is anyone else in Bexar County allowed to do traffic stops without your knowing about it?"

"Nope. We didn't arrest McDonald. The FBI did. Once we picked up McDonald's wife and daughter at their house, we took no further action. The FBI specifically asked us not to. They had jurisdiction and we were squeezed out."

"So, why does the press think that SAPD arrested McDonald at a traffic stop?"

"Don't know, but it wasn't us."

"Did the FBI have a dragnet around the city?"

"It's possible. You'll have to ask them. It would have been outside Bexar County if they did. If they had it inside the county, we'd have been involved, or at least have an incident report on file. We have none."

"Thanks." Ag rang off the call, but his mind kept working. *More secrets in the secret files. Work fast, Merit.*

31

Merit checked in by phone with her office and Betty, then drove north to the Live Oak Federal Campus. She parked in the designated parking lot and hung the security tag she'd been issued on her rearview mirror. She left her phone in the glove box, as she was not allowed to have a camera on campus, and proceeded inside.

The receptionist unlocked the sterile windowless conference room, and Merit continued the tedious work of reviewing and redacting documents from the file box on the table.

On her first visit, she'd found nothing of interest, mostly statements taken by agents from various witnesses at the scene of the bombing. She'd failed to see how that was much more than a duplication of the work by the San Antonio Police Department. She'd already reviewed the SAPD files with Ag that had been sent to hers and Jerry's offices and had found nothing particularly impactful to McDonald's case.

Just the facts. There was a bomb, it blew up. Nothing in those files pointed a finger at the defendant, McDonald, nor was there any exculpatory evidence to help him either. Glaring them all in the face, and the major point of circumstantial evidence for the prosecution, was that all four men were communicating. McDonald, Walsh, and the two dead alleged co-conspirators all had phone calls on their cell phones to each other. Phone calls aren't evidence of guilt, but it added a lot to a circumstantial case.

If anything else was to be found to help or harm McDonald's case, it would be included in the FBI files provided in this room. That made her job even more important in the service of justice.

Merit did a quick scan of the remaining documents in the box. Satisfied that there was nothing new, and not having a phone in the room, she went to the receptionist's desk and asked for Agent Rachel Ward to arrange for the second box.

Merit decided to check-in with her office and grab a bite while the FBI agent swapped out the document boxes. She went out to her car, grabbed her phone, and proceeded to the Campus Cantina, a fast-food counter not much bigger than the breakroom in her office. There were a couple of cafe tables and a bar with three barstools along one wall. She bought a premade chicken fajita salad and an iced tea from a wrinkled Hispanic woman behind the counter, snagged a plastic fork and knife, and perched on one of the barstools to eat and check her email. Satisfied, with a quick scan of correspondence, that nothing needed attention until she returned to her office, she called Betty.

"Hi there. Just checking in. Any messages you didn't send through email?"

She listened to a long one-sided conversation while stuffing her mouth with iceberg lettuce, tomato, and grilled chicken, all doused in buttermilk ranch dressing.

"Okay, I'll run by the office tonight when I leave here. No need to wait for me. Thanks, Betty."

When Merit hung up, she took a sip of her tea and noticed she was not alone. Duke was sitting right behind her at one of the cafe tables, drinking a cup of coffee and looking at his smartphone. Only thing, Merit saw that the screen was black. He wasn't looking at anything. She pretended not to notice him, split her food and recyclable plastic into the appropriate trash bins, and left.

As Merit approached her car to store her iPhone, she saw Duke walk from the Cantina area across the campus toward his car in the parking lot. He appeared to get something out of it, then returned to his office building. He paused beneath a crimson crepe myrtle tree and looked her way. She pretended to be busy, looking for something in the glove box, while she observed him through the windshield.

Merit's armpits prickled and she had a shiver.

He waited. She held her phone up to her ear and moved her lips. She waited.

Merit felt it was becoming obvious she was stalling, so she stowed her phone, locked the car, and walked back toward the building. She desperately wanted to take her Ruger into the conference room with her.

What are you going to do? Shoot him?

When she started up the sidewalk, Duke was gone.

32

Ag and Chaplain met for a beer after work at Scholtz's Beer Garden on San Jacinto in downtown Austin. It was hotter than hell out, so they sat inside at the bar and ordered a couple of draft beers and pretzels the size of frying pans with bier cheese, garlic butter, and Dusseldorf mustard.

Ag took a long draw on his Live Oak Hefeweizen, then wiped the foam from his upper lip. "This McDonald case is stinky. Everywhere I look there's something stinky."

Chaplain dunked his pretzel in the mustard. "Everything around these extremist organizations is questionable."

"What's the difference between an extremist and a terrorist?"

"Hell if I know. What do you mean stinky?"

"Can't talk about specifics, as you know, but there seems to be a lot of false information and conflicting facts around several steps of the arrest."

"What did Haas say? You thinking SAPD screwed something up, or is in on some shenanigans?"

"No. Their actions seem to be pretty cut and dried. The FBI arrested McDonald, but the press thinks SAPD got him."

"Could just be fog of war. What does McDonald say?"

Ag gave Chaplain an I-can't-say look.

"Okay. Has there been an ID of the bombers' organization?"

"No, and I have no idea which group to look at. White supremacists? Posse Comitatus? Boogaloo movement? Garden variety militia?"

Chaplain took a bite of his pretzel sprinkled with big chunks of salt. "White supremacists usually target Blacks, not Hispanics, though not always."

"Right."

"Almost all of the domestic terrorist groups have Nazi-inspired backgrounds."

"That's what my research shows as well. Do you know much about the Oklahoma City bombing?"

"Had a seminar way back when. Timothy McVeigh bombed the Murrah Federal Building in April of 1995. He and Terry Nichols were brought up on murder and conspiracy charges. McVeigh got the death penalty, and Nichols got life in prison."

"Yeah, seems they had a beef with the federal government. Do you understand the motivation of those guys?"

"McVeigh was a disaffected veteran, but that's not the whole story. The case was solved, but investigators never knew the exact origin of the plot or how many people carried it out."

"Did they ever find out if it was a specific group or just a few individuals?"

"The indictment against the two made specific mention of 'others unknown.' The presiding judge urged the FBI and all law enforcement agencies to keep investigating, but the plea seemed to fall on deaf ears."

"The facts of the case must have led the judge to believe there were others involved."

Chaplain grunted. "It would seem so."

"What type of group would you think might want to hurt Hispanics in particular? My research shows that Boogaloo boys wear Hawaiian shirts and are preparing for a second American Civil War."

"Yeah, they call that the boogaloo, the next war. They're into violent uprisings against the federal government or left-wing politics. They think the government is going to take away their guns."

"That doesn't seem to fit our case."

Chaplain nodded. "The Posse Comitatus is far right conspiracy minded, anti-government white Christians for the most part. They, too, think their rights are in danger."

"Aren't they mostly survivalists forming armed militias, like David Koresh in Waco?"

"Right, so that might or might not fit."

Ag drank and thought. "Since this bombing was in San Antonio, on Cinco de Mayo, that seems a fairly particular statement unless they were just targeting a large crowd with low security."

"Doubtful it was nonspecific. These things rarely are. I agree. It was probably racially motivated. Anti-Latino hate crimes are up over twenty percent with all the new anti-immigration politics. Attacks against Muslims peaked in about 2016 when foreign terrorism was the concern. Crimes against Blacks just dropped to about twenty-seven percent, the lowest since the FBI began tracking data. Now, Latinos and transgenders are being targeted."

Ag considered this information. "Political agendas pushed the rise?"

"Seems so. It's a democratization of hate. There is a reshuffling of who's in the crosshairs. My intel shows the targets are people, more than property. That could explain your large crowd attack, especially involving Latino families and kids."

"You think it could have spun out of the white nationalism movement? Who?"

"Pick your haters. Any neo-Nazi or militia group that believes in white supremacy will target anyone who is other than they are. There are a variety of names. American Freedom Party, American Renaissance. American or freedom combined with any other words will do."

"Wouldn't the FBI be tracking these groups and have a bead on the ones that are most radical or become more active or violent?"

"Sure, but the militants hide in the shadows. They watch out for each other, and often one part of the group or cell doesn't know about another cell. That keeps the chatter down online and at the gatherings. They also speak in code to avoid key words on cell phone scanners. It's hard to get a handle on their actions until it's too late."

"Then how did all the participants in the San Antonio bombing get rounded up or killed in less than a day?"

Chaplain took a swig of beer. "Don't know. Sounds like above average police work."

Ag nodded. "Or a miracle."

Chaplain grunted.

33

Jerry ran east along Lady Bird Lake on the hike and bike trail on the south side, away from Austin High School. He didn't think Merit would try to speak with him, now that the trial had officially started, but he didn't want to run into her so he changed his usual pattern.

He ran up the embankment along Barton Springs Road and stopped at South Lamar Boulevard at the traffic light. He ran in place to keep his heart rate up until the light changed and he trotted across Lamar. He turned onto the Pfluger Pedestrian Bridge, named after James D. Pfluger, a notable Austin-area architect who had designed parts of the city's hike and bike trail system.

Tourists took pictures of downtown Austin and the lake from the bridge's unique vantage point. Couples sat on the many park benches dotting the span, over the water, looking toward the city skyline. Several runners used the railing to stretch and prepare for their jog. The activity provided the perfect cover for the hooded runner following Jerry who dodged walkers and gawkers as he picked up speed to match Jerry's pace.

About halfway across, Jerry looked over to a lamppost along the west side and remembered an evening he and Merit had strolled across the bridge when they were dating. They had enjoyed the downtown lights and magical night air as she teased him about being three years younger and, therefore, her boy toy. He'd told her that term required at least a ten-year age difference, but she wouldn't have it. He remembered her laugh and her sparkling blue eyes.

When they stopped at the lamppost for a kiss, it was the first time he'd thought there could be a future for them. Even though his divorce wasn't final, her presence in his life made him hopeful that there could be a better future. He'd actually thought she might be the one. But it wasn't meant to be. Life happened. His nasty divorce and father's death intervened and the thread between them was broken.

As Jerry ran and reminisced, he could feel her softness, her lips pressing against his, her body warm in the tangled sheets after their lovemaking. In his reverie, he never sensed or saw the bald man behind him.

Merit sat on the balcony of her high-rise condo looking out over downtown Austin. Still in her yoga clothes, she had a half empty bottle of a nice red blend on the table before her and a wine glass with a bowl so big a bird could take a bath in it.

The yoga had not relieved her stress. She was full of anxiety and considered calling Ace at school, but her semi-lit condition and motherly instincts to spare him her stress prevailed. Instead, she took a picture of Pepper, Ace's dog, who was sitting at her feet, and posted it on her Instagram page. She was sure

Ace would take a look when he finished his studies, or night out in Houston, or whatever he was doing to make his teenage years fun and meaningful to him. It consoled her that their monthly visit was coming up and she could wait for contact until then.

As the darkness grew and the lights in all the downtown buildings shone brighter, she was swept up in a memory of Jerry when they were dating. She remembered their walk over the Pfluger Pedestrian Bridge after an intimate dinner at The Paggi House, their favorite restaurant. It had since been torn down as part of the high-rise epidemic along South Lamar.

About halfway across the bridge, she and Jerry had stopped at a lamppost along the west side of the bridge and enjoyed the view of the downtown lights and magical night air. She remembered teasing him about his being three years younger and, therefore, her boy toy. When they shared a special kiss at the lamppost, it was the first time she'd thought there could be more than just friendship and sex between them. It was the first time she'd actually considered a real relationship since Tony's suicide.

Merit could feel Jerry's arms around her and his lips on hers as the kiss lingered. It was a moment she'd never forgotten, but their relationship wasn't meant to last. Life happened and it had ended abruptly when his highly publicized divorce followed on the heels of his father's death. Fortunately, their secret remained between them.

She came back to the present, sighed, and nuzzled Pepper's ears.

34

Ag made yet another trip to San Antonio to investigate Bowie Street, the location where McDonald's car was purportedly found. He flipped to the page in his notes where he had written down the location while he was at the impound lot where McDonald's Hummer was stored. He drove to the 300 block, parked on the street, and took pictures of the entire block and all the businesses facing the street. He made a list of the six most likely places that McDonald may have been and started at the north end of the block.

When in doubt, knock on doors.

Ag first went into a custom boot shop and inquired as to whether the clerk remembered seeing McDonald or anyone driving a Hummer on the day of the bombing. Ag showed the clerk a photo of McDonald and also the vehicle. It was a dead end, as the clerk was not working that day and had not been there when they towed the Hummer.

Ag went to the next business, a knitting shop with skeins of yarn displayed in the window. He did not have that business on his list. He decided to skip that venue as unlikely and double back if he didn't find anyone else who was helpful. It went that way for a few more shops until he came to the Posse Restaurant. The neon sign showed 'OPEN,' so he went inside and surveyed the layout. It was a casual place that looked like it had once been a diner. Maybe a Howard Johnson's or an IHOP.

A waiter came over with a menu. "Just one?"

"Not eating today. I'm looking for some information. Were you here when the black Hummer was towed by the police on the day of the bombing?"

"Yes."

"And?"

"And what? You're the second person who's been in here asking about this."

"Yeah? Who else?"

"Some lawyer from Austin."

"Lawyer from Austin? What did you tell him?"

"Just that the guy was in here having breakfast with some other dude. Both the same color—white. Both the same sex—male. Both had the same thing—coffee. Both left at the same time—around 11:00 a.m."

Ag opened the picture of McDonald on his phone and showed it to the waiter. "Was this one of the guys?"

"Yep."

Ag googled a picture of Walsh and showed it to the waiter. "Was this the other guy?"

"Nope. That's the bomber I saw in the news. I'd remember if it was him."

"Was anyone else with them? Did they talk to anyone?"

"No, just me. It was the off time between breakfast and lunch. Hardly anyone was around. I waited on them. Big guy paid and left me a lousy tip as I recall."

"A big guy. Anything else you remember?"

"He had on a suit. Looked like a corporate type. I remember

because not many people wear suits in San Antonio, much less in this neighborhood."

Ag mentally crossed his fingers. "Did you get some CCTV footage from that camera?"

"Yep, but it's gone. Records over every few weeks."

Ag pulled up a State Bar of Texas photo of Robert Riley on his phone. "Was this the lawyer from Austin who asked you these same questions?"

"Yep. That's him. Now, if you want to know anything else, you need to buy something."

"Okay, I will. Just one more thing. Does your manager store anything in the Cloud or have any other copies of that camera footage?"

"Nope, Austin lawyer asked the same thing. He didn't buy anything either. Now, eat or go."

"Why don't I just tip you without eating?" Ag laid a ten-dollar bill on the counter.

"That'll do."

Ag took extra pictures of the Posse Restaurant and the street in that part of the block. He returned to his F-150 and called Jerry.

"Hey, I found the spot where McDonald's Hummer was parked. Seemed he met a guy for coffee the day of the bombing. No CCTV footage."

"Militia type?"

"No, suit and tie type."

Jerry responded on the other end. "That's odd. I wonder what was so special about that meeting?"

"Doesn't appear they met anyone else, just coffee and a chat, then they left."

"Okay, write it up and I'll see if I can get Merit …"

"One more thing. The waiter identified a picture of Robert Riley as an attorney from Austin who came in asking the same questions that I asked today."

"What?"

"He was obviously following the same clues that we are."

"You think Riley found out something that raised a red flag?"

"Don't know. Just keeping you informed."

Jerry replied. "I'd hate to think that's what led to his death. We still don't know if it was suicide or foul play."

"Hmm."

35

There could not have been a better or worse time for Merit to go out of town for the weekend, but she hadn't seen Ace in a month, and it was time for their scheduled mother/son visit. Seeing him at least every three to four weeks was a rule she never broke. Phone and Skype only took them so far in their relationship until it was time for a face-to-face. She was never exactly sure how he was doing until she could look him in the eyes.

She consulted with Judge Ginsberg by phone, and he told her that if she was going to leave town for a weekend to do it before the trial started.

Merit went into the garage at her condo, packed her SUV with a small suitcase, Pepper Dog, and a tin of Betty's world-famous lemon squares and headed to Houston. In the hatch was a large box of files that Betty had put together for her to review on her not-so-leisurely vacation.

Ace had been boarding in Houston at Rawson-Saunders School for Dyslexic Students for over two years. It was an adjustment, living apart, but there was no school in Austin that came close to what the Houston school could do for him. Truthfully, Betty had often reminded Merit that she was such a workaholic, it was better for her to see him for concentrated periods of time rather than missing dinner and leaving him at loose ends most nights. Merit thought Betty was just trying to make her feel better about a hard parenting choice.

The plan was to spend a long weekend in Port Aransas. Merit intended to work each morning, at their beach house, as Ace did his usual teenage sleep-in until noon. It seemed he was always catching up on rest at his age, or maybe he just liked sleeping in his own room at the Port Aransas house.

Pepper Dog was laying on the black leather passenger seat next to her, snoozing away. Merit drove along, listening to the Paul English Quartet, a small ensemble jazz band out of Houston, on XM radio. She'd heard them with Joy and Tucker at the Mucky Duck last time she'd visited Ace and stayed with her friends.

She only had to make one stop on the way for gas and a potty break for herself and Pepper. Merit exited the freeway and drove into Bucc-ee's, the Texas amusement park of gas station/convenience stores. She pulled up to a pump and started the gas, locked the car, and led Pepper by the leash over to a grassy area provided for doggies needing to go.

When she returned to the car, she noticed a bald man she thought was looking at her, but he walked by and entered the store. Merit topped off the tank, pulled the car forward to a parking spot, left the engine running to provide cool air, and locked Pepper inside. She entered the store past meat smokers, fire pits, ice chests, and all manner of other items needed or wanted by travelers. She cut through the aisles, went into the toilet, found a stall with a green vacant sign on the lock, and finished her business.

On the way out, she paused to look at Texana art, books,

and bluebonnet souvenirs. She passed by a long line of hanging candies, grabbed a bag of beef jerky because Ace loved it, then grabbed a second bag for his school roommate. All the while, the bald man watched her from the corner of the store where the cold case housed every beverage known to man and womankind.

She checked out at the register, then the bald man followed her out the front door and continued his surveillance all the way to Houston. She never realized he was behind her.

There were a lot of people on the road, but traffic was moving. The remainder of the two-hour drive allowed Merit time to think and sort her jagged thoughts.

Was she being paranoid about Duke?

Was Jerry able to handle a case of this magnitude at his age and level of experience? Why would his firm give him so much responsibility? Why would Judge Ginsberg give me so much responsibility?

Is Ace handling his father's suicide? Is he performing as well in school as his teachers are reporting?

The floating ride of the BMW and the lyrical music overshadowed the worrying thoughts and occupied her mind. She smiled at the windshield as calm and relaxation finally swept over her.

Merit and Ace had a brief dinner in Houston with Merit's best friend, Joy, and her husband, Tucker, before the two planned a late departure for Port Aransas. During dinner, Pepper Dog stayed at Joy and Tucker's home with their pet, a white Westie, named Willie.

The four chose Ouisie's Table on San Felipe for their upscale southern cuisine as it was one of Merit's favorites from her undergrad days at Rice, when the restaurant was on Sunset.

The four shared mushroom risotto-filled jalapeños as an appetizer, then each ordered an entrée. Merit and Joy opted for lamb while Tucker went for seafood and Ace had Julia Child's poulet au four roti. Ace just called it roasted chicken and mashed potatoes.

Merit saw a man sitting at a small table near the kitchen, wearing a dark suit and sporting a totally hairless head. She turned to Joy. "Do you know that guy? He looks familiar."

"Nope. Looks like your average businessman-in-town-for-a-meeting type."

"Yeah. I guess. Tell me what you've been up to?"

Merit flashed on an image of the same bald man in Buc-ee's filling the gas tank of a four-door sedan while she walked Pepper along the grass. *That's a big coincidence.* Her armpits prickled ever so slightly.

Joy looked at her friend of many years. "What's wrong?"

Merit looked over at Ace. "Not a thing. All's right with the world." Merit made a mental note and smiled at her table mates.

Merit and Ace arrived at the house in Port Aransas late that night. They were met with all the lights on, the air conditioner working overtime, and the fridge stocked to the brim. Merit was thankful that Betty had alerted the housekeeper to air out the house and set things up for their arrival.

Ace and Pepper hit the sack before Merit could get the car unloaded. When she tucked them in, they were sound asleep. Ace had his head on one pillow, and Pepper had her head on the other.

The next morning, Ace slept in, as expected, and Merit setup a workspace on the outdoor deck, looking over the Gulf of Mexico. She had a pot of tea, a box of files, and her laptop. She opened the John and Ariana Sanderson documents on her computer, then accessed several recent emails. She read a memo with various information, including the fact that the warehouse property had been designated as St. Elmo Studios, LLC. Now that she had a name, she could fill in more of the lease documentation and hopefully send another version of the draft to the attorneys in Los Angeles before she went back to Austin.

The Sandersons' studio property lease was not the type she habitually worked on. There were only two other film studios in Austin, and Merit had not prepared those documents. However, a lease on a building is a commonsense thing for most transactional lawyers. There's a building, a landlord, and a tenant, for a term of years, with certain perks and, most importantly, rent paid. Beyond that, it got complicated quickly. There were all types of pitfalls the uneducated could fall into, and Merit began to work on those clauses very carefully. She also made sure that there were no issues omitted that needed to be there. She'd learned in law school that often it wasn't what was in a document that was important, but also what was left out and, therefore, covered by common law and statutory law.

Occasionally, she drank her tea and looked out across the dunes to the beach and the water. After she was satisfied with the lease, she typed a memo to Betty with some office details for the next week, attached it all to an email, and hit send.

She heard Ace and Pepper moving about inside and slapped down the lid of the laptop. "Time for some fun."

36

It was a fine day in Port Aransas, so Merit and Ace took Pepper for a walk on the beach and looked out over the blue Gulf of Mexico. It was a beautiful sunny day, so little clothing was needed. All three were barefoot.

What they couldn't see was a small black dingy being dropped from a dark silent helicopter about two miles past the line of offshore drilling rigs that made a line along the Gulf Coast from Mexico to Florida. Also, into the water dropped a lone swimmer who pulled himself into the rubber boat and started a small trolling motor attached to the rear. The dingy contained two plastic cartons, one port and one starboard, that balanced the boat. Each had a small switch on top connected through a hole in the plastic to small bombs nestled in their interiors.

The design and materials were similar to the explosives used in San Antonio. The debris would be easy to identify and connect to the market bomb. That was part of the plan that Merit knew nothing about.

Once the occupant of the boat started motoring toward

the closest offshore rig, the helicopter left the area as silently as it had arrived. No patrolling Coast Guard copters were in sight.

In the boat, Robby Hickson's chest puffed with pride. He was afraid, but he was more excited to finally be on a valiant mission. He was doing something to stop the decline of America. With an IQ of less than eighty, Robby had no clue that he was being used. He banged the dingy on each rise of salty water as he sped toward the southern-most pylon of the nearest offshore rig, happy to be doing God's work on this beautiful day.

Robby spoke out loud to his deceased brother who had died in Afghanistan, telling him he would soon be joining him in heaven. "I'm a soldier, too. See the helicopter I got to ride in? I've been trained, just like you."

Robby had no idea that the bombs he carried couldn't possibly topple an eighteen thousand pound drilling rig. It would be like an elephant being fucked by a mosquito. The elephant would not even notice. Robby had been selected, groomed, then brainwashed into thinking this was his big moment. He had cleaned guns, drank beer, and made friends with strong men in the American Freedom Militia. He had finally been noticed and appreciated. He was the chosen one. Little did he know that he had been played again, as he'd been duped and used his entire life.

Robby followed the instructions of his handlers and lined up on his target. No one saw him. Not the men working on the rig, not the sunbathers on the beach, not even the fish in the water paid attention to him. He flipped the activation buttons on both bombs, pushed up the lever on the motor to full strength, aimed, and plowed directly into the huge round pylon.

Bang! Robby was gone, but the rig was barely affected.

Debris and burning flotsam floated around Robby's remains in the water as workers on the platform yelled and pointed.

Merit and Ace heard a sound, looked out over the Gulf, and saw a bright fire burning orange against the blue sky and water.

Ace squinted. "What was that?"

Merit shaded her eyes with her hand. "I don't know, but it's odd."

Within minutes, half a dozen U.S. Coast Guard helicopters streaked toward the platform, then hovered over the fiery scene.

Merit looked up at the whirly birds. "What the hell?"

Ace pulled on Pepper's leash and headed toward the board-walk over the dunes back to the house.

"Let's go turn on the news."

By the time Merit and Ace walked across the dunes to the beach house, NNN had the story. Ernest Anguish reported from New York about the Port Aransas offshore bombing.

"Today in the Gulf of Mexico, near the town of Corpus Christi, Texas, a bomb was exploded at the base of a Dexon offshore drilling platform."

The screen was split between Anguish's face and the buzzing of helicopters over the platform. The footage must have been shot from a local news helicopter with a zoom lens, as it was from a downward angle and somewhat jerky and grainy at times, going in and out of focus.

"So far, no one has taken credit for the bombing. It appears as if the bomb exploded early or missed its mark. There was little damage to the rig and no deaths or injuries on the platform.

"Authorities say it was lucky that no one was hurt. They are gathering up debris from the water to try to piece together the source of the bomb and clues to its maker."

Merit and Ace kept an eye on the story off and on throughout the rest of the day and into the evening. That night, Ernest Anguish came back on the air with more information. He flashed his charismatic smile at the camera and began.

"We have with us FBI spokesperson, Agent Archibald Duke."

Merit, standing in the kitchen, jerked her head around when she heard the name. Pepper's ears perked up as she laid on the floor near Ace's chair in the living room.

The screen was split between the two talking heads.

Merit looked at Ace. "That man is an agent in the office where I work. He's monitoring the document redacting and supervising security."

Ace looked up from a video game he was playing on a handheld device. "What's he doing on the news?"

Merit wiped her hands on a kitchen towel. "Let's see."

Duke answered several lead-in questions tossed to him by Anguish, then landed the information he seemed to want to get out into the public. "The debris in the water indicates that the origin of the materials used are the same as the San Antonio Market bombing."

On Anguish. "Have any of the militia taken credit?"

On Duke. "No one has contacted us at this early stage."

On Anguish. "Do you have any idea who might be responsible?"

On Duke. "Obviously, the American Freedom Militia is our primary suspect since the evidence in the San Antonio bombing points to them as well."

On Anguish. "What is their motivation, if you know?"

On Duke. "This is just another incident in a long line of actions by domestic terrorists in our country. We've petitioned Congress for an increase in our defense budget to try to get out ahead of these attacks."

Merit considered the information Duke was selling. "Hmm. I'll get dinner going. Why don't you setup a new jigsaw puzzle on the game table?"

"Oh, Mom. I'm in an online tournament here."

"Well, hurry up and win. Setup either a puzzle or a game. Something we can do together besides watch television."

Merit clicked off the TV and returned to the island in the kitchen.

Ace looked at the glass of chardonnay Merit was pouring. "Do I get some wine if I do it?"

Merit laughed. "No. How about a Dr. Pepper?"

When Duke wrapped the interview, he walked outside and called Tank on the appropriate burner phone. "Did you see the news?"

Tank grunted. "I did. It was perfect."

"That should divert attention away from Waco and keep Homeland Security busy."

"Should put the fear of God in Merit Bridges, too."

"Yep, two birds, one stone."

"Are you sure she saw the bomb go off?"

"Yeah. Baldy has been keeping an eye on her. He coordi-

MANNING WOLFE

nated the timing to her walk on the beach with her kid and the dog."

"Poor Robby never knew what was going on, but he was a hero."

Duke scoffed. "He served his country well. May he rest in peace."

"Peace, brother."

Duke grunted. "How's Four Leaf holding up?"

"She's in a daze. Sometimes I doubt she knows her name."

"And the troops?"

"They're holding together so far. This morning, the religious faction had a sunrise service to bless the parishioners' firearms."

"Ha! Who's acting as minister?"

"Moonie, that dingleberry from San Saba has them all mesmerized. He's quoting Revelations 2:27. Believes the AR-15 is the same as the iron scepter in the Bible verse."

"Good. Keep him close, but let him think he's in control."

"No problem with that. He thinks he's channeling Jesus."

170

37

Merit looked up as Judge Ginsberg sat on the bench in U.S. Criminal Court, Western District, in Austin, Texas, and banged the gavel. Court clerk, Hattie Mae Townsend, said the same thing she'd said on every court day for over thirty years. "Court is called to order. Honorable Judge Harold Ginsberg presiding. Please be seated."

The room hushed before the intimidating man wearing a black robe and sitting on a throne on a riser with flags and seals behind him. Judge Ginsberg had been appointed during the administration of George Herbert Walker Bush many years ago. He was a legend known to be a hard hitter, but fair dealer, who didn't tolerate a lot of shenanigans in his courtroom.

The prosecution and defense tables had been pushed farther apart to allow the insertion of a third table between them for Merit as special counsel. She sat with perfect posture in a navy suit with a pink silk blouse peeking out underneath.

On Merit's right at the defense table was Jerry Webb sitting next to his client, Bobby Ray McDonald. The difference between them was striking, Jerry tall, tan, fit, and full of vitality. McDonald shrunken, sullen, jaundiced, and hunched over.

Their clothing provided further information about their circumstances. Jerry wore a Tom Ford double-vent navy suit ensemble with crisp white shirt and cuff links in the shape of a horseshoe. The cuff links had belonged to Gerald Webb Sr., and Jerry was counting on them to bring him the spirit of his father for good luck. McDonald wore a polyester brown saggy bag of a suit that even tailoring would not have saved. The mugshot taken of his cocky, vigorous demeanor on the day he was arrested was long gone.

On Merit's left was the prosecution, Robert Bowser, known as Bob. He was about fifty years old with an impressive resume in criminal law. His list of courtroom wins was almost as long as the rap sheets of the defendants he prosecuted. Bowser sported a no-nonsense black suit and white shirt, as did the assistant prosecutor sitting next to him. Eleanor "Ellie" Frank was a dark-skinned woman of middle age, possibly chosen as second chair for her politically correct color as much as her legal expertise.

The judge banged the gavel once more for good measure and began. "We are convened here today to hear the charges in the matter of The United States versus Bobby Ray McDonald. The clerk will stand and read the charges."

Hattie Mae stood in her cubicle, to the left of the judge, so she could be seen and heard behind a large computer screen. She held in her hands a printed docket sheet from which she read the charges from the indictment that had been handed down by the Grand Jury in San Antonio. Hattie Mae sat down, and Judge Ginsberg took over. "Does the defense waive a reading of the full indictment?"

Jerry stood and addressed the court. "We waive the reading, Your Honor."

A cacophony of whispers passed through the gallery that was full of reporters, families of the deceased, and gawkers.

Lyle Ryder was in the first row, on the defense side, behind the bar separating the attorneys from the populace. Packed in-between other attendees, he struggled to use a notepad and balance a tape recorder on his lap, as there wasn't an empty seat in the house to hold his belongings. He finally turned the recorder on and slid it into his shirt pocket so he could write and hold the notepad at the same time.

FBI special counsel on the case, Richard Dell, sat directly behind Prosecutor Bowser. His job was to monitor the use of the information obtained from the FBI files and to protect the agency, and its agents, at all costs.

The judge cleared his throat and continued. "Before we begin, let's get one thing clear. There will be no disruptions and no extraneous activities in my courtroom. Anyone who crosses the line will be removed and will not be allowed to return. No second chances." The judge nodded his head, first to one corner of the back of the room, then to the other, where armed security guards stood at the ready to remove anyone brave enough to defy Judge Ginsberg.

The gallery hushed.

In the far-right corner of the room, directly in front of the first security guard, was Archibald Duke and his right hand, Rachel Ward, both wearing their FBI-style black suits. In the very back by the door stood the bald man in a business suit. Duke nodded to him, and he nodded in return.

Judge Ginsberg seemed pleased that everyone had settled in. "Today is about organizing the trial and preparing to bring in the jury panel tomorrow. I see we have two motions for hear-ings from defense counsel, and one motion from special coun-sel. Let's dispense with the easy one first. Mr. Webb?"

Jerry stood and addressed the court. "Your Honor, we have

filed a motion for dismissal of the charges in light of the fact that my client was not near the site of the bombing on the day in question and had no criminal connection to Mr. Walsh, the alleged bomber. None of the evidence in the San Antonio Police Department files shows any connection between my client and the domestic terrorist attack." Jerry sat back down beside his client.

Judge Ginsberg nodded to Prosecutor Bowser who stood. "Your Honor, the people plan to show a definitive connection between the three bombers and the defendant, Mr. McDonald, creating a conspiracy. It's absurd to think that this matter can be dismissed without a full airing of the evidence and the facilitation of the judicial process."

"Okay, that's enough. Mr. Webb, you've done your obligatory duty and your motion is preserved for appeal, but the court's ruling is that the request for dismissal is denied."

Jerry didn't look surprised and neither did Merit or anyone else in the room. It was a perfunctory motion to get it on the record, but it didn't stand a snowball's chance in Texas of being granted.

The judge nodded at Merit. "Next up, Ms. Bridges. Please proceed."

Merit stood at her table and took a deep breath. "Your Honor, I have been presented with six of eight boxes of documents by the Federal Bureau of Investigation. I have been reviewing and redacting them as quickly as possible in order to relay the pertinent materials to Mr. Webb. However, I have not completed the process and, therefore, may not have provided everything that is needed by the defense team to represent Mr. McDonald. I request a short recess of a few days in order to complete the task."

Duke masked a sly smile and glared at the back of Merit's head.

The judge rubbed his chin and looked pensive. "I understand your concern. How many days do you think you will need?"

Merit considered. "Depending on what I find in the remaining two document boxes, possibly three to four days is my best estimate."

Jerry stood. "May I speak, Your Honor?"

"Speak."

"Even if we get the documents this week, we will need time to process the information and add it to our trial strategy. We can't conduct trial by ambush. We have no idea what we might face in terms of evidentiary material."

Judge Ginsberg indicated toward FBI counsel, Richard Dell. "Can you shed any light on what might be in the remaining files?"

Dell stood. "Your Honor, we presented the most relevant and important documents first. What remain are merely perfunctory files in order to dispel any doubt that the federal government was not forthcoming. We expect no further pertinent evidence to surface."

Judge Ginsberg looked at Merit. "Ms. Bridges, tomorrow starts voir dire. That will take at least two days. You don't need to be here for that as you have no input during jury selection. Why don't you take those two days. That will bring us to Thursday. I'll dismiss court on Friday so that Mr. Webb will have the long weekend to examine any further documentation that you choose to send over to him."

Merit looked disappointed but nodded. "Yes, Judge."

Jerry stood again. "But, Your Honor."

"It's done, Mr. Webb. We'll all reconsider the timeframe on Monday. If anyone has any further issues or questions, we'll address them at that time."

All three attorneys mumbled, "Thank you, Your Honor."

Dell looked back at Duke. He and Rachel quietly stood and left the courtroom as the judge ended the hearing and the crowd dispersed.

The next day, Judge Ginsberg called the room to order and directed the bailiff to bring in the first set of twenty-four jurors to be vetted for possible trial service. The table that had been provided for Merit had been conspicuously removed.

Prosecutor Bowser addressed the jury first. "Hello, ladies and gentlemen. I'm sure you're aware that this is a trial about terrorists and conspiracies. Not conspiracy theories, mind you, but true back door hiding out in dark places, plotting to do evil in the world conspiracies. In order to serve this court and the cause of justice, you will need to go into the blackest places in your mind and heart. I'm going to ask a series of questions that allow us to decide whether you would be a good juror for this trial. It's important that you answer honestly, as this will be a long ordeal, and finding twelve committed and law-abiding individuals is essential to the process."

Judge Ginsberg looked as though he was about to prod Bowser, but the prosecutor moved on.

"First, I'll pose the question, then I'll ask each of you individually for an answer. Do any of you have an issue with the death penalty under the federal laws of the United States of America, or the State of Texas, as you understand it to be? Candidate number one?"

"Nope."

And so it went, the prosecutor went through all twenty-four asking for their answer to this and several other questions, all tailored to bringing in a final verdict of guilty and the execution of McDonald.

When it was Jerry's turn, he stood and addressed the same twenty-four citizens. "My questions will be brief. My primary concern, at this stage, is not the end of the trial, but the process. I need to know if each one of you can maintain a fair approach and open mind through the entire series of witnesses and presentation of evidence, before you decide on your verdict. There is a presumption of innocence regardless of what you've heard on the news or assume to be true. It is not enough for you to presume my client is guilty, but, in order to bring in that verdict, the prosecution must prove that my client is guilty of conspiracy and you must be convinced beyond a shadow of a doubt. Conspiracy is a very specific term under the law. It requires action on the part of the co-conspirators that fits a very distinct criterion. The fact that people merely know each other is not proof of a conspiracy."

Some of the jurors nodded. Jerry smiled and continued. "For example, if your neighbor committed a crime and you didn't participate, you would not be a co-conspirator. You would simply have lousy neighbors."

The jurors laughed, and Jerry seemed pleased.

"But, what if you baked cookies and delivered them to a meeting at your neighbor's but didn't know what was going on and didn't stay for coffee? Next day you learn that the gathering was for the purpose of plotting a crime. It gets into the gray area of the law that requires a great deal of focus and determination to evaluate."

The jurors seemed to realize the gravity of their role in the proceedings.

Jerry continued. "Now, I'm going to ask each one of you in turn whether you can one, keep an open mind through the trial and, two, carefully evaluate the evidence as it's presented, paying special attention to detail. Candidate number one?"

"Yes."

The process evolved, each juror responding as Helen Sharp took notes for Jerry at the defense table and the prosecution watched and noted as well.

Both the prosecution and defense filed preemptory challenges and challenges for cause, finding only nine jurors out of the twenty-four that were satisfactory to both sides for service.

After lunch, Judge Ginsberg had the second twenty-four juror candidates brought in, and the attorneys went through the exact same process. Several more jurors were found in group two to be unsatisfactory to one or both sides of the aisle. When the final jury, with two alternates, was approved by both prosecution and defense, Judge Ginsberg declared the jury empaneled. He then dismissed the panel until the next morning.

McDonald watched as four white men, three white women, three Hispanic men, one Hispanic woman, and one black man, all between the ages of thirty and seventy, filed out of the room.

Jerry looked at McDonald and thought, *There is a jury of your peers.*

38

Merit once again sat in the windowless office at the Live Oak Federal Campus for what she hoped was the last day of FBI document review. She'd done little since Judge Ginsberg's order but sort, redact, and evaluate evidence for the McDonald defense. Her office work was falling further and further behind, but she was close to reaching her goal of completing the review of the final boxes. Having the full overview allowed her to begin to see the holes in the evidence. She asked the receptionist to call Rachel Ward and request that she drop by at her convenience.

Agent Ward entered wearing her gun on her hip, hidden under her suit. "You asked for me?"

"Yes, thanks. Just a quick check-in to make sure I've received all the documentation related to the case. This is the eighth box and I'm almost finished with it. Tomorrow will be the first day I'm back in court and I want to be able to report to Judge Ginsberg that I've completed the work as he defined it."

Rachel pointed to the box on the desk. "That's it. This is the last box that Duke authorized."

Merit picked up a stack of papers in front of her. "If this is it, I have some questions about holes in the evidence. There's not enough here for anyone to piece together a series of events making up a logical story."

"From my understanding, it's not your job to evaluate the information, just to redact what's irrelevant for the defense to see."

"Of course, but if I don't understand the context, I can't decide what's relevant. This doesn't make sense with what's being presented here."

Rachel raised an eyebrow. "Like what?"

Merit reached for the laptop she was using to list on a spreadsheet the documentation she'd sent over to defense counsel. She then pulled a corresponding document from the stack of copies she'd made. "I'll give you an example. There's a report here showing that the call came in from SAPD that they'd received the tip on the storage unit and had gone to McDonald's home. It shows the police took Faye McDonald and their daughter, Lucy, into custody."

"Right."

"But there is nothing that shows how Bobby Ray McDonald was apprehended. Nothing about a roadblock as these summaries indicate. No backup details with officers, times and locations, and nothing about his vehicle except that it was impounded. I only see an arrest report saying he was arrested and detained on that date."

Rachel took the first document from Merit and scanned it quickly. "This is probably a report summary. The full report would have been over a dozen pages."

"Well, I'm supposed to decide what's useful, not someone who prepares a summary. I need to see the full report. And, if there are any other summaries relating to the documents in the eight boxes, I need to see all the original reports for those as well."

Rachel looked at Merit like she was a pain in the ass.

"I'll see what I can do."

Merit, Jerry, Helen Sharp, Prosecutor Bowser, and FBI counsel, Richard Dell, appeared before Judge Ginsberg in chambers for a hearing on the evidence requested by Merit. The judge had granted the in-chambers hearing in order to move things along through the weekend.

The purpose of the meeting was to address the problem with summaries and missing information from the FBI files. Merit had filed the motion for the hearing on the evidence and was joined in the motion by Jerry as primary defense counsel for McDonald. All very technically correct to preserve the record, much to the chagrin of Richard Dell, FBI counsel.

Judge Ginsberg turned to Merit. "Ms. Bridges, you asked for this proceeding. Let's hear it."

Merit stood and addressed the judge. "Your Honor, as asserted in my motion for the hearing, I've found irregularities in the FBI documentation that you've assigned for my review and redacting. There are documents referencing reports and information that aren't in the files. I've requested that the additional material be made available, and it has not been fully provided. In order to do my job properly, I demand to see those documents."

"I see, Ms. Bridges. How do you know that the additional information is necessary to your review?"

"Parts of the story are being left out, Your Honor. For example, there is a report summary showing that Mr. McDonald was arrested, but the full report showing where and how he was arrested is missing. Another example, there is no documentation of how the self-storage facility was identified by the FBI, only that it was located and searched. I could go on."

"How much is missing?"

"Just to clarify, Your Honor. The information is lost in the gap between the San Antonio Police Department reports and the FBI reports. It's as if there was an investigation that occurred somewhere in the space between the two legal authorities that is not being revealed in the documentation."

The judge looked at Prosecutor Bowser, then at FBI counsel, Dell, as if he was deciding who to call on next.

Richard Dell stood. "If I may, Your Honor? Since I represent the FBI's interests with regard to the Chinese Wall, I'd like to be heard on this issue."

"Mr. Dell, do you have information regarding the missing documentation?"

"Yes, Your Honor. Our agents had to boil the relevant information down to a few boxes for Ms. Bridges' review. Under my supervision, they did the best they could, but we may have erred on the side of frugality. It was our intention to provide only what was necessary to the defense."

Jerry sat beside Merit before Judge Ginsberg's desk. When the judge nodded at him, Jerry spoke. "Your Honor, Ms. Bridges is to decide what is necessary to the defense, not Mr. Dell. We are already handicapped in our representation of Mr. McDonald by the Chinese Wall, causing an intermediary to redact and evaluate what should be passed on to us. Having that information edited even before it is given to Ms. Bridges provides a double wall to our use of what may or may not be necessary for us to properly defend our client."

Merit piped up. "I was told that the only things removed from the documentation were the real names of the agents who work undercover."

The judge seemed to contemplate the issue. "Mr. Bowser, do you have anything to add to this discussion before I rule on the motion?"

The prosecutor stood up. "No, Your Honor. I am willing to prosecute this case with the information Your Honor deems relevant to the charges."

Jerry cleared his throat. *Kiss ass.*

The judge, seemingly unimpressed, addressed the group. "Mr. Dell, perhaps you'd like to review the documentation again and consider whether there are indeed gaps in the story as Ms. Bridges describes it."

Mr. Dell nodded. "We'd welcome that opportunity, Your Honor."

As welcome as a tick on a hound's back. Merit channeled her inner Betty.

On the FBI campus, Merit received several additional files from Rachel Ward after the order from Judge Ginsberg and facilitation by Attorney Dell. With each document she reviewed, Merit asked herself the same question: *Is this information relevant to the case and do I need to pass it beyond the Chinese Wall?* She combined the additional pertinent information into her spreadsheet by date and event.

She placed several redacted reports into the box to be copied and sent over to Jerry Webb. She was not allowed to highlight passages in the documents, but she hoped that Jerry and his team would see the patterns and ferret out additional parts of the story as she had. The chain of events was starting to become clear, and Merit didn't like what she was seeing.

The first point of concern was that the FBI still had not revealed how they knew who McDonald was, and where he would be, on the date of the bombing. It was also unclear who picked him up on I-10 during his supposed escape from San Antonio to Houston. As far as Merit could document, that event never happened.

The second issue was the evidence that appeared in McDonald's car after it was impounded. The original SAPD report showed only children's books, a blanket, and emergency supplies normally carried in a vehicle. The FBI report showed extremist pamphlets, a Glock 17, and propaganda tying McDonald to the American Freedom Militia, a domestic terrorist group that had not been located or identified as to members.

39

Duke watched Merit on-screen through a camera hidden in the conference room. He saw her flipping through the new documents that Judge Ginsberg had ordered and Rachel Ward had delivered for review and redacting.

He had clearly underestimated Merit. *Why couldn't she have just done the perfunctory review that a guilty man deserved and be done with it?*

Duke wasn't trying to convict an innocent man; he knew McDonald was guilty of helping to facilitate the attacks. He was just making sure that the buck stopped there, and that McDonald was blamed for the planning and financing as well.

With each document that Merit redacted and placed into the outbox, Duke grew angrier, hotter, and more concerned for his plan.

So much for the long-term version, might have to switch to the short-term plan.

Duke left the FBI campus after Merit finished her review and had gone to her car. He saw Baldy, as planned, pull out behind her.

Duke drove across old Airport Boulevard and out of Austin toward Bastrop. After turning in and out of several farm-to-market roads, he wound up on a dirt drive. He stopped and unlocked a gate, drove through, and relocked the gate behind him. He looked around and made sure he was alone.

All clear.

Farther down the dirt drive, he skirted around a disheveled farmhouse and pulled up to a barn behind it. An old outhouse was falling down behind the house beside a bone pile of old tractor parts with cactus growing between them. Several head of cattle roamed in a pasture next to the fenced property line. Duke had bought the farm in his uncle's name after his reprimand for attacking the Muslim prisoner when he'd been transferred from international terrorism to domestic terrorism.

He'd seen the handwriting on the wall. Everything was becoming more and more politically correct, to the point that he knew he could not effectuate the change he desired from within the agency. Going outside the FBI and the law, he knew it was inevitable that at some point he might have to flee, and he was ready.

Duke opened one of the two large double doors to the old barn. Inside was a brand-new compact Class C RV with bed-over cab. On the bumper dock was a Kawasaki motorcycle beside a ladder that allowed access to the top of the vehicle where a small canoe was strapped on with bungee cords. On the side of the RV, beside the door, was a rolled-up awning designed to protect a summer kitchen built into a slide out. He could spend months, if not years, on the road in this getup if he stayed in the shadows and woods across the U.S. and Canada. He could make it all the way to Alaska if he wanted to.

Inside, Duke unlocked a small safe built into the top of the closet that looked like a false cabinet. He added an extra twenty thousand dollars in cash that he'd brought with him. That made a total of six hundred thousand and change that he'd accumulated. Also in the safe was an assortment of identification and passports with pictures of him in various looks—with a beard, with long blond hair, and clean-cut with glasses.

He also had gold, diamonds, and other untraceable, but negotiable, assets hidden under the boards of the bathroom floor. Beneath the sofa seat was a small arsenal of guns and ammo, covered by extra bedding.

Visiting his escape plan calmed him.

He went inside the old farmhouse and located the freezer being run off a small generator. He swept old boxes off the top, unlocked the lid with a key from his ring, and examined a large male corpse without hands. The body was outfitted with a duplicate of Duke's dental work, his deceased father's antique watch, and a wallet full of his credit cards, ID, and family photos.

The poor soul had been part of a recent case investigated by Duke, as was the contraband in the RV. All of his escape assets had been gleaned slowly from one case to the next without anyone being the wiser.

I'm ready when it's time. They might figure out it's not me, but it will take a while and I'll be long gone by then.

40

Jerry ran on his usual route around the Lady Bird Lake shoreline, past a crew of eight skulling at a rapid pace, and a young couple on paddle boards that looked like ironing boards. He needed exercise more than ever with the mounting pressure from the trial, his firm, and the FBI.

As Jerry turned the corner near an outcropping of rocks near Lou Neff Point, Lyle jogged past Jerry and a family feeding some ducks at the water's edge. Lyle was wearing standard running attire and a black baseball cap that hid most of his face. He slowed to a walk beside Jerry.

"I need to talk to you."

Jerry jogged on, forcing Lyle to run again. "I think I'm being watched. You need to stay away from me."

"You've been watched all along. Consider yourself lucky you're watched and not dead like your old buddy Riley or those guys at the oil platform in the Gulf."

"What does that have to do with Riley's death or my case?"

"It's all smoke and mirrors. Anything to pull attention away from what actually happened in San Antonio and dilute law enforcement resources."

"And you know this how?"

Lyle kept the pace although he looked like he might faint. "My paper has been getting messages from someone. I don't know who it is, but every few days we get a small bit of information. Someone in the FBI or very close to them is leaking."

Jerry picked up the pace. "Sounds like Deep Throat stuff to me."

Lyle stopped in his tracks and gasped for air. "You need to listen to me."

Jerry stopped as well and looked at Lyle. "What do you expect me to do? I have a case to try. That's my focus."

Lyle put his hands on his thighs, leaned over, and continued to pant. "The FBI is all over this case. They're running you through the information they're feeding Merit Bridges. They want McDonald dead and buried."

Jerry grimaced. "If that were the case, wouldn't they have taken him out by now?"

Lyle looked around furtively. "They might have, but now it's public and there must be a trial. The country has to have someone to blame."

Jerry looked at Lyle. "What proof do you have?"

"The FBI must have a trial to have a guilty verdict. And they are assigned the duty to protect McDonald and his family in their custody. They're in a bind and people are becoming erratic."

"You're guessing."

"Don't wait until he's convicted. I wonder if his family will be safe. I bet that's the deal. I can't get to your client, but you can question him. I need you to confirm my research before I go to press."

Jerry paused for a moment then decided to trust Lyle, a little.

"I've found out that Riley's death most likely was murder."

Lyle nodded. "I assumed that but have no proof."

"I have the medical examiner's report. I'll get it to you. That's as far as I'll go. That's not part of the case against my client. No attorney/client problem."

"I understand. I'll be very careful with the information."

Jerry thought about revealing Lucy but decided not to. "Someone is playing with all of our lives here."

"I know. I'm heading to D.C. tonight to meet with my editor. I'm going to run what I have in the paper next week. If you can help me any further, please call."

Jerry jogged on.

41

Merit and Jerry entered the interview room at the detention center where McDonald was being held. Jerry had asked for the session under the guise of preparing trial strategy, but he had an ulterior motive. He had some questions for his client that needed to be answered. Merit wondered what Jerry was up to, but her own suspicions informed her silence.

McDonald was brought in wearing his usual orange jumpsuit that bagged so far down his arms, the sleeves were rolled up. He appeared to have given up eating altogether. If this went on much longer, Jerry might have to petition the court to put in a feeding tube to keep him alive and healthy enough to stand trial.

Jerry stared down his client who didn't flinch.

"You're not as tough as you think you are."

Merit was startled, but McDonald didn't respond.

Jerry's eyes flashed with anger. "I know you're keeping things from us and that can get you killed. The press thinks you're being blackmailed."

McDonald held Jerry's gaze. "I've decided to testify. You can ask all the questions you want in court."

"Why? What could you possibly gain? It's only going to hurt your case. I strongly advise against it."

"It's been decided."

Merit supported Jerry's call. "The FBI has very little directly tying you to the bombing. It's all circumstantial."

"I want to testify in court. I want to show my face. I am not ashamed of my actions."

"What actions? As far as the jury will know, you were working in San Antonio, someone rented a storage unit in your name, and then you were arrested on the way to a legitimate visit to Houston. You had some phone conversations with hunting buddies. All circumstantial. So far, the FBI documents don't show much more than that. What more do they have on you?"

McDonald went mute.

Merit looked at Jerry, then McDonald. *What the hell is going on here?*

42

Jerry crawled out of bed in his blue plaid boxers and went into the kitchen of his condo. He put on a pot of dark roast coffee and clicked the remote on the television across the room in the living area. The TV was tuned to the National News Network and Ernest Anguish was reporting. A photograph of Lyle Ryder was on the left side of the screen and Anguish's talking head was on the right side. Jerry recognized Lyle immediately and turned up the volume.

"*Washington Times* reporter, Lyle Ryder, was killed in a hit and run accident on Dupont Circle in D.C. today," reported Anguish from New York.

"What the fuck?" Jerry said to the screen.

The crawl along the bottom of the screen showed: Young Reporter Killed in Hit and Run! The photo of Lyle dropped to a small insert and Anguish's serious face took the full screen.

"Witnesses say that a yellow cab, license number unknown, appeared to accelerate and jump the curb, killing Ryder and wounding two tourists. Although there were many witnesses, authorities report that no one was able to identify the driver.

"Our hearts go out to Ryder's family and friends. We go now to Jana Williams who is back in D.C. with her coverage for us in Texas. Jana, what do we know from the sources at Ryder's newspaper?"

Jana stood before a monolithic building with 'Washington Times' chiseled into the granite over the doorway. She moved her microphone closer to her mouth. "Apparently, Ryder was on his way to this *Washington Times* office where he was based. He had been writing about the McDonald terrorist trial on location in Texas and had traveled to D.C. to meet with the *Washington Times* editorial board."

Anguish's face split the screen with the reporter. "Jana, do we know the nature of the meeting that was planned to take place?"

"No, Ernest, the *Times* is being very close lipped about what Ryder was working on or had discovered during his coverage of the McDonald story. We see from his recent stories that he had begun to question some of the facts of the case, but exactly what he had discovered is unknown to us at this time."

Duke was watching the same news coverage at his Austin office. He picked up his second burner phone when it rang, muted the sound on the TV, and said, "Speak."

The voice on the other end of the line said, "It's done. The little reporter reports no more."

Duke smiled. "Excellent."

"Accidental. Per your instructions."

"I see on TV he tangoed with a taxi."

"More like the twist."

Duke grunted. "And the lawyer?"

"He's next."

"And Four Leaf? Has she been convicted yet?"

Tank laughed. "Almost. We have some long-winded Perry Mason wannabes in the group. They love listening to themselves talk. They walk before the jury and pontificate as if they'd been to Harvard."

Duke laughed. "How's Four Leaf holding up?"

"We've kept her tied and drugged at night as a precaution. In the daytime, the troops bring her into the main barn for the trial. The yahoos have a jury box made out of reclaimed lumber with folding tables and chairs for the prosecution and defense teams. No one wanted to defend her, so they drew straws. Guy who drew the short straw is mounting her defense, but his heart's not in it."

"I bet."

"Every now and then Four Leaf says something to defend herself, but mostly she nods and tries to stay awake."

"Alright. Let's keep them busy as long as possible. Let me know if they start to grow bored with the process. And don't let them hurt her too much. We'll need her later."

"Roger that."

"Out."

43

Merit and Betty worked through a huge stack of files, sorting, signing, and tossing pages into the recycling bin. Betty's goal was to have all the paperwork in the office under control before the McDonald trial started, and she'd sweetly goaded Merit into getting it done.

They watched the television on the credenza in Merit's office as Ernest Anguish reported from New York to interested parties around the world. "Monday morning will be the first day of trial in the matter of The United States of America versus Bobby Lee McDonald. The jury has been selected and is ready to hear the case."

The screen split between Anguish and the mayor of San Antonio. "We have with us today Mayor Manuel Sincero from San Antonio. Mr. Mayor, we are sorry for your loss. We know that your wife was caught in the bombing and that you have been grieving along with your city."

On Mayor Sincero. "Thank you, Ernest."

On Anguish. "We understand that the final death count in

the market bombing was over five hundred souls. How is your city faring in their recovery from these unlawful acts?"

"San Antonio is a city made up of brave citizens with a strong constitution. Although we are still in our grief over the loss of our loved ones, we are starting to rebuild and are looking forward to finalizing the trial of Bobby Ray McDonald in Austin."

The screen split three ways and another talking head popped up. "We are now joined by Texas Law School criminal law professor, Jacob Lerner. Professor, we understand that the trial will be based largely on circumstantial evidence and that conspiracy charges are difficult to prove. What can you tell us about the nature of this proceeding?"

"Thanks for having me, Ernest. This trial is one of the most visible in recent history. Historically, members of the Colombian drug cartels, members of organized crime, and former Enron executives have one thing in common. They all have federal conspiracy convictions. The essence of a conspiracy is an agreement of two or more persons to engage in some form of legally prohibited conduct."

Anguish's face filled the screen. "So, the co-conspirators have to agree to break the law?"

On Lerner. "That's right. The crime is complete upon agreement, although some statutes require prosecutors to show that at least one of the co-conspirators has taken some concrete step or committed some overt act in furtherance of the scheme. Because many joining together in crime pose a greater danger than the lone offender, co-conspirators may be punished for the conspiracy and any completed offense which is proven to be the object of the plot of all co-conspirators."

On Anguish. "So, even if the co-conspirator didn't actually set the bomb, he's responsible for the death of the victims because he is part of the overall scheme?"

On Lerner. "Correct. If the prosecution can show that Mr. McDonald knew or could have foreseen that the bomb would kill the victims in San Antonio, he's as guilty as if he placed the bomb himself. And he's also responsible for any other foreseeable offenses that one of the co-conspirators commits in furtherance of the plan."

On Anguish. "Such as?"

On Lerner. "For example, if someone was shot or injured in the course of the detonation, all co-conspirators could be held responsible even though that wasn't part of the original plan."

On Anguish. "Does the prosecution have enough evidence to prove a circumstantial case against McDonald? Do you foresee a guilty verdict in this case?"

On Lerner. "I never try to get into the minds of an American jury, but the evidence seems compelling."

44

The first day of the trial of Bobby Ray McDonald began in a flurry of activity around the federal courthouse in Austin. Barricades and police held back crowds, and a long line formed at the security entrance as each person was scanned for weapons and phones before entering the courtroom.

The press used every advantage to gain footage of the spectacle, including placing cameras on the roofs of nearby buildings and having parked vans overnight, in strategic positions, along the nearby streets.

Protestors on both sides of the issues carried signs and chanted slogans either for McDonald's release or calling for him to be put to death. Both sides agreed on one thing: No justice, no peace.

Once all participants were successfully seated in the courtroom, Judge Ginsberg wasted no time getting things moving.

"Come to order! Same admonitions are in place. Anyone disrupting these proceedings will be removed."

The entire room of attorneys, court officers, and attendees released a collective sigh. Only McDonald seemed to be holding his breath as he once again sat sandwiched between Jerry Webb and Helen Sharp.

Faye and Lucy were not allowed to attend the proceedings as they were to be called as witnesses and weren't allowed to hear other witness testimony. McDonald looked around the courtroom and didn't appear to recognize anyone. Merit looked at his face and almost felt sorry for him. Almost.

Judge Ginsberg called for opening remarks. "Mr. Bowser, are you ready with your opening statement?"

Prosecutor Bob Bowser stood. "Yes, Your Honor." He turned to the jury. "We are here today to prove the guilt of Bobby Ray McDonald. The prosecution will show that Mr. McDonald planned, financed, and assisted in the execution of the crime of murder in the first degree.

"We will further show that the charge of mens rea is pertinent here in that Mr. McDonald joined with other co-conspirators with the intention of committing these heinous crimes and did proceed to commit those crimes in conjunction with Messrs. Walsh, Cobb, and Trigger."

Merit ticked off the elements of the case in her mind as Bowser droned on and on. He didn't seem to be aware that the jury members had lost interest in his pontification and were fidgeting in their chairs. Merit was dying for a bathroom break when the prosecutor finally ran out of steam and sat down. The judge must have needed to go as well because he immediately called a twenty-minute break.

When everyone returned to court and settled in, Judge Ginsberg called for the defense opening statement. Before he stood up, Jerry looked back at the spot where Lyle Ryder had sat before and felt a jolt of horror when he thought of what happened to him. Jerry rose, buttoned the top two buttons on his jacket, and cleared his throat.

"Ladies and gentlemen of the jury, I will be brief. My name is Jerry Webb and I represent Bobby Ray McDonald."

Jerry put his hand on McDonald's shoulder before moving around the table and standing closer to the jury box. "Your job as jurists is to listen to all of the evidence, as you promised during voir dire. We all heard the prosecution sum up a tidy story asserting my client's guilt. But you're all smart enough to know that things are never that cut and dried. In order to prove mens rea, or co-conspiracy, the court must show that my client agreed to commit the crime, never withdrew his participation if it had occurred, did not believe he was acting outside the law, and did not commit any furthering of the crime that may have been discussed. Although we could take full advantage of all of these defenses, we plan to focus on the first, that my client agreed to commit the crime. There is absolutely no evidence of that. When the witnesses testify and the documentation is introduced, you will hear only that my client was friends with Messrs. Walsh, Cobb, and Trigger. What you will not hear is that the four planned anything other than a hunting trip. What you will not see is any evidence tying my client to the other three alleged co-conspirators. What you will not see is any proof at all that my client even knew of the events that unfolded on Cinco de Mayo in San Antonio."

Merit looked at her legal pad and ticked off the defense position as she had outlined it. Jerry had delivered it perfectly and she didn't think she could have done it better herself.

When Jerry finished, Judge Ginsberg thanked both the

prosecution and defense teams for their comments and adjourned court for the day with a loud bang of his gavel.

Merit stood along with the rest of the room as the judge left the bench.

What does the prosecution think they have? Phone records are not enough. There's still something we're missing here.

45

The stress was building on Jerry. He needed to think and clear his mind, but the days were so full of the trial he had no time. After prepping for the next day's witnesses, he went for a nighttime run. The trail around Lady Bird Lake was well lit, and there were runners and walkers almost twenty-four hours a day somewhere along the path.

He parked near the statue of Stevie Ray Vaughan and ran toward the Congress Avenue bridge where the tourists were watching the bats fly out. He ran over the bridge, then turned left, intending to run all the way to Austin High School, but fate had other plans.

Jerry exited the north end of the bridge, took a left, and jogged to the corner. He had the green light, so he paused to check the traffic and trotted on across the street and south. He felt movement on his left and jumped to his right as a bicyclist in a black helmet bumped into his left shoulder.

Jerry yelled. "Watch where you're going!"

Jerry couldn't stop his momentum and he stepped into the street in front of oncoming traffic that had been stopped at the light. Traffic continued and several horns blared, drivers swerved to avoid hitting him. The bicyclist looked back over his shoulder but didn't stop.

A white Tesla sedan swerved, but still clipped Jerry on his right thigh. Jerry went down and his head banged the curb and his shoulder hit the pavement, hard. The Tesla's quick stop set off a pileup of screeching tires and crunching rear-ended cars, filling the night with noise.

Moments later, as Jerry looked up from the street, he could see shapes of people all around him. He could hear people yelling and an ambulance siren in the distance. *Probably coming from Brackenridge*, he thought, just before he lost consciousness.

Jerry lay in the hospital under the influence of some very heavy drugs. He woke up to see his law partner, Adam Alistair, sitting in the corner, reading something on his phone.

Jerry looked around at the institutional style room, that seemed to blur at the edges, and mumbled something incoherent.

Alistair looked up with a smile. "Hey, we almost lost you."

Jerry tried to speak but couldn't seem to make his mouth work. He almost gagged on the strong smell of antiseptic.

Alistair took a cup of water with a straw inserted in the lid and offered it to Jerry. "This should help."

A few sips seemed to revive Jerry and his brain engaged his mouth to talk with a slur. "What happened?"

"Looks like you fell off the sidewalk in front of a fairly large car. The car won."

"Very fucking funny." It came out more like "therry thucking unny."

Alistair smiled. "I thought running was supposed to make you healthier, not kill you."

Jerry almost mustered a smile at the joke. "Injuries?"

"A car hit your thigh, you fell and hit your head and shoulder. Nothing is broken, but you have serious muscle bruising and a concussion."

A nurse came into the room and took Jerry's pulse. She increased the drip on the bag, hanging by the bed, that was connected by a long plastic tube to Jerry's vein. She gave Alistair a warning look on her way out the door. "Not too much longer. He needs to rest."

Jerry's eyes began to flutter. "How long?"

"How long have you been here? Just since last night. How long will you stay here? The doctors want to watch the concussion for a couple of days. We've notified Judge Ginsberg. He's ordered a delay in the trial until you can either get on your feet or we substitute someone else from the firm. He said something about lawyers dropping like flies from Alistair, Riley & Webb."

Jerry didn't try to laugh this time. He spoke in short, clipped sentences with much effort. "No. Don't do that. Buy me some time. I have to ..."

"Your father would want you to be safe. Maybe it's best if someone else takes over."

That's an odd thing to say, Jerry thought as he slipped back into a dream state, remembering Robert Riley's purported suicide and Lyle Ryder's hit and run.

Alistair left Jerry's room per the nurse's orders. Since she'd increased the pain meds, he was asleep and wouldn't know if visitors were there or not.

When Alistair walked out of the room, Duke stood at the end of the hall by the stairwell, avoiding the cameras and medical personnel. "Is he going to make it?"

Alistair nodded. "Yes. You should have finished him. He'll never give up and he'll wind up ruining my law firm."

Duke laughed. "I thought you two were asshole buddies. Now you want him out of the way?"

The attorney frowned. "I'm friends with everyone until they cut into my income. Speaking of income ..."

Duke nodded. "Everything always comes down to money, doesn't it?"

"And you're in it for the fun of it?"

Duke grunted. "I'm in it for my own reasons. You'll get your money."

46

Ag waited for Merit in the parking garage at her condo. He sat in his blue F-150 listening to "Chitlins con Carne" by Stevie Ray Vaughan and Double Trouble.

Ag had his head back and his eyes closed as Stevie's grinding guitar transported him to a time when Austin was classic Austin and keeping it weird meant more. He opened his eyes to peek when he heard a car coming down the ramp, but it wasn't her.

After about half an hour, he was rewarded when he saw Merit's red BMW SUV round the corner and proceed to her parking space.

He waited for her to get out of the car so as not to startle her. Merit wore a suit of pale lavender with a dark purple blouse beneath and black strappy high heel sandals that showed off her legs. A Louis Vuitton tote completed the outfit.

Ag admired her through the windshield of his truck. *Such a beautiful woman*, he thought.

He allowed himself a few more seconds to enjoy the view, then lightly tapped the horn.

Merit looked up, smiled, then looked confused. She walked over to the truck. Ag turned off the music and rolled down his window.

"Climb in."

"I can't. What are you doing here? You know I can't confer ex parte with the defense team. How many times do you think we can get away with this?"

"I know, but this isn't actually about the case. I'm worried about you. Besides, don't you think we've passed that threshold?"

Merit looked up and down the garage then walked around to the passenger side. Ag reached over and pushed open the door and she climbed in.

"What's happened?"

"Jerry is in the hospital. Running accident. He could have been killed."

Merit sucked in her breath and her armpits prickled full on.

"He's going to be okay. Jerry thought there was probably foul play surrounding Robert Riley's demise, then that reporter is killed, and now this."

"I had no idea about Riley."

"The McDonald matter was the only file Riley was working on, so it follows that his death might have had something to do with the case. I had to warn you."

"It could be a coincidence with the reporter. Even if Riley's death wasn't a suicide, it doesn't mean anyone is coming after me." Merit's armpits prickled again.

"I know. But there's more. Lyle Ryder warned Jerry on a couple of occasions about unusual things he suspected were going on behind the scenes. He was a young journalist but did seem to have a nose for things."

"I'll be careful. You shouldn't be here."

"I know, but it looks like someone's cleaning house, and you could be in the crosshairs."

"I appreciate your concern, Ag. I really do, but there are cameras all over this garage. You have to go."

Ag looked at her gently. "I will. But, if someone is killing lawyers, I don't want you to be one of them."

Merit approached the nurses' station at the hospital where Jerry was recovering. She waited for the duty nurse to leave the desk and slipped into Jerry's room.

When she first looked at him, she felt a jolt. His eyes were closed, and he was so gray she thought he might be dead. She looked at the monitor beside the bed and saw a graph showing his vital signs.

Oh my God.

She moved to the bedside and put her hand on his, lying limp at his side. His eyes fluttered and he looked at her, then closed his eyes and drifted away again. Merit leaned over, kissed his cheek, and left the way she'd come in.

47

W hen Jerry made it out of the hospital, Judge Ginsberg gave him a few days to get his case back together. In preparation for calling his witnesses, Jerry went, at the appointed time, to meet with McDonald's wife, Faye, and daughter, Lucy.

It was the reason Faye and Lucy had been moved to Austin when the change of venue was granted by the San Antonio federal court. They were needed nearby to assist in the preparation of the case, and also to be protected from those seeking possible revenge for McDonald's actions.

Jerry's plan was to put Faye on the stand in defense of her husband. Jerry hoped he could elicit testimony from her that would shed light on McDonald's relationship with the cell that caused the bombing. Of course, she could not be compelled to testify. Jerry wanted to evaluate her ability to be helpful or harmful to the case. He hoped that if Faye testified on her husband's behalf, he could convince McDonald not to testify.

The FBI agents who escorted Jerry from downtown Austin to the safehouse stayed in their cars on the street to make sure the transport group had not been followed. The protective team of FBI agents opened the door to the safehouse and frisked Jerry.

Jerry raised his arms. "I need to talk to them. I don't want to kill them."

Where were you when a bicycle was mowing me down?

Jerry went into the modest living room with sparse furnishings where Faye and Lucy sat on a long beige print sofa. Lucy watched a large television, sitting on a console at the end of the room, showing an American sitcom. As all three introduced themselves, Lucy surreptitiously peeked at the TV show from time to time.

Before starting his questions, Jerry sat in a matching beige chair, placed near the end of the sofa, and sized them up. Both mother and daughter wore jeans and T-shirts, Lucy in a rosy pink and Faye in dark green. Where Faye seemed shy and reserved, Lucy seemed almost like any American kid, curious, outgoing, and healthy, but with a cloud of sadness surrounding her.

Jerry went through a list of questions covering their family history. "How did you come to be in Texas in general, and San Antonio in particular?"

Faye thought for a moment. "We came to San Antonio for my husband's work. He had been a butcher at his uncle's shop and when he left that place, a friend of his in San Antonio offered him a job doing similar work. I don't know the friend's name or how it was arranged."

"Has that always been Bobby Ray's profession? A butcher?"

"No, he's had lots of jobs. Mostly handyman. In the last few years, that's what he's done for work."

Jerry flipped a page on his legal pad to the next questions. "How could he afford the Hummer and your home on a butcher's salary? I know there are butchers and shop owners who make more money, but your husband didn't seem to be on that level."

Faye nodded. "I don't know."

Lucy seemed to take an interest. "A friend of his in Houston got the Hummer for him. We drove it to San Antonio."

Faye gave her daughter a warning look.

Jerry didn't see it. "Do you know the friend's name?"

Lucy looked toward the kitchen as movement revealed a shadow of someone in the next room. She gave Jerry a worried look and shook her head. "No."

Jerry got up and looked around the corner, but no one was there.

Faye answered most of the remaining background questions, with Lucy filling in very few details from her perspective.

"I'd like to know more about the arrest. How the family was taken into custody by the FBI so soon after the bombing."

Faye answered. "We were surprised by a shout at the door by the FBI. We had no idea a bombing had occurred as we'd been in the back yard gardening all morning."

Lucy looked surprised but nodded her agreement.

Jerry made a note. "And where was Bobby Ray at the time of your detainment? The documentation I've seen merely says he and the family were detained. He was not in the news footage at the time you were picked up at home."

Faye hesitated, then said, "He wasn't there."

It was like pulling teeth to get a straight and full answer from them. When Jerry focused on questions surrounding their detainment and the bombing, both mother and daughter showed signs of nervousness and anxiety.

"I'm here to represent your husband. I don't know how much I can do, but I certainly need your help. You do want to help him, don't you?"

Lucy's eyes softened. She looked at Jerry and smiled.

Jerry smiled back.

Lucy locked eyes with him, then shifted her gaze to the corner of the room where a lamp, possibly housing a video camera, was reflecting a red light against the metal base.

Jerry caught the hint and made a mental note. *The FBI is watching.*

Jerry modified his questions to less sensitive subjects than the bombing and arrests, and the mother and daughter seemed to relax.

After another few minutes, asking pretend questions he already knew the answers to, he wrapped it up. "That about does it for now."

Lucy looked over at the television as the sitcom ended and the local news began. The opening showed a series of photographs around Austin and settled on a torrent of rain over the Texas Hill Country.

Jerry nodded at the television. "Looks like we're in for it."

Lucy moved over to the screen. "It does. I'll turn up the volume."

The radar showed multiple colors of weather cells moving into the area. "Another wave of thunderstorms is approaching from the north."

She turned up the sound with her back to the lamp camera, as the newscaster reported on the inclement weather that had damaged many buildings in town the night before.

The newscaster had switched to the Broken Spoke and the damage to the roof of the honky-tonk by golf ball sized hail. Lucy tapped on the screen so Jerry could see, but not Faye or the camera. The spot Lucy was tapping was the sign over the entrance to the bar.

Jerry looked at his watch and looked at Faye. "I didn't realize I was keeping you so late." Then to Lucy, as he tapped his watch and winked at her. "It's almost nine o'clock."

The next night, Jerry drove to the Broken Spoke a little before nine, circled the block, and backed into the garage of the beer parlor across the street so he could see the entire parking lot and establishment before him. He was sure Lucy had picked up on the double entendre and the wink he had given her about the time of a possible meeting. He was certain that she had tapped on the sign for the Broken Spoke.

What wasn't certain was whether she could get out of the house undetected by the FBI and possibly her mother. If she did get out, how would she get from the safehouse to the Broken Spoke about fifteen miles away?

After sitting in his car for over an hour, he looked at his watch. It was nine thirty, he'd gotten nothing for his trouble and his head still hurt from the accident. He gave up and went home.

48

D uke met Tank at a biker bar called Sally's on the outskirts of Waco. Both wore leather jackets, boots, and Baylor Bear caps pulled down over their eyes. None of the drunk, rowdy bikers seemed to notice them or the bulges under their clothing from the guns they toted. Half the bikers toted guns, too.

They took a booth in the far corner, Duke with his back to the wall and Tank reluctantly in the vulnerable spot with his back to the room. They ordered a couple of burgers and beers from the bleach blonde waitress wearing a Sally's T-shirt showing a bull rider on the back of a Harley. The handlebars had been replaced by wide longhorns and the printing stated: Watch This, Hold my Beer.

Duke looked around one last time, then turned to Tank. "How are the troops?"

Tank grunted. "They're getting bored and restless. They're undisciplined and anxious for some action."

"Figures. How's Four Leaf holding up?"

"She's about to lose it. I don't think she'll make it much

longer. The homeboys want to lynch her now that she's been convicted in the faux trial."

The waitress slammed a couple of frosty longnecks on the table. "Food will be right up."

Duke waited for her to clear out. "How much longer will they follow orders?"

Tank took a swig from his longneck. "My two guys are good, but the rest are not really military. I'm running out of things to tell them."

"I'm planning a dramatic event to give them some new energy, get them stoked up again. Can you buy me more time?"

"I'll work on it."

49

Duke went to meet with Faye and Lucy at the safehouse. He addressed the agents on duty. "Go ahead and take a break. I need to talk to them." Duke jerked his thumb toward the living room.

The two agents went outside on the deck, one lit up a cigarette. When Duke was sure they were out of hearing range, he nodded at Lucy and addressed Faye. "I need to talk to Lucy about her testimony."

"I can help her remember what she needs to say."

He looked at Faye then went over to the lamp and switched off the camera control behind it.

Duke grunted. "Understand what will happen if you don't."

"We're well aware of your tactics, Duke. Tell us what you want."

"Lucy, you'll be asked questions about who you saw with your dad and what they said."

"I did see him with Walsh and Trigger, but I don't know what they said. I never saw Cobb."

"You identify the men, then tell the court that you heard

them discuss the bombing, but you didn't know the place or date. You can say you weren't sure what was going on until after the event in San Antonio."

Lucy bit her lip. "I don't know if I can remember all that."

"Keep it simple. Just stick to the men with your father, talk of the bombing, and you don't know anything else. You never saw him with anyone else. Remember that."

Faye looked at Duke. "You know that will get him the death penalty."

Lucy looked shocked. "I won't kill my own father."

Duke locked eyes with Lucy. "Your father or your mother. Which is it going to be?"

Duke postured his large body in a menacing way in front of Faye. "Remember that you haven't been arrested, but that could change at any time."

Faye looked at Lucy. "I know my place."

Lucy looked at Duke with defiance, then to her mother and smiled. "Don't worry, Mama."

Duke glared at Lucy. "Now look, you little brat. You want to help your parents, you'll keep your mouth shut about the rest. You start spreading lies and getting all chatty with the lawyers and we'll put you in separate jail cells. You'll never see either of your parents again."

Lucy looked angry. "I know the deal, Agent Duke." *Rhymes with puke,* she thought.

Lucy took her handheld game player off her nightstand and pretended to play a game. She clicked around on the buttons and jerked around like she was killing bad guys. After she was pretty sure she was boring the FBI watchers downstairs, she went to the window and opened it. She couldn't be sure the FBI wasn't onto her, but she had to risk it. She turned her back to the camera, propped her elbows on the windowsill, and held the game out the window as if she were still playing, gesticulating, and saying things like 'take that' and 'gotcha.'

Lucy waited until she saw two small bars appear on the game player WiFi and latched onto the signal from the neighbor's internet. She logged into her father's bank, clicked on the bank statements button, and downloaded the bank records with evidence of the deposits from the FBI to her father's account. Next, she plugged in a flash drive and loaded the statements on it. She saved the information in a file marked 'Math Test,' logged out, and closed the website.

She heard one knock on her door, then it flew open. Rachel Ward stood there with a suspicious look on her face. "What are you doing?"

Lucy pulled the flash drive from the game player, let it drop to the grass below through the open window, and turned toward the door.

"Just playing my game. It's hot in here."

Rachel examined a rheostat by the light switch near the door. "Close that window. I'll turn up the ceiling fan."

Lucy smiled at her sweetly. "Thanks."

Rachel didn't smile back.

50

Duke stared at his computer screen. He knew someone had started to suspect the FBI's role and was leaking information. He was certain that they had not yet identified him as an active participant since he still had full access and was running the case. He mentally formulated a plan and began an email from one of his many faux accounts.

Two can play the leak game.

He knew the *Washington Times* as well as NNN would read the Huntingdon Report, an online political blog, written by a left-wing political hack with connections. It was the perfect place to leak information. He composed the email as if it were from an anonymous source in the inner circle of law enforcement, which technically it was.

"The FBI has been working under the assumption that the terrorist cell is bigger than they had first believed. They've tied the bombing materials to several other smaller attacks around the country, including the offshore rig bombing near Corpus Christi, Texas."

Duke thought for a few more minutes, then added another paragraph.

"There have been several failed attempts that were thwarted, but kept secret, by the FBI in an effort to capture the perpetrators and possibly the ring leaders of the domestic terrorist group. The FBI has narrowed its search to the American Freedom Militia, a web of constitutional activists loosely connected across the United States by the dark web through a site on which they communicate in code."

Rachel tapped on the door. "I'm heading home. Need anything before I go?"

Duke jerked his head up. "No. Uh. No, thanks."

"Sorry to interrupt. You must have been deep in thought there."

Duke smiled his best smile. "Just trying to catch a few bad guys."

"Anything I can do to help?"

"No. I'll see you tomorrow."

When Rachel left, Duke returned to his fake news email. "The American Freedom Militia, which is rumored to be encamped near Waco, is suspected of having connections to gun running, the income from which supports their terrorist efforts."

That should do it.

Next step in the plan, Duke called Tank on the burner. "Someone talked. There's been intel about the militia's location. I can't contain it. We'll have to move up the timeline."

"A fuckin' leak! Shame. How much damage do you want?"

Duke rubbed his chin and thought of all the work he'd done going down the drain, but it couldn't be helped. "All the way. Follow the plan. You have three to four hours. Be sure you get out before then."

"I want to take a couple of the Sincero guys and the Four Leaf extraction team with me. I trust those guys. They're mine. They're not the leak."

"We can't take the risk. No loose ends. I'll clean up my end. You handle yours."

"They don't know your name or that you're my contact. I know these guys. How about just Six-pack and Cupcake?"

"They know your name, and you know mine. Wrap it up. All the way."

Tank grunted. "It's a shame. It takes years to train these guys, and I consider them friends."

"Can't be helped. Understood?"

There was a long pause.

"Tank, I said do you understand?"

"Roger that."

Three hours later, Duke led a fleet of FBI vehicles down Interstate 35 past Waco and onto a small farm-to-market road with bullet holes in the highway markers. McLennan County sheriff squad cars joined in behind them, and they all arrived at the militia encampment at once. They were just in time, as the first explosion that Tank had set went off in one of the bunkhouses behind the main building.

Reacting to the noise, militia members took cover around the camp and began to fire on law enforcement who dropped down behind their vehicles and returned fire. The majority of the militia fired from windows and doors of the main building as a second timed explosion ripped through it, killing everyone inside. Three more explosions followed in each of the remaining close-in buildings, taking out the last of the members bearing automatic weapons.

Five members bearing handguns ran out the back of one of the outbuildings toward the small shed on the far perimeter of the property. Duke shot one, signaling to his FBI team to take them out. The fastest runner in the militia fired into the shed as his brothers in arms fell one by one on the path to the shack.

Duke ran down the path, jumping over dead bodies, into the shed behind the main building and found Clover Thibodeaux bound, gagged and sitting in her own urine on the grubby wooden plank floor.

"I'm Archibald Duke with the FBI. You're safe now." Duke untied her hands and pulled off the gag, a Lone Star State kerchief. Her clothes were dirty and tattered. Her bare feet were almost black with soil.

Duke waited until he could hear the helicopters overhead, then told Clover it was time to go. Clover shrieked and wrapped her arms around his neck, sobbing as Duke lifted her and carried her out into the sunshine while the helicopter cameras above filmed the ostensibly heroic act.

The scene looked like something out of an apocalyptic movie. After the explosions and gunfire ceased, the crackling fires continued to pop and hiss. The main building and all the outbuildings, except the shed, continued to burn to the ground. Within minutes, the entire camp and its members were wiped out. Duke rounded up his crew and barked orders to gather evidence and take photographs, but there was little left to verify.

Merit, Red Thallon, and Kim Wan Thibodeaux arrived at the McLennan County Hospital in Waco at almost the same time and were hit with the smell of institutional cleaner. Red had picked up the report of the raid from her news sources and grabbed Merit on the way out of Austin for the one-hour drive to Waco. Kim Wan had been called by an FBI staffer who was guarded as to Clover's condition.

News vans had moved from the flaming encampment to the hospital and setup a perimeter that pushed the legal limits allowed by the county. Duke gave the nod to allow Merit and Kim Wan through, but Red had to stay behind with the press. Merit gave her a knowing look as if to say, *I'll fill you in shortly*.

Kim Wan looked as though he would faint, and Merit grabbed his hand to steady him as they wound their way through the institutional corridors and followed Duke into a room with sheriffs guarding the door.

Clover sat on an examining table in a hospital gown. Her face was dirty, her hair matted. Her feet were so dirty it was impossible to tell what color her skin was. Both Kim Wan and Merit burst into tears.

51

Jerry drove to Thom's Convenience Store on Barton Springs Road. He went in and found a rack of burner phones, looked around to make sure he wasn't seen, and bought two. Next, he went to the Office Depot on South Lamar at Oltorf and used the business office to design and print out several flyers with a picture of a Cairn Terrier he'd found on the internet. He bought some supplies and paid for all of it with cash.

He got in his car and drove back to Lady Bird Lake and parked on the south side near the Pfluger Pedestrian Bridge. He sat in his car and programmed the two phones, left one in the glove box, and walked halfway across the bridge to the lamppost where he and Merit had shared their special kiss.

He taped the flyer to the lamppost. It had the picture of the Cairn Terrier, the words 'missing dog' in large font, and the phone number of the burner phone that he'd left in the glove box. He concealed the second burner phone beneath the flyer and went round and round with the tape to hide the bump beneath. Satisfied that the phone was concealed, he returned to the car and texted Merit:

FOUND YOUR DOG. MEET ON PFLUGER BRIDGE.

Merit sat at the desk in her office going through client files and catching up on correspondence left by Betty in her IN box. Her phone went off signaling a text from a number she didn't recognize. It stated that her dog had been found. She started to hit reply, but she knew that Pepper could not have gotten out of the condo. Instead, she called the security desk at her high rise.

"Hi, Jack. Just checking in. Did you take Pepper out for her afternoon walk today?"

Jack replied, "Yes, she was happy to have a potty break. I let her take a few turns around the dog park, gave her a treat, and locked her back in around 4:00 p.m. Any problem? Want me to run up and check on her?"

"No, just wanted to be sure all was normal. Need to run. Thanks."

She looked at the text again, studied it for a long while, then got up, grabbed her jacket and handbag, and left.

Merit drove to her condo, parked in the underground garage, and took the elevator up to her unit. When she let herself in, Pepper came trotting up to greet her with a big doggie grin, then rolled over on her back. Merit leaned down and rubbed her tummy.

"You're just fine aren't you, Pepper Dog? Want to go for a walk?"

Pepper rolled over onto all fours and ran to the hall closet where her leash was kept.

Merit laughed. "Give me a minute to change, girl."

Merit went into her bedroom, switched into her running gear, transferred her phone, house keys, driver's license, and some cash into a waist pack, and went back to the living room. Pepper was still sitting and facing the closet door.

"You're my disguise."

Merit got the leash, hooked it on Pepper's collar, and away they went.

Merit and Pepper trotted from her condo through the Warehouse District downtown and over to Lady Bird Lake. They moved into the foot traffic running and biking along the Butler Hike and Bike Trail and eventually onto the Pfluger Pedestrian Bridge.

Merit slowed to a walk as she approached the special lamp post, then she saw it. A missing dog poster with a Cairn Terrier pictured that looked a lot like Pepper. She examined the flyer, pressed around the back side, and finding nothing, pressed the front and felt a bump. She ripped the top then the bottom of the paper flyer, as she could not tear the duct tape or remove it. When she cleared the paper, she was able to stretch the tape until she worked the hump out from under it. It was a burner phone. She looked around, but no one seemed to care about her or Pepper.

She slipped the phone into her pack, zipped it shut, and jogged back the way she'd come and to her condo.

Back in her condo, Merit waited, then got hungry. She looked up her grandmother's pasta sauce recipe and waited some more. The burner phone was on the island in the kitchen, but it didn't ring. No text, no nothing.

She put a large red Le Creuset pot on the gas stove and sweated onions, bell pepper, and garlic. Then, she browned a pound of ground round and added two cans of tomatoes. While the water for the pasta boiled, she went onto the patio and harvested two big bunches of basil from a pot of herbs. It smelled wonderful, but she was too nervous to eat much. She put most of it in the refrigerator and finished the glass of Malbec she'd started with the meal. Still no text.

She paced, turned on the news, turned off the news, and finally sat down on the sofa, put the burner phone on the coffee table, and stared out the window.

The burner buzzed and Merit grabbed it.

The text read: Can't talk on phone, must meet.

Merit: Can't. What's wrong?

Burner: Danger. Meet.

Merit: Okay. Where?

52

Lucy went up to her room for bed around 11:00 p.m. She was sure the FBI agents were watching her from the camera she'd found in her room when they'd first come to the safe house. She had wanted to sneak out the day after she and Jerry made their silent agreement, but a female FBI agent had come by every night to tuck her in, and she was certain she'd be found out if she left. Today, there were only male FBI agents in the house, and they had never come into her bedroom before.

She made a big deal of saying goodnight to her mother in front of the camera in Faye's bedroom, then went to her own room, presumably to get ready for bed. She opened the bathroom door to block the camera. In the bathroom, she pulled a jean jacket over her pajama top and popped a Spurs cap on her head. Her pajama bottoms had a small flower print. She hoped anyone she ran into would think they were just pants. Next, she bunched pillows and blankets to make it appear that she was under the covers asleep. She turned off the lights so that the room was dark and closed the bathroom door, allowing viewing to the camera again.

Lucy slid on her belly along the foot of the bed out of the camera angle, then opened and climbed out the window. She slid down the side of the house using her Nikes to grip a rain gutter to the ground.

She cut through the neighbor's yard near a wooded area and over to the street at the end of the block. She made her way to the bus stop and, before she could say cat burglar, she was on a bus to South Lamar and Ben White Boulevard.

Merit walked into The Tavern and let her eyes adjust to the darkness. After a few minutes, she saw Jerry at the end of the bar wearing a Yale law school cap. She went over and sat on the stool beside him.

"We should not be here. What's so important?"

"You must see what I'm seeing in all those documents."

"I can't say. You'll have to tell me what you mean."

"Aren't we past that? McDonald was working for the FBI at the time of the bombing. He was their CI and something went wrong. They either didn't stop the cell or McDonald didn't pass on the intel, but they made it possible."

Merit winced. "Can you prove that?"

"McDonald won't admit it, but I know it's true. That's what the FBI is trying to hide."

Merit studied the table. "If we're going to do anything with this information, we must prove it first."

"They got Riley, it wasn't suicide, and they got Lyle Ryder. Next, they'll get me. Don't give them a reason to get you, too."

Merit nodded. "I have an idea, but I need your help. We can bring out the truth in open court to protect McDonald and us. We can't openly breach the oath, but we can let the court do the work for us."

"You mean introduce enough of the documents into evidence to show the FBI connection?"

"Yes, and, once it's out, they have no further reason to come after us."

"We need more evidence."

"Yes. Where can we get it?"

Around nine, Merit and Jerry circled the block around the Broken Spoke several times, looking for Lucy. They were just about to give up when Jerry saw someone he thought was her, behind a large oak tree, peeking out at him.

Jerry walked over, looking around to make sure no one noticed. "Hi, Lucy. You made it."

"I had to wait for the lady agent to have a day off. The men never come in my bedroom at night."

"Do you think they'll miss you?"

"Maybe, but they already know I don't like being told what to do. If they do miss me, they'll never guess I'm meeting with you."

Merit joined them.

"This is Merit Bridges. She's another one of your dad's attorneys."

Merit nodded. "You have something you need to tell us about your dad?"

"How do I know I can trust you not to hurt us?"

Merit smiled. "I guess you'll have to trust your instincts."

Jerry smiled too. "If you need help, I promise I will do everything in my power to assist you and your mother."

Lucy looked at Jerry and seemed to make a decision. "I have a flash drive with some things about my dad."

Jerry sucked in air so loudly he surprised himself. "What are you saying?"

"My dad was a confidential informant for the FBI. He was getting in wire transfers and giving government money to the militia."

"How do you know for sure?"

"He talked to the FBI agent on the phone every week. Lately, all the time. I have the bank records."

"How much money are we talking about? Enough to pay the bills or more?"

"Lots more. Hundreds of thousands of dollars."

Merit sucked in her breath.

"I have to go back now. My mom will be put in jail if I don't cooperate. They might even hurt her. Agent Duke is all over me lately."

"Why are you on their witness list?"

"Duke is making me testify against my dad. I'm supposed to say I saw him with Walsh and Trigger, who were killed. He knows I know something else, but he doesn't know what. I don't want to testify. I don't want to go to court at all."

"Give us some time to work on this. Do you want us to drive you back? Drop you in the neighborhood?"

"No, I'll take the bus back. If they catch me, at least they won't know I talked to you."

"Lucy, I'm really worried about you. You are brave, but you're very young to have all this on your shoulders."

Lucy began to cry. "I have to help my mom."

Merit started toward the bar. "Okay. Let me run in here and get a drink. You can douse yourself with it. The FBI agents will hopefully think you're a willful teenager who went out partying with friends."

"I wish I were."

Jerry looked worried. Merit went inside the Broken Spoke

and got a shot of whiskey. When she came back out, Lucy and Jerry were hiding behind the tree again. Lucy came out and Merit handed her the shot.

"If you're caught, just act drunk. They won't be able to get a straight answer from you and will hopefully put you to bed."

Lucy nodded and took the shot glass from her and poured the contents on her pajama bottoms.

Jerry took a piece of paper from his pocket and wrote on it.

"I have a burner phone. Here's the number. Memorize it. If you need us, text and we'll meet you here. Just know they're probably monitoring your phone."

"I know. I won't be able to call or text without them knowing."

"If you're in real trouble, it won't matter if they know."

Lucy swallowed hard, turned, and started jogging toward the bus stop in her liquor-soaked pants.

Merit and Jerry drove back downtown, mulling over what they'd learned from Lucy.

Merit stated what they were both thinking. "That's a lot of money from the FBI to McDonald."

"Yep. More than what's needed to pay his bills. They were financing his operations within the militia."

Merit's shoulders sagged. "The bomber killed all those innocent people with taxpayer money."

Jerry's head swiveled on his neck. "Riley found out. When Riley got close, I think they killed him and made it look like a suicide.

"McDonald was part of the American Freedom Militia. They're watched by the FBI all the time. His actions would not have been missed. Riley may have had evidence of that."

"McDonald was clearly their confidential informant, but who was handling him?"

"Duke most likely. Could there be another explanation?"

"Either McDonald double-crossed the FBI or the cell suspected him and tricked him into taking the heat. No wonder the FBI is so upset. They fucked up. The FBI has to have a scapegoat and see this through until someone pays."

Jerry nodded. "The local tip off would have gone to SAPD and the cops went straight to the house before putting it out where the FBI could have known. The family was under arrest before the FBI could get to them. So, the agents had to cover it up."

Merit puzzled. "They can't all be dishonest, but they're all fucked if it comes out."

"That's about the sum of it," Jerry said.

53

Jerry met with McDonald one more time before he and Merit decided what to do. He had to be sure that what he was thinking was true, and he was willing to take a risk to find out. Jerry entered the facility and asked that his client be brought to him in the attorney interview room. Jerry sat at the metal table and looked at his watch.

What's taking so long?

When McDonald arrived, Jerry gave him a no-nonsense look.

"The FBI has evidence from your car that shows you had a weapon and pamphlets in it. SAPD found none of that, according to their reports, at the time it was impounded. How can you explain that it wasn't there, now it is?"

"Maybe they didn't look good enough the first time."

"Are you telling me that the evidence is legit? You really were foolish enough to have that type of paraphernalia in your vehicle?"

"I don't know."

Jerry was astonished. "This is one element of the case we can call into question, and you're not going to confirm or deny the validity of it?"

"I don't know."

"Who were you meeting at the restaurant? How can you explain going there before you left for Houston?"

"I can't."

"Were you a confidential informant for the FBI? Is that how you traveled so freely from one place to the next? I need answers to my questions, and I'm not going to dance with you this time. I know you were informing for the FBI, so don't deny it."

McDonald squirmed in the chair and seemed to be thinking fast.

"Tell me the truth. We know about the bank transfers. Did you know about the bombing or were you tricked? Did the cell hide it from you because they found out you were informing, or did you know about the bombing and not tell the FBI? It can only go one of two ways, which is it?"

McDonald blinked. "How the hell?"

Jerry stared him down. "No matter how the hell. I know you were informing to the FBI. I know you were part of the American Freedom Militia. Now, I want to know just what brand of monster you are. Did you help kill those people or just fail to prevent it?"

"I don't have an answer for you."

"Is it your family? Does someone have more on you? Why are you going like a sheep to the slaughter?"

McDonald put his head on the table. When he raised his head again, he looked into Jerry's eyes. It was a cold-blooded evil look that Jerry had never seen before. He knew McDonald was not the innocent he tried to believe. He knew.

An evil laugh caught in McDonald's throat. "You don't have a clue. You think you've figured it all out, but you haven't."

"Double talk. Always double talk. What do you mean I don't have a clue?"

.

54

D uke stood outside the detention cell where McDonald was being housed during the trial. Inside the cell, the accused sat on a single bed attached to the wall across from a one-piece toilet and sink appliance. Duke smiled at McDonald and nodded toward the observation camera in the corner of the ceiling. The red light was not on.

Duke grinned. "Nobody here but us terrorists."

"Where's my lawyer?"

"He's interviewing your wife and daughter. Besides, you don't need a lawyer, the die is cast. You've made your deal."

"I'll keep my end. I'll testify in open court. My attorney won't have anything to say about it. I'll do it in front of God and everybody. Webb can't force me, and neither can the judge. It's just between you and me. The two of us have a deal. I've already agreed to the plan, so why are you here?"

"Well, my friend, things have changed a bit since we made that deal. Your daughter is getting very squirrelly. Sneaking out at all hours. Drinking and whoring, for all we know. She's not

being cooperative anymore and your wife doesn't seem to be able to control her."

"Let me talk to them. I know Lucy will do anything to protect her mother. She knows what she has to do, whether she wants to or not."

"Well, that brings me to the reason for my little visit. Sometimes we all have to do things we don't want to do."

McDonald looked into Duke's evil eyes and grew stiff and cold. "What? I won't tell my lawyers or the court about the information I gave you, or the FBI money you gave me. My house and my Hummer can't be traced to you or the confidential informant cash. I'll never see my family again without bars between us. Isn't that punishment enough? What else can I do for you? What?"

Duke let out a wicked laugh. "Well, there's only one way to make sure that you never talk in any court at any time. Who knows, someone may come along and make you a better deal."

Realization swept over McDonald's face. "No, that wasn't our fuckin' deal. I'll go to prison for life. I'll never talk. Not to anyone."

"Your do-gooder attorney and his girlfriend lawyer have gotten wise. We can't afford to have them in open court anymore."

"That's your problem. I didn't tell them a thing."

"It's your problem now."

"I'll tell Webb to back off. He has to do what I say."

"Maybe. What about down the road? What if you really meet God this time instead of that radical dictator of a savior you claim you found?"

"Don't talk about my religion. You could use some fuckin' saving of your own."

"Maybe, but right now, I'm judge and executioner. There's only one way to stop the trial and stop the questions. You have until witnesses are called in court to meet your maker, or Faye and Lucy will meet theirs. No testimony on the record."

McDonald's shoulders slumped, and he looked up at the camera which was still off. "I'm on suicide watch."

"Don't worry about that. Even guards have to pee, especially on the three to eleven shift."

McDonald couldn't swallow his mouth was so dry.

"I want to see my family first. If you want me to do this thing, I want to tell them goodbye. Alone."

"You're not in a position to make demands."

"You're not in a position to deny me."

Duke setup a time for McDonald to meet with Faye and Lucy. Neither of the women knew it was to be their last visit. Duke was reluctant but things were unraveling, and he needed to start tying up loose ends.

The cover story was that they were needed to prepare for the defense. As if a cover was needed. No attorneys were present. In fact, Jerry didn't even know about the meeting, so legal prep was a thin excuse. Faye and Lucy were so thrilled to see McDonald, neither of them took time to consider how things had been arranged or might play out.

At the detention center, the family didn't meet in the usual place with surveillance cameras to monitor them. They met in a small vending machine room near the lockers and showers of the detention officers. Duke put a sign on the door indicating that it was closed for cleaning and sent for McDonald to be brought in.

By design, the meeting was set in the midst of the three to eleven shift, so all workers were at their stations and the locker room was empty. The two detention officers Duke needed to pull off the meeting were rabid militia sympathizers and well paid, although they would have done it for free to help the cause.

Duke had placed three chairs amongst the machines vending Coke, Doritos, Snickers, Rice Krispy Treats, and every other tempting snack known to modern overweight America. The colorful background of the advertisements on the machines was a stark contrast to the somber faces of the three McDonalds.

McDonald looked at Duke. "Take off my fuckin' handcuffs. Our deal was that I talk to them alone."

"We don't have a deal. Handcuffs stay. This is a courtesy. Make it fast." Duke stepped out into the hallway and closed the door behind him.

McDonald hugged his family as best he could without using his arms. "I don't think there are microphones in here. Duke doesn't want a record of this any more than we do, but we should be careful what we say, just in case."

Lucy's lower lip began to quiver. "Daddy, they want me to testify in court about you, Walsh, and Trigger being the bombers. They say they'll hurt Mama if I don't."

McDonald leaned over and put his cheek against Lucy's. "It's going to be okay. You won't have to testify. Just keep doing what they say. Agree to everything and you'll be alright."

Faye looked at her husband with a question mark in her eyes. "What do they know about me?"

Lucy looked alarmed.

McDonald looked at Faye. "Nothing yet. If I do what they say, they may never find out."

Tears began to puddle in Faye's eyes. "Is there no other way?"

Lucy jerked her head toward her mother. "No. No. What are you saying?"

McDonald looked at his daughter tenderly. "You have to be brave and strong. Protect your mother at all costs. I'm counting on you."

Faye bowed her head. "Let's pray."

Lucy looked at her mother and father as McDonald went into a long prayer about the sacredness of their family, triumph of the militia, and their rewards in heaven for their just deeds on earth.

Lucy did not pray with them. She remembered all the Sundays in church when her father and mother had pledged allegiance to a vengeful god she never understood. It was always in the days after church that they had violently hurt people and were proud of it. That was not a god she wanted to know. The only time she'd found peace was when she was in the woods walking through the trees or swimming in a pond or river. She thought of that now and prayed her own prayer. She asked for help from anyone or thing who might be out there, of a peaceful nature, and inclined to come to her aid.

That night around ten, McDonald knelt on the floor of his cell with his elbows on his bed and his hands folded in prayer. His lips moved silently as sweat poured down his face and dripped onto the striped ticking of the bare mattress. He looked up at the observation camera. The red light was not glowing as it usually did, in the dark, after lights out.

He whispered. "Father, you know I come to you with blood on my hands, but the cause was your cause and it was just. I ask your forgiveness for failing you in my quest to rid your beautiful world of the perverse, miserable, and abnormal vermin and animals that are taking it over."

The sweating stopped and resolve swept over him. He

looked at the torn sheets tied and knotted to the bars beside him. He closed his eyes one more time.

"I ask your blessings on my family. Please protect my wife from those who might harm her. Please lead my daughter into the path of her salvation in you. I ask the gift of a place in heaven with you for the good works I did in your name and for what I'm about to do here. In Jesus' name, amen."

Less than ten minutes later, McDonald's blood vessels began to dilate as he tightened the noose around his neck by slumping against the bars and sliding to the floor. He experienced visceral congestion of the venous blood vessels and blood stasis, petechiae, cyanosis, and fluidity of the body. Small veins broke from high intravascular pressure on the surface of his heart and organs, skin and scalp. His eyes bulged, his breathing stopped.

He may or may not have been at peace, only he and his god were privy to that information.

The three to eleven shift checked out, and the 11:00 p.m. to 7:00 a.m. shift started in the detention center where McDonald was jailed. A fresh guard viewed each high-security inmate, in turn, on the observation cameras. An alarm went up when the guard viewed McDonald's cell and saw his body slumped against the bars with the sheets tight around his neck.

Guards on the floor were dispatched to assist but when they arrived at McDonald's cell and checked his pulse, he was dead.

Duke had already been called by the corrupt three to eleven guards, at about 10:30 p.m., before the body was cold or officially discovered. As far as he was concerned, it was over.

55

With McDonald dead, Ag was officially off the clock on the case, but his intuition had been working overtime and he needed to tie up a loose end for his own benefit. He arrived at the Posse Restaurant on Bowie in San Antonio for the second time. He stood at the door until he spotted the waiter he had spoken to, and bribed, on his earlier visit. Ag motioned him over and started to ask a question.

The waiter held up his hand like a stop sign. "No. This time, you eat first."

"Alright, alright. Seat me in your section."

The waiter showed Ag to a booth and handed him a menu.

Ag selected the first thing he saw. "I'll have a club sandwich and an iced tea. Happy now?"

The waiter wrote down the order. "Okay, now ask your questions."

Ag scrolled through the photos and screenshots on his phone. "You told me that when the man who drove the Hummer was in here, he met with a big white man."

"Right."

Ag showed him a photo of Archie Duke from the press conference. "Is this him?"

The waiter took the phone and studied it carefully.

"Yep. Maybe. It might be. Hmm. I think so. Yeah."

"Thanks. I'll take that sandwich to go, please."

56

Early that morning, Merit and Betty went through the details of the case. As they worked in her office, they had NNN muted on the television. Betty looked up and saw the news crawl along the bottom of the screen: San Antonio Bomber commits suicide.

"Quick. Turn up the volume."

Merit hit the mute button just in time to hear Ernest Anguish reporting.

"Breaking news! In a disturbing turn of events in Austin, Texas, Bobby Ray McDonald died by suicide in his detention cell late last night. The alleged domestic terrorist and co-conspirator was awaiting trial on charges in the San Antonio Market bombing, for which he faced death or life in prison."

The screen split between Anguish's face and an aerial shot of the federal detention facility.

"Multiple sources told NNN that McDonald was placed on suicide watch, a monitoring process that is designed to prevent someone from taking their own life."

Back to full screen of Anguish.

"We have, as our guest today, Joseph Bircher, a former correctional treatment specialist for the Federal Bureau of Prisons and author of *Inmate Suicide*. Dr. Bircher comes to us from Arlington, Virginia. Welcome to the program and thank you for joining us."

The screen split between Anguish and Bircher who sat on camera in front of a bookshelf filled with at least two dozen copies of his book.

"Thank you for having me."

"Dr. Bircher, there has been no statement from the detention facility as to how or why the suicide watch failed. Can you tell us how a man on suicide alert would be able to take his own life?"

"So far, with the information that's been released, I don't see a breach of protocol in this instance. Suicide watch does not usually involve constant monitoring of an inmate. If someone is really determined to die, it is very difficult to prevent that. I don't see an egregious issue here."

"What is involved in monitoring high-risk inmates in correctional facilities?"

"Good question, Ernest. There are two main levels of suicide watch in detention facilities. The first is called constant observation or one-on-one, which means a staff member is assigned to sit outside the inmate's cell and provide continuous uninterrupted observation. The resources are usually not available for that, as it's very time and staff intensive. This method is used only with the most acutely suicidal."

On Anguish. "Obviously, that was not in place at the time of McDonald's suicide."

On Bircher. "Correct. The second and more common level to monitor those at risk is close observation. In most cases, inmates under this level are checked at fifteen-minute intervals via CCTV or walk-bys."

On Anguish. "Doesn't the prisoner get wise to the timetable and act accordingly, if they are really motivated to kill themselves?"

On Bircher. "It's best to stagger the walks, so the first-time officers would go by at around fifteen minutes, the next time ten minutes, then twelve, and so forth. That way, the inmate does not anticipate the observation happening. With CCTV, the timing is unknown to the prisoner, but most prisons either can't afford the equipment or only have the budget for one camera to cover several cells."

On Anguish. "We're told that there were no provisions for McDonald to kill himself in his cell. No sharp objects, eating utensils, ball point pens, shoelaces, that sort of thing."

On Bircher. "That's correct, Ernest. Inmates on suicide watch, or safety watch, should be kept in a suicide-resistant room. That means there are no protrusions for the inmate to hang himself on, like a vent, sprinkler head, doorknobs, bars, or bunkbeds, for example."

On Anguish. "What about sheets and pants?"

On Bircher. "Inmates can be given limited access to things they could potentially tie around their necks such as tear-resistant bedding and clothing. Nothing they could stuff down their throats. No toilet paper, no towels. They can be forced to wear a safety smock which can't be torn or wrapped up into a ligature."

On Anguish. "If all this was in place, how did McDonald kill himself?"

On Bircher. "We won't know the answer to that for certain until the autopsy is released, but most likely a mental health professional determined that the risk was moderate, advising monitoring and minimal suicide precaution. If that occurred, a limited number of items, such as sheets and clothing, may have been reinstated."

On Anguish. "In a case such as this one, with the accused being the center of national, even worldwide attention, why not keep the maximum suicide watch in place?"

On Bircher. "Being under this kind of watch is very restrictive. In some facilities, it can make inmates even more dejected, despairing, and hopeless. It would be unreasonable and inhumane to keep an inmate who appears to be stable on suicide watch indefinitely. It might even be considered cruel and unusual punishment."

On Anguish. "We know these criminal trials can take months and sometimes years to prepare for and orchestrate."

On Bircher. "Right. Often making their lives more restrictive doesn't make them less suicidal. It actually makes them more suicidal."

On Anguish. "Based on your best-selling books, *Inmate Suicide* and *Dangers During Incarceration*, there seems to be a body of evidence on this issue."

On Bircher. "Thanks for the plug, Ernest. Yes, although everyone pays attention to this issue when it happens to a celebrity or notorious criminal, suicides in jail happen every day."

Merit looked at Betty. "Stinks to me. What do you make of that?"

Betty frowned. "Looks like he loaded the wrong wagon."

Merit texted Jerry on the burner phone.

"Can you talk?"

"No. Text."

"We have to hurry."

"Agree."

"Meet and strategize?"

"Where?"

"I have a client who might help. I'll pick you up at your office."

"Garage. Third floor entrance. One hour."

Merit nodded at the phone and walked out of her office to Betty's desk. Guilt swept over Merit when she saw a stack of photos of wedding cakes.

Betty scooped up the pics and slid them in a drawer. "This is not important right now. What can I do to help you?"

"I'm worried about what's happening. I'm being followed. I need to stay away from home for a few days. Can you take care of Pepper?"

"Of course, but where will you go? How will I find you?"

"I'll call you as soon as I sort it out."

Betty warned. "Be careful out there, darlin'. There's a lot of law enforcement with horns holding up their halos."

"Don't worry."

"You know me. I'll worry if I want to. I'll run by and get Pepper right away. Check in when you can."

Merit promised, grabbed her bag, and left to get Jerry.

Merit drove her BMW out of the office garage. She knew that she was probably being watched but didn't see anyone behind her. She decided to take a diversionary route until she could determine if she was being followed. The last thing she wanted was to lead anyone who might harm her or Jerry to their hiding place. She needed to talk to Jerry, think things through, and formulate a plan.

Merit zigged and zagged through downtown. There was a lot of traffic, as usual, so she wasn't sure if she was being followed. She hoped the traffic would help her hide, not hide her pursuers. She drove out of downtown on South Lamar and pulled into a Valero gas station. She pretended to need gas, but barely topped off her tank as she looked around for anyone who might look familiar and there he was.

Merit recognized the bald man she'd seen at the gas station on the way to Houston and then again at Ouisie's Table at dinner. Baldy had on a Dallas Cowboys cap, sunglasses, gray sweatpants, and a white T-shirt, but she was sure it was him in spite of the thin disguise. His car was different, but that didn't dissuade her from what she knew to be true. He looked more like law enforcement than militia, but who knew what passed for an activist these days?

She pretended not to notice him, replaced the nozzle, and drove out and onto the street, watching him in the black sedan behind her via the rearview mirror.

How do I get rid of you?

Merit took several streets south and entered the ramp onto I-35 North. Traffic was heavy but moving. She worked her way into the middle lane and kept pace with the traffic around her. Eighteen-wheelers populated the right lane as they did almost twenty-four hours a day on I-35.

She checked the huge green and white highway signs overhead showing which exits were coming up next. She waited for the law school exit, which she knew well from her days at UT. She stayed in the middle lane, gauged the distance, and shot into the gap between two eighteen-wheelers traveling in the right-hand lane. She could hear the air brakes behind her, but fortunately, the trucker didn't honk at her.

Merit waited until she saw the sedan in the middle lane in her side mirror. It was about a car length behind her but couldn't get over because it was blocked by the trucks. When she saw the law school exit, she swerved onto the off ramp and down the frontage road. The sedan was caught in the middle on the other side of the trucks, unable to exit. Merit was shaking, but she was free of him. She cut across the campus on MLK, down the drag, out Enfield Road, and wound her way across the dam on Redbud to the back side of Westlake. Only then did she pull over amidst the cedar trees to catch her breath and stop shaking.

Ag parked his blue F-150 in Merit's garage and setup surveillance on her condo parking spot. He had no idea where she was, as no one answered at the office and Merit didn't answer her cell.

Things were heating up too much to take a chance on her safety any longer. Jerry Webb was not reachable either and his office did not know where he'd gone. People had been killed. The McDonald trial was derailed when the defendant committed suicide. Ag didn't know if the extremists could reach Merit or if law enforcement was watching her. He wasn't leaving her safety in anyone's hands but his own.

He had backed into a space that allowed him to see Merit's parking spot and the glass doors entering the elevator lobby and called Betty's mobile. "Did you find out where Merit is yet?"

"No, I hoped you were calling to tell me she was okay. I'm as nervous as a whore in church."

"I'm watching her condo. Her SUV isn't here."

"It won't be. She's gone to hide out. I don't know where. I have Pepper. She promised to check in."

Ag grunted. "We need to reach her. I have some information about Duke."

"I've left messages. Her phone finder shows the mobile is off. If she turns it on, I'll get a fix on her."

"Keep checking and let me know if you locate her, please."

"Will do. We must find her, Ag. That woman will charge hell with a bucket of ice water. I admire that, but she doesn't always think before she acts. I want her at my wedding."

"You know I'll do my best."

Ag waited in Merit's garage for her to return or Betty to call until around 2:00 a.m. Merit's parking spot was still empty. She had never come back. Ag started his truck and went to look for her.

57

Merit pulled into the garage on the third floor of Jerry's office building. She could see him pacing behind the glass in the elevator lobby. When she pulled up, he ran toward her BMW and jumped in.

"They're onto us. Let's go."

Merit threw the SUV in reverse, but before she could back out, Baldy, in the black sedan, blocked her exit. She could not pull forward because of a concrete wall. With cars on both sides, they were trapped.

Merit tapped the console between them. "I've got my Ruger, but I don't think I should pull it."

"Agreed. Let's see if we can talk our way out of this. There are cameras all over this facility. Surely he won't try anything here."

Merit and Jerry got out of the vehicle and walked back to the sedan. Baldy got out and stood by the door.

Merit kept a safe distance from him. "I saw you at Bucc-ee's, at Ouisie's Table in Houston, at the Valero, and now here. Why are you following me?"

Baldy stood mute. He was probably armed, based on the bulge at his waist under his clothes, but did not pull his weapon.

Jerry addressed him. "Move your fucking car. This is unlawful detention. My next step is to call the cops."

Duke drove into the garage, got out of his car, and walked over to them. "We are the cops. You are the ones breaking the law. You two have been sharing information on the case from the beginning. That's called treason by my definition. You signed a confidentiality agreement, remember?"

Merit grimaced. "You never intended to provide what we needed for a fair trial. This has been a setup from the beginning."

"That's right, and we chose you two as part of our plan. We know about your affair, and we know you didn't reveal it to the judge."

Merit stared at Duke. "I did not break the confidentiality agreement until you threatened our lives."

Duke scoffed. "No one will believe that. Remember the appearance of impropriety is just as lethal as doing the thing."

Merit didn't bite. "What do you want? You didn't come out here to arrest us."

"I don't need to arrest you. You either drop this whole thing or both of your careers will be ruined. You'll lose your law licenses, and you'll never work in your field again."

Merit was riled. "Maybe you're the one who'll never work in your field again."

Duke frowned. "Well, there are other options. You might just disappear, or ..."

Jerry pointed to the ceiling. "Or what? See those cameras?"

Duke looked at Jerry. "What do you think happened to your lawyer buddy, Riley, and Lyle Ryder? Cameras aren't everywhere."

"Judge Ginsberg will hear about this."

"You going to tattle on me, Jerry? Going to tell the judge I was a bad boy and broke the rules?"

Merit bristled. "Who do you think you are? There are laws that even you have to follow."

"Haven't you learned by now that you're outnumbered, outwitted, outplayed?"

Jerry scoffed. "This isn't an episode of *Survivor*. You're dealing with people's lives here."

"That's right, and I'm about to tell you what's going to happen to your life if you don't drop this whole line of questioning. That bicycler won't miss next time."

Merit looked astonished that Duke would reveal so much.

Duke looked at Jerry. "Think about it. Best thing you can do is keep your confidentiality. You were his lawyer."

Jerry bristled, and Baldy perked up into ready position.

Duke turned to Merit. "You, Ms. Bridges, are finished with this whole mess. Your job is done. Go home and shut up if you know what's good for you."

Baldy backed his car into a parking spot, releasing Merit and Jerry from captivity in the garage. They wasted no time getting into the BMW and peeling out of the parking garage.

Duke walked over to the driver's side window of Baldy's sedan. "They're not going to let it go. Take them out. Call me when it's done."

"Roger that."

58

Merit and Jerry left the parking garage and drove to the wooded area of Westlake on the west side of Austin. Merit had taken at least a dozen turns and twists, watching all the while in her rearview mirror.

She turned to Jerry. "My phone is off. Better do the same."

"Right."

When Merit was sure they hadn't been followed, she drove them to Ariana and John Sanderson's house, turned into the drive, and stopped at the double gates of the estate. She pressed the intercom button and when Ariana answered, she said, "Ariana, this is Merit. I need your help. A friend and I need a place to hide and figure out some things. Can you help us?"

Without a word in response, the gates opened.

Merit drove through the gates and up to the compound. The five-acre grounds were filled with a large house, pool with guest house, attached and detached garages, maintenance shed, and putting green. A fence enclosed the entire estate, the back perimeter heavily wooded.

Ariana walked out the front door to greet them.

Merit made the introductions. "Thank you so much for your help. I didn't know what to do. My office is probably being watched, along with my condo."

Jerry shook Ariana's hand. "I'm pretty sure my office and home are under surveillance as well."

Ariana smiled. "You're safe here."

Merit hugged Ariana. "If we could just stay for tonight and figure out what to do in the morning."

"No problem. Security cameras are aimed at the entrance gates, and the alarm is wired into the Westlake Police Department. There is no other ingress or egress."

Merit looked relieved, but Jerry looked unsure about the police, although he didn't say so.

Ariana was a gracious hostess. "The pool house is always setup for guests. Stay as long as you like. John will be home any minute and he can help too, if you need it."

Merit looked relieved. "We appreciate it so much. We were careful not to bring danger to your door."

Jerry nodded. "I'm exhausted from looking over my shoulder, but I don't think we were followed."

Ariana showed Merit and Jerry to the one-bedroom guest house. "You'll be comfortable here. Everything you need. Get settled and I'll send some food over in a bit."

Ariana walked beside the kidney-shaped swimming pool the size of a small lake and entered the main house. One end of the pool had a gradual slope for in-water sunbathing and at the other end was a waterfall. Natural stone and rocks comprised an abstract dome cut out of a limestone embankment about ten feet high and up lit by soft spotlights. The water poured over the top rocks and snaked its way down to the pool, creating a lovely babbling sound.

Merit and Jerry looked around the guest house and simultaneously flopped on the sofa.

Merit kicked off her shoes. "I just need a few minutes to calm down and think."

"Can you think in the water?"

Merit's eyes lit up.

They found swimsuits and robes in the bathroom, dressed, and got in the pool. The water was refreshing. Merit dipped her head in, swept back her wet hair, and let out the first easy breath of the day.

After they cooled down and gathered their wits, they stretched out on water lounges in the sloped end of the pool and watched the waterfall. Both were silent. Neither knew what to do next.

Little did Merit know that more than one person was watching and waiting. Betty pinged her BMW's location at the Sandersons'. She googled the house on satellite mapping and saw the estate. She was pretty sure she knew who lived there.

Betty went onto the law firm's server, searched the firm's client list with the address in Westlake and found what she thought she might. Up popped the Sandersons' home from the lease file on the St. Elmo film studio.

Betty texted the address with a note to Ag and started waiting again.

That girl is giving me a big ol' headache.

Ag drove to Ariana's address and circled the estate several times, checking to see if there was another way in besides the

front gate. Since Ariana was a client of Merit's according to
Betty, it was probably safe inside, but since Ag didn't know the
Sandersons, he didn't want to take a chance that Merit was
being held there against her will.

Memories of finding Merit hanging from a meat hook in a
warehouse, owned by a Russian gangster named Browno Zars,
made Ag shiver. He intended to make sure that never happened
to her again, even if she hadn't asked for his help.

Ag circled the streets, marking the boundaries of the
estate one last time. He was satisfied that the fence around the
property had only one entrance because of the dense woods
in back. The double gates had security cameras focused on
them, and the driveway up to the house looked quiet and
normal. He parked his truck out of sight in the shadows of the
trees near the front gates. He checked his Glock 17, stuck it
back in his holster, and took a pair of binoculars from the
glove box.

Ag got out of the truck and set out on foot to try to find a
vantage point to view the property through the woods in back.
After skirting the fence for a few minutes, he was rewarded
with an opening where he could see the back of the house, a
large swimming pool, and a pool house.

Sitting on the steps leading into the pool were Merit and
Jerry Webb. Merit looked so beautiful in a one-piece turquoise
swimsuit that it took Ag's breath away. Jerry looked trim and fit
from all the running, in black swim trunks, but Ag didn't dwell
on that.

A lovely, elegant woman, he assumed to be Ariana Sanderson, brought out a tray of beverages and set them on a glass-
topped table with an umbrella over it. She pointed at the tray,
said something to Merit and Jerry, and went back into the main
house.

Ag let out a sigh of relief. They did not seem to be being

held against their will. They were not under guard or being threatened.

Ag focused the binoculars on their faces, which were both very serious looking. He tried to read their lips, but he couldn't make out more than an occasional word. He thought he saw the use of FBI and McDonald several times. After a long conversation between the two, Merit touched Jerry's cheek in a way that made Ag bristle with jealousy.

He walked back around the wooded fenced area toward his truck and saw a parked black sedan near the entrance gates. Ag drew back quickly into the shadows of the trees and watched. The driver, a bald man, was also surveilling the property with binoculars. talking on the phone at the same time. Ag couldn't fully see his face, but he didn't recognize him. Dark sedan, man in a dark suit. He must have followed them or tracked her somehow, or tracked Jerry.

Maybe law enforcement?

Ag walked backward in the shadows of the trees, then turned and trotted all the way back around the Sandersons' estate to his truck. He quietly climbed in, gently closed the door, put his Glock on the passenger seat beside him, and texted Betty that Merit was safe.

Ag alternated focusing his binoculars between the front gates and the black sedan. The bald watcher was now being watched.

After their swim, Merit took a shower in the pool house. She then laid down to rest on the king-sized bed with her wet hair wrapped in a towel, while Jerry took a turn in the bathroom. She was asleep in minutes.

Ariana had sent her cleaning lady out with bread, cold cuts, and assorted condiments which were sitting untouched on the island in the kitchenette.

When Jerry returned from his shower, with a towel wrapped around his waist, he saw Merit on the bed. Her blond hair had fallen out of the towel and around her face. She looked so peaceful, like a sleeping angel. She opened her eyes and looked at him, then raised her hand inviting him into the bed with her.

When Jerry slid in beside her, his towel dropped to the floor. He circled her warm body with his cool arms and looked into her eyes. He saw tenderness there and remembered what that was like.

The heat they had once shared returned as the spark between them was reignited. Jerry rolled onto his back taking Merit with him. She straddled him and slid him inside her in one motion.

The two rocked in harmony until Jerry was close to the finish line. In unison, they rolled over with Merit on her back while Jerry stayed inside her. He smoothed her hair back from her face and looked into her eyes as they finished together.

From his truck, Ag watched the house and the sedan long into the night. Except for what appeared to be a maid leaving around dark, nothing moved.

Around midnight, Ag watched to see the lights go out first in the main house, then in the pool house.

The sedan must have decided they were in for the night because the driver did a three-point turn and headed out of the neighborhood.

Ag's shoulders slumped. He knew Merit, and he was fairly

certain he knew what she was doing with Jerry in the pool house.

He texted Betty again that Merit was safe and sound for the night, and that he was going home and would be back before dawn the next morning. He drove out Bee Cave's Road to Lakeway and onto Briarcliff for a well-deserved shower and fretful rest.

59

Around 3:00 a.m., Merit woke to the sound of something odd. She didn't remember where she was, but quickly oriented herself when she heard the pool waterfall outside. She looked over at Jerry, snoring softly beside her. She gently slipped out of bed, went into the bathroom, and pulled on Jerry's shirt.

When she came out, she saw shadows moving around the walls of the main house, interrupting the reflection of the water. She went to the glass doors and peeked out, but no one was there. Further movement caught her attention and pulled her eye to the top of the waterfall rocks where the bald man was starting to work his way down. The fence at the back of the property was about the same height as the rock wall. It would not have been difficult to climb over.

Merit went back into the bedroom, woke up Jerry, and put her fingers to her lips. "Shhh."

She grabbed her Ruger from her handbag and crept over to the glass doors again, remaining in the shadows. Jerry pulled on his boxers and joined her.

Baldy worked his way about halfway down the rock pile. It was slow going as the rocks were slippery and the water was hitting his shoes and pant legs. His gun was in its holster, as he was using both hands to make his way.

Jerry looked at the pistol. "Give me the gun."

Merit looked at him, incredulous. "I'm not giving you my pistol. When was the last time you went to the firing range?"

"Good point."

Merit held the gun out ahead of her, and the two of them pushed open the glass doors and ran out to the pool. Jerry yelled over the sound of the water, "Stop right there."

Apparently, the Sandersons were wise to what was going on as well because John came out of the big house with a shotgun and pointed it at the bald man just as he went for the gun in his holster. John shot first, hitting him in the chest. When Merit shot, seconds later, the impact from the shotgun made Baldy jerk, causing her shot to miss him by inches. Baldy dropped his pistol into the pool, lost his footing, and fell all the way into the deep end. He did not come up. Ariana ran out behind John. Jerry dove in from the side of the pool and pulled Baldy over to where John and Ariana were standing. They rolled him out of the water, while Merit ran around the shallow end to join them.

John took the bald man's pulse, but he was obviously dead.

John reloaded his shotgun and said, "You better get out of here. The neighbors must have heard the shots. I'll handle the Westlake police. I know most of them."

Jerry looked relieved. "I feel you need representation just to be sure."

Merit nodded. "I agree. Please call my friend Kim Wan Thibodeaux. He's an excellent criminal defense attorney. I'd call him for you, but I don't want to create a trail."

John stood the shotgun against the side of the house. "Will do."

Jerry added, "Maybe if you lawyer up you can avoid telling them we were here until we can sort out what to do next."

Merit looked at the rocks. "They're going to find the bullet from my pistol."

John nodded. "Maybe, but not tonight. Get going."

Ariana patted Merit on the shoulder. "Go to the St. Elmo warehouse. There's a bathroom with a shower and a small breakroom. I'll get towels and food for you while you pack. I don't know where you can sleep if you're there for long. There are no beds."

"Thank you so much. Don't worry about sleeping arrangements. We'll sort something out. Hopefully, we won't be there long enough to worry about it."

"Take my car. It's in the garage."

Ariana handed Merit a ring of keys. "Check in when you can. We'll maintain silence on our end as long as we can."

Merit hugged her and ran into the pool house to dress.

60

Merit watched the rearview mirror as they left John and Ariana Sanderson's home and drove across Austin in Ariana's silver Mercedes sedan.

When they felt secure, they pulled into an all-night big box store and bought sleeping bags, bedding, clothes, and toiletries. Most importantly, they bought new burner phones. Merit destroyed the burner Jerry had left for her at the bridge by driving over it in the parking lot. Jerry kept his, although turned off for now, in the event that Lucy tried to contact him later. It was the only active number Lucy had for Jerry.

After all that was sorted out, Merit drove them toward St. Elmo. Jerry sat in the passenger seat, staring out the window. "I need food to get my brain to turn back on. Coffee would help, too."

"Magnolia Cafe, okay? It's open twenty-four hours."

"Yeah. No one will be looking for us there."

"Or this car."

Merit drove them down South Congress and parked on the

side of the all-night diner toward the back fence. They looked around for a while and, seeing no one, went inside.

After they were seated and had coffee and tea on the way, Merit looked at the menu. "We need to discuss a plan. How can we help Lucy and Faye? Do you think Duke, or the FBI, will harm them?"

Jerry made his choice and closed his menu. "Yes, I do. I think Duke will harm us now, too."

The waiter came back with their beverages. "May I take your order?"

Merit closed her menu. "I'll have the spinach and swiss omelet, side of fruit."

Jerry looked at the waiter. "Grilled ham and eggs. Plain toast."

"Coming right up." The waiter wrote down their orders, took the menus, and left them to strategize.

Jerry took a sip of coffee. "What if we contact Duke, tell him we'll make a deal. If they protect Faye and Lucy, we'll keep our mouths shut and do as we're told."

"Can you sell that to him? He doesn't look like the type to buy into promises without leverage."

"What else can we offer them?"

"Lucy has the flash drive with evidence of bank deposits."

"If we give that to them, they'll not only know she knows, but they'll also have even more reason to kill her and Faye."

They went quiet, both contemplating and hoping for their brains to start working. Their food arrived and they both dug in.

Jerry swallowed a big bite of ham. "What if we tell them we

have the flash drive and it's in a safe place. If anything happens to any of us, it goes public."

"You've been watching too many TV shows. They'll kill anyone we trust to keep it, and they may threaten Betty and my office even if we don't leave it with her. I'm not taking that chance."

"True. Got any better ideas?"

"Well, first of all, it might help if we actually had the flash drive. How do we know they haven't found it and taken it from her already?"

"Good point."

"We need to talk to Lucy."

Merit had a fitful few hours of sleep in a sleeping bag at the St. Elmo film studio. Jerry was across the room in his own makeshift bed.

The idea was to get some rest to clear her head, then take the next step in their plan that wasn't really a plan, as they didn't know how to get to Lucy without being outed. Merit tossed and turned until she finally gave up and went into the kitchenette for a bottle of water. She took it back to the main room, sat down on a folding chair pulled up to a rough-hewn wooden worktable, and thought.

How do I get myself out of this mess?

No answers came. She abandoned her strategizing and went into the communal bathroom lined with shower stalls. No curtains were hanging on the rods. She did her best to clean up and get dressed, pulling jeans out of a bag, and removing the tags before she put them on. When she came out, she was greeted with the smell of coffee and Jerry in the kitchenette.

"Hey."

"Hey yourself."

"Couldn't sleep?"

Merit yawned. "Not much. Trying to decide what to do next."

"There's no tea, do you want coffee?"

Merit walked over to the small refrigerator, opened it, looked inside, then closed it. "Sure."

Jerry pulled a couple of cups from a metal cabinet above the counter and blew in them to make sure there was no dust. "Did you figure anything out?"

"No, and I've had it. This corruption so deep inside the FBI is unconscionable. Who's minding the store over there? Can Duke just do whatever he pleases with no consequences?"

Jerry measured coffee into the filter of the machine. "I've been thinking about that, too. They can't all be corrupt, but we don't know how far it goes and who's involved."

Merit shook her head. "Seems to me, we save our careers or save Faye and Lucy. If all this comes out, we'll be screwed either way. Might as well go down with a little integrity."

Jerry laughed the nervous laugh people use to release tension. "It would be funny if it weren't so tragic. We need some help."

"I agree. Ag will help us. Maybe Chaplain, his friend at APD."

Jerry poured the coffee and passed a cup to Merit. "We need to get Faye and Lucy out of the city before the FBI finds out about the evidence that Lucy has on Duke."

"How do we get them from the safe house?"

"If they're still in the same place, it's guarded by two agents all the time and there are security cameras. They would know it was us, even if we were able to get them out."

Merit took a sip and burned her tongue. "Hot. Maybe we can grab them at McDonald's funeral, if they go."

Jerry nodded. "That's a better idea. There will be a lot of law enforcement around there. At least if the plan fails, maybe we won't get shot."

"Maybe."

61

Duke drove alone to the safe house to address his problem with the rest of the McDonald family. He entered the house and greeted the agents on duty. "I'll hold down the fort until the next shift arrives. You guys go ahead and get some dinner. I'm sure you're hungry."

"Thanks, Archie. Faye is in the living room and Lucy is upstairs in her room."

The agents wasted no time getting out the door. "Goodnight."

Duke went through the kitchen to the dining room, which was a makeshift surveillance area for both inside and outside the house. There were a dozen TV screens, each monitoring a different room, the front door, and the back yard. Duke watched the agents leave, then checked the screen in Lucy's room and saw her sitting on her bed, legs folded, playing her handheld video game.

Next, he went into the living room and found Faye watching the news. It was a morbid scene, with every channel dissecting the ins and outs of her husband's suicide. Duke stood for a moment and stared at her.

Faye looked up under the impact of his gaze. Her eyes searched the door to the kitchen for the other agents. "What are you doing here? What do you want now?"

"It's time to move you and Lucy to a more permanent location. Go get her and we'll head on over. The agents will pack up your things and bring them later."

Faye's eyes jutted around the room, seeking an answer that wasn't there. "Sure. I'll go tell Lucy." She stood and moved to the end of the sofa away from Duke, even though it was the long way out of the room.

Duke continued to stare at her as she climbed the stairs, then went back to the dining room and watched the screen that monitored Lucy's room. He saw Faye speaking with her and grabbing a backpack and putting clothes, books, and school supplies inside.

Upstairs, Faye spoke to Lucy with her back to the camera.

"Try to look normal. Duke is downstairs. Now that your daddy is gone, I don't think that Duke needs us anymore. He says we're moving to another location, but there are no FBI agents with him. I'm afraid he's up to no good."

Lucy sucked in air. "We can run."

"Not together. He'll catch us before we clear the yard. We need to split up. I'll go down and distract him. I want you to go out the front door behind me. If I get away, we'll meet at the central library downtown. These boneheads haven't read a book in years."

Lucy almost laughed, more from nerves than amusement.

"It'd be better if I go out the window and down the drainpipe. I've done it before."

Faye looked surprised, then relieved. "Can you do it without being seen?"

"If he's watching the cameras, he'll see me. I've only done it in the dark before."

"Okay, I'll go down and distract him. As soon as you hear me talking to him, head out. Run. Don't look back."

Lucy looked afraid. She had already lost one parent. "I can't leave you. I promised Daddy I'd look after you. What if he hurts you?"

"He won't. He knows he can control us by using the other. If we're apart, I'm betting he'll keep us alive, at least for a while, to lure the other back in. He'll need the other agents to help him search, so he won't risk killing one of us."

Lucy started to object.

"If you get away, that's how you save both of us. I'll try to think of something better, but you have to go now."

Lucy grabbed her denim jacket and her Spurs cap.

"I'm afraid."

"Me too. Now get ready."

Faye got her purse from the master bedroom across the hall and went downstairs. Duke was still watching the security monitors in the dining room when Faye walked in. Onscreen, Lucy continued to pretend to add items to the backpack and put on her Nikes.

"I told you the agents would pack for you later."

Faye made a point of showing her purse on her shoulder. "Just a few things. You know young girls. She doesn't want to go without her books. She'll be right down. Where are you taking us? I want to make sure we stay in Austin so we can go to Bobby Ray's funeral."

Duke smiled. "That's all arranged."

Faye walked toward him. "I don't believe you. Where are you taking us?"

Duke looked up from the screens at Faye, who began to gesticulate wildly. "I don't want to go with you." She elevated her voice to a high-pitched scream. "Nooooo. Leave us alone. We did everything you wanted and you killed Bobby Ray. I know it was you. Nooooo."

Duke stared at her for a moment, then jerked his head around to look at the screen of Lucy's room.

When she heard her mother's screaming voice from downstairs, Lucy took a deep breath, opened the window, and slid down the drainpipe. She scooped up the flash drive she had dropped from the window into the bushes and ran toward the end of the block at full speed. Duke came out of the house and ran after Lucy. She was faster, cleared the corner, and turned toward a yard full of trees.

Duke looked back and saw Faye running out the front door in the other direction. He made a decision, pulled his gun, pointed it at Faye, and let Lucy go. "Halt! I will shoot you."

Faye stopped and threw up her hands, dropping her purse on the ground.

Duke walked toward her with the gun out before him. "Nice move."

62

In the St. Elmo warehouse, Merit left her iPhone off and opened one of the new burners from the big box store. It took only a few minutes to set it up and she was in business.

First, Merit called Betty to let her know she was okay and to check on Pepper. Thankfully, nothing eventful had happened since they last spoke except for Betty's persistent worry.

"I need to get to Ag and ask him to contact Chaplain. Will you handle that for me and also keep checking on Ace through the school?"

"Of course, darlin'. How should I have him get the information to you? Where are you?"

Merit went into shorthand mode with Betty. They had been speaking in code for years and she hoped Betty would catch on. "I don't want to say, just in case. There could be a television show recording us. There might be zombies."

Betty was silent for a brief pause. "Oh, yeah. That would be a bad idea. I'll send Ag over to your place in about an hour."

Merit knew she had picked up the hint as to their location and that Ag was on his way. Hopefully, if anyone figured out that they were speaking jibberish, at least they wouldn't know what it meant. "That sounds good."

Less than an hour later, Ag pulled up to the St. Elmo studio and parked his truck around the back side of the main warehouse. He walked halfway around the building until he found a side door marked 'Deliveries' and tapped on it. No one responded, so he walked another quarter round and tapped on a door marked 'Actor Entrance.'

Seconds later, Merit opened the door and let him in. She looked both ways outside, then closed the door and they hugged. Merit looked relieved. "It's so good to see you."

Jerry came over and shook hands with Ag. "Thanks for coming. We are desperate."

Ag followed them into the main warehouse area where the three sat on folding chairs at the rough-hewn table.

"Betty said you want me to talk to Chaplain. What about?"

Jerry nodded. "You're going to hear the news soon. A bald man we think is an FBI agent was killed by John Sanderson while we were at his house."

Ag silently rebuked himself for leaving them unguarded when the bald man in the sedan had pulled away. As he listened, he looked around the huge warehouse and familiarized himself with his surroundings. Old habits die hard.

Merit continued. "We think Faye and Lucy McDonald are in danger from the FBI. We're trying to get more proof of Duke's involvement. Duke has threatened us, and we've probably violated the law fifteen ways from Sunday."

Jerry looked at Ag. "We need an honest FBI agent to talk to. Someone outside of Duke's inner circle."

Merit nodded. "Do you think Chaplain can get you the

name of someone we can trust, if there is such a thing as an honest FBI agent."

"I can try."

Ag left them to twiddle their thumbs while he tried to make contact with a reputable FBI agent through Chaplain. He drove his truck away from the warehouse before dialing as a precautionary measure.

Jerry decided to take a shower as he was still in the sweatpants and T-shirt he'd slept in. He ripped the tags off a pair of jeans and a T-shirt. He'd forgotten to buy boxers, so he rinsed out the ones he had on, hung them on the empty shower curtain rod, and went commando while they dried.

Merit explored the warehouse to see what was available for their use in case they had to stay for a few more days. First, she went through the food that Ariana had packed for them. The night before, they had put the whole bag on a shelf in the refrigerator. Merit took the items out and sorted them as appropriate. Cold cuts back into the fridge and non-perishables around the kitchenette. Bread, she left out on the Formica counter. Tea, she put by the coffee in the metal cabinet.

Merit circled around the perimeter of the warehouse where there were doors opening onto the main room. The warehouse buildings were over an acre in size and connected by hallways, so walking all the way around was about a quarter of a mile. Most doors were labeled. Laundry contained two washers and two dryers along with a wall-mounted service utility-type sink. She twisted the laundry faucet, the water was working. Against the far wall was a large metal rack on wheels with about a dozen items hanging on it. There was a pile of dirty-looking clothes on the floor, more like rags than wearable items. She knew from her legal files that the film studio was going to shoot not only glamour scenes, but also scenes involving zombies, gangsters, the homeless, and others who would wear less than pristine costumes.

The door next to the laundry bore a sign that said 'Wardrobe.' Inside was an especially large room filled with mostly casual clothes for all ages and a selection of business-type costumes for men and women. One entire wall housed shoes in every style, color, and size. Merit was peeking behind the curtain of the film and television business. It was fascinating. She might have enjoyed it if she wasn't so afraid of Duke.

She walked back out into the warehouse and past the communal showers where she could hear the water running as Jerry cleaned himself up. She walked on past a short hallway leading to the men's restroom. Another longer hallway led to a women's restroom with a sign that said 'Out of Order' on the door which she had found the night before when they first arrived. Merit opened the door and found that the toilet did not flush.

Guess I'll be sharing the men's room from now on.

Merit went back out into the main warehouse and crossed over to a corner full of cardboard boxes, some taped shut and some open. She found last year's calendars with colorful photos, an assortment of novelties and toys, and some party decorations in the open boxes. She remembered that Ariana had said that the last tenant was a calendar and novelty gifts company.

She proceeded around to the longest wall which was cut in the middle by a large loading dock with a roll-up door that was closed and a huge concrete slab jutting out of the metal surround. She assumed the concrete continued out the other side for ease in unloading large trucks of equipment, cameras, and more wardrobe items.

Merit's latest burner phone rang. It was on the rough-hewn table, and she had to run across the building to answer it. She was happy to hear Ag's voice. He had gotten what they needed from Chaplain, and Merit scribbled down the name and number on the border of an old calendar with a novelty pen from one of the tenant's boxes. It had a pink flamingo on the top that bobbled when she wrote. It reminded Merit of the cranes in Port Aransas, and she longed for the freedom to go there, be with Ace, and soak up the sun.

Jerry returned to the main room from the shower.

Merit held up the number she'd written on the paper. "Ag called with the name and number for the FBI agent. How do we want to handle contacting him?"

"I guess we just call, lay it out, and see if he has any ideas. Maybe he can get to someone higher up than Duke and do us some good."

"Agreed."

Jerry used Merit's burner phone and called the number for Agent Edward Johnson. Whoever answered the phone said he was out. "I'd like to leave a message. I'm Jerry Webb. I represent a client sensitive to the FBI, and I need to speak to Agent Johnson immediately. I was referred by Detective Chaplain at the Austin Police Department." Jerry left Merit's burner phone number.

While they waited, Merit filled Jerry in on the status of the provisions. "We have food for about two days. There are lots of clothes around that we can borrow. If we don't want to wear those, we can wash what we have. There's no laundry detergent, but we can get by without it. The toilet in the women's room isn't working, so we'll be taking turns in the men's room. I guess you noticed there are no shower curtains."

"Yeah, I managed. Kitchen appliances work. But it sounds like you think we'll be here for a while."

"I hope not, but we have to get to Lucy and Faye. That could take some time. The funeral isn't set yet. I don't want Ag and other people in my office coming in and out of here. It's too risky."

"Agreed. I could see if Alistair could help at my office, but I don't want to incriminate him. He has a license to protect, too."

"So, we're left waiting on Agent Edward Johnson. Whoever he is."

At that moment, the burner phone rang. "Speak of the devil."

Jerry picked it up. "Yes?"

Merit came around the table and put her ear to Jerry's head so she could hear.

"This is Archie Duke. I got a message that you wanted to talk to the FBI."

Jerry didn't know what to say, so he didn't respond. Obviously, Agent Edward Johnson had ratted them out without even a return call. *Bastard.*

On the phone, Duke continued. "What? No wiseass remarks counselor? I'm in charge of this case. What did you think was going to happen?"

"We were seeking a neutral third party to make a deal."

"You can deal with me."

"We haven't found you and your henchmen to be exactly trustworthy. Last time we saw you, you threatened our careers and our lives."

"Well, things have changed. Give us the girl and we'll call it even."

"What girl? Lucy? We had no idea she was missing. You were supposed to be protecting her and Faye."

"I don't think I believe you."

"You can believe us or not. We don't have her."

Duke laughed. "Then, no deal." He hung up.

Jerry and Merit looked at each other. "So much for that plan."

Merit touched Jerry's arm. "We still have some cards to play. They don't have Lucy, but she's going to need help."

Jerry nodded. "She has texted the burner before, but we can't be sure she still has the number. Let's go to the Broken Spoke at nine tonight and see if she shows up. It's the only common contact point we have."

Merit looked hopeful. "Yes, that's what we'll do. In the meantime, we can't use this burner again. Duke may not be able to ping the phone, but he can triangulate it based on cell tower use. We can't risk his getting another coordinate."

"We'll buy another one when we go out." Jerry put the phone on the rough-hewn table and looked at it suspiciously. He picked up a piece of wood from the corner of the room and smashed the phone to bits. Then he put his old burner phone on the table.

Merit didn't know whether it was a lifeline for Lucy, or a death trap for Jerry and herself.

63

The minute Duke hung up from talking with Jerry, he regretted his words. *Damn. Now they know the girl is out there.*

He picked up the phone on his desk and buzzed Rachel. "Come to my office. Now, please."

When she entered, Duke didn't bother with a greeting. "We need to find Lucy McDonald."

"We've been searching all the tween and teen hangouts. We've looked through the homeless tent cities and underpass areas. She doesn't have any money that we know of. We're watching hotels and motels, but it's not likely she'll show up there. We don't know where else to look."

"Expand the search to CCTV cameras around town and try facial identification. Maybe someone is helping her."

"We're doing that, but we'll do more. How about her mother? Does she have any ideas?"

"Faye has no desire to assist us in locating Lucy."

"Why? You'd think she'd be worried about her. It's likely

Lucy will try to contact her mother even if Faye doesn't know where she is. That's our best bet. Watch Faye."

Duke lied. "I don't know why Faye is doing what she's doing."

"Lucy can't do any harm to anyone but herself. She's probably acting out about the death of her father."

Duke turned angry. "These people are all crazy. Just find her."

Rachel left the room with a puzzled look on her face.

Lucy bought a Cedar Bank money card from the Valero gas station and convenience store on South Congress. She only had ten dollars, so she put five dollars on the card, paid the fee, and kept the rest. The clerk at the register looked surprised at the small amount.

Lucy smiled her most charming smile. "It's a birthday gift for my brother. I want to add money on it from time to time. This is just a start."

The clerk smiled back, seemingly satisfied with an explanation that was none of his business anyway.

Lucy used her bus pass to get downtown and walked the last few blocks to the Austin Public Library on Cesar Chavez Street. It contained six floors and over two hundred thousand square feet. Lucy had visited most of it on a school field trip from San Antonio during the opening in 2017. She checked around to see where the cameras were, but doubted anyone would look for her there, other than her mother. She was certain that Faye was still being held by the FBI. More prisoner than protected.

She entered the building, snugged her Spurs ball cap down over her eyes, and went to the fifth floor and signed in, using her best friend's name, to wait for a computer station to open up. There were many machines provided, so she didn't have to wait long.

Lucy went online and found the bank login page. She took her algebra book from her backpack and flipped to a worksheet at the back. Between the lines of the algebra formula was a long number and a few lines down another shorter number with some letters. She used the first number to get to the bank account where her father had deposited the money from the FBI. Then, she used the second number as the password to login.

Unbeknownst to Lucy, most of the money had been used to finance the San Antonio bombing. Lucy felt her father would want her to have it and use it to save herself and her mother or he wouldn't have given her the account number and password. She hoped the FBI hadn't snatched the money back. Since they didn't know she had access, and her father was dead, she would bet her last dollar that the money was still there. When she entered the password and checked the balance, she found there was about seventy-five thousand dollars left.

Lucy swallowed hard and looked around to see if anyone was watching. She calmed herself, logged into the website for Cedar Bank, and took the money card out of her pocket. She loaded the card information into the online box provided and tapped the small dollar sign at the bottom of the screen.

When prompted, she added the banking code information from her father's account. Next, she clicked over to the move money screen and moved nine thousand dollars to the bank card. She wasn't sure why she chose nine thousand except she had heard or read that sums above ten thousand dollars were monitored or reported or something that sounded like Big

Brother or taxes to her. She was rewarded with a screen that popped up showing 'Transaction Complete.'

Lucy closed out of the websites and looked at the card. *Let's see if it works.*

Lucy took the elevator to the Cookbook Cafe on the next floor down. She walked between over five hundred shelved cookbooks to the counter. She perused the menu and silently prayed that the card would work. Her stomach growled. When it was her turn in line, she approached the counter clerk, took a deep breath, and ordered.

"I'll have the Farmer's Breakfast grilled cheese and a large half coffee and half hot chocolate. Uh. And some French fries."

The clerk rang up the sale and Lucy slid the card through the machine by the register. 'Transaction Approved' appeared on the tiny screen, and Lucy had to contain her excitement.

The clerk handed Lucy a receipt. "Thanks, your order will be right out."

Lucy turned toward a stack of cookbooks and silently clapped her hands with delight.

When her order number was called, she took the food outside to the cafe patio. She sat down at a table away from the only security camera she could see, and dug in. When she was finished, she let loose a long, satisfying burp, then went back, ordered the same thing again, and ate it all just as fast.

Fueled by the sustenance, and emboldened by her Cedar Bank money card, Lucy left the library, walked to a convenience store, and purchased a burner phone. She found a Starbuck's nearby, bought an iced mochaccino, and found a table where she unboxed and activated the burner. She typed in Jerry's phone number from memory and texted. "It's LM. I need help." She waited.

A few minutes later, she heard a ding from the phone. "I'm here. I can meet you."

She texted back. "I need to be sure it's you."

The screen showed, "Did you go home drunk last time we met?"

Lucy texted. "Didn't have to, wasn't caught."

The screen showed, "Can you get to the same place we met last time?"

Lucy texted. "Yes."

The screen showed, "On my way now."

Lucy took the bus to South Lamar and got off at the stop nearest the Broken Spoke. She walked across the property and lurked around the side of the building. The bar was closed and the parking lot was empty, so it was easy to see Merit drive Jerry in Ariana's Mercedes into the entrance past the hitching post fencing. Lucy waited until Jerry got out of the car and walked over to the oak tree where they had chatted the last time. She watched for a few moments as the sedan pulled out of the lot and parked on the street on the north side of the bar. Confident that Jerry was not under duress or followed, Lucy made her location known to Jerry.

"Who's in the car?"

"It's Merit Bridges. Let's get out of here before someone sees us. We have a safe place."

Lucy reluctantly climbed in the back.

Once the three were driving back toward St. Elmo, Merit looked in the rearview mirror at Lucy. "Are you alright?"

"Yes, Duke almost had me, but my mom lured him back to the safe house."

"Where did you spend the night?"

"I hid in the Waller Creek Boathouse. It's not hard to get in there. The Austin Rowing Club isn't that good with security. It's right down from the library and has bathrooms. I wanted to be at the library early this morning so I could access the internet to get some money to buy a burner phone."

Jerry turned in the front seat and looked back at Lucy. "How do you get money at a library?"

"I loaded up a money card from one of their computers. It's a long story."

"Merit has a client with a warehouse. We are setup there. The FBI is looking for us, too. Let's get over there and you can tell us what you want to do."

"I need to get my mom away from Duke."

"We agree. Let's work on that."

Ag met Merit, Jerry, and Lucy at the St. Elmo warehouse. He brought a video camera, laptop, and printer from Merit's office. "Betty said to tell you to get this problem handled and get back to the office. Your work is piling up. She also said to be careful, and she loves you."

"Tell her I'm doing my best and I love her too."

Ag smiled at the dynamic between the two women that he'd witnessed for almost a decade.

Merit pointed to an empty area of the warehouse. "Would you please setup the camera over there."

While Ag setup the tripod and camera, Merit typed up a document on the laptop.

Lucy came over to watch. "What's that?"

"This is an affidavit for you to sign affirming the information you gave to Jerry about Duke's association with your father, the militia cell, and the San Antonio bombing. Once we make sure it's accurate, we'll print it and you can execute it."

"It says here I was with them at a meeting. I wasn't. I took a video on my cell phone from my dad's Hummer without Duke knowing I was in there. Dad said he'd be right back, but he wound up taking a long time."

Jerry's head jerked around. "A video? Showing them together?"

Lucy nodded. "You can't hear them talking. I'm sorry I didn't tell you when I told you about the bank account. I was deciding how far I could trust you."

Jerry smiled. "Understood. Didn't the FBI take your phone?"

"Yes, for a while, but I had already moved the video to my Instagram page. I just saved it and didn't publish it. I deleted it from my phone in case the FBI or my mom looked at it."

Merit and Jerry shared a look. Merit took a breath and put her hands on the keyboard. "Okay, let me change this section. Anything else?"

Merit and Lucy went back and forth on the details of the affidavit with Jerry's input while Ag setup the printer.

Merit gave Lucy a script to memorize while she finished typing. Once the document was to everyone's satisfaction, Merit turned to Lucy. "Sign here and raise your right hand."

Lucy looked afraid.

Merit patted her shoulder. "It's okay, this will help keep you safe. You won't say anything that's not the truth or that you don't feel comfortable with."

Lucy signed and raised her hand.

"Repeat after me." Merit administered the oath as a notary public for the State of Texas. "Do you, Lucille Agatha McDonald, solemnly swear and acknowledge that you are the person who executed this document for the purposes and consideration therein expressed?"

Lucy nodded. "I do."

Jerry smiled reassuringly at Lucy. "Good work. Let's get it on tape."

Ag worked the camera, and Lucy stood against the wall and read the affidavit. Next, a few prompts from Merit and Jerry got some questions and answers on tape without stopping the recording and interrupting the feed. No need giving anyone any doubt about it's being doctored and spliced.

Lucy looked directly into the camera and answered their questions. "I am not being coerced, and I am giving this statement openly and freely."

Merit nodded at Ag. "That should do it."

"Wait. I want to say that my mother has done nothing to deserve being detained by the FBI or imprisoned. She has cooperated through this entire process, as have I. My father is dead, and I'm concerned for my mother's safety. I beg you to let her go."

When Lucy teared up, Merit had to fight to keep her emotions under control. "You are a brave and extraordinary young woman."

After the work was done, Merit, Ag, Jerry, and Lucy all grabbed bottles of water from the kitchenette and sat at the rough-hewn table in folding chairs.

Merit smiled at Lucy. "Now, let's discuss how we get your mother."

64

Merit and Jerry left Lucy in Ag's protection at the warehouse and drove by the Live Oak Federal Campus where Merit had reviewed the documents. She wove Ariana's Mercedes in and out of the cars in the parking lot until she saw Duke's vehicle, or what she assumed was his, from the day he'd watched her after lunch.

"We can't be sure he's in his office, but that's the car I saw him get something from."

"We'll have to risk it. We go while he's here at work."

"Agreed."

Merit dropped Jerry at the corner near the safe house where Faye was being kept and found a place to wait in the shade a few streets over.

Jerry knocked on the door and was greeted by an FBI agent he'd not met before. He could see through the house to the back yard where a second agent was smoking a cigarette. Jerry could hear the television on in the living room and assumed Faye was in there.

"I'm Jerry Webb, the McDonald's attorney, and I'm here to see Faye McDonald."

The agent sneered. "The case is over. McDonald hung himself, in case you didn't hear."

Jerry lied. "I still represent Faye and Lucy. I'm here to confer with my clients."

The agent did not reveal that Lucy was not there. "You're not supposed to come here without an escort. You're not following protocol. You could get them killed."

"I wasn't followed. I just need a few minutes with Faye. Could you get her please?"

"I need to call Duke. He's in charge of this operation and we're under strict orders here."

Faye peeked around the corner and listened to the conversation.

"What if I make it worth your while? Just five minutes for five hundred dollars. A hundred dollars a minute. Not a bad day's work."

"What?"

"It's important I get answers to my questions right away. I'll give you five hundred if you'll just look the other way for five minutes."

Faye slipped up behind the agent. "What do you need to ask me?"

The agent sized them up, knew he could take them both out with one punch if things went south, and made his decision. Greed won out.

"Make it six hundred. Five minutes, but if you do anything suspicious, you're out of here."

Jerry took all the money from his pocket and handed it to the agent. "I have five hundred and thirty dollars and some change."

"Okay." The agent didn't move.

"In private, please."

"Go to the living room. I'll wait in the kitchen."

Jerry and Faye went to the sofa and sat close together. Jerry whispered, "Lucy is with me."

Relief visibly swept over Faye.

"We need to get you out of here. Can you slip out?"

"No. They watch me all the time since Lucy left. Maybe with a distraction, but not alone."

"Be ready after dark tonight. If you get out, run to the corner of the street with the woods. A man named Ag in an F-150 truck will be there to pick you up. If you can't get out, you're no worse off than you are now."

Faye looked terrified. "I'm afraid time is running out."

Jerry patted her hand. "So are we. Duke is cleaning up his mess and a lot of people are getting hurt."

That night, a little after nine, Merit and Jerry returned to the safe house followed by Ag in his truck. Merit drove past the end of the block with the wooded area and pointed out the window for Ag to wait there. She parked a few streets over, and Jerry went to the door of the safe house and knocked.

The agent who'd taken the money earlier answered the door. "You had your five minutes."

Jerry shrugged. "I forgot one last question. It won't take long. Please."

Faye had dressed in jeans, a T-shirt, and sneakers good for running. She had emptied the necessary items from her purse into her pockets. She sat on the sofa pretending to watch TV, straining to hear. When Jerry knocked, she moved to the edge of the sofa, alert and ready to react. She could hear Jerry arguing with the agent at the door.

The second agent came around the corner from the dining room, looked at Faye and then toward the front door. "What's going on here?"

The dirty agent waved him off. "I've got this. Go back to the screens."

When the second agent left the room, the dirty agent looked back at Jerry. "I'm going to have to call this in."

Jerry spoke in a low voice so the other agent couldn't hear. "If you do, I'll tell them about the money you took."

"Your word against mine."

Faye worked her way around the sofa and under the stairs. When Jerry saw her at the ready, he pushed the dirty agent, catching him off guard. The agent went down on the floor and Faye ran out beside Jerry and toward the wooded area, as instructed, where Ag waited.

Jerry stood in the doorway for three seconds giving her a head start as the second agent ran in from the dining room and the agent on the floor found his balance and got up. Jerry slammed the door in the agents' faces and ran toward the other end of the street as both men came out the door behind him. They were no match for Jerry's regular running regimen, and he reached Merit in time to jump in the door which was open and waiting.

Merit pulled out with squealing tires, leaving the FBI agents confused and disoriented. Jerry hung on for dear life as Merit took the corner and shot out of the neighborhood.

Faye was invisible in the wooded area as she looked out the edge of the trees searching for the F-150. She spotted Ag and sprinted out of the woods toward him. The agents had not seen her exit, and were not behind her, but she and Ag peeled out of the neighborhood as if they were being pursued. When she and Ag felt safe, they made introductions.

"Nice to meet you. I'm Faye McDonald, Lucy's mom."

"I'm Ag Malone. I was on your husband's defense team."

Faye went quiet, letting her heart rate slow and her breathing return to normal. After about ten minutes of driving, she turned to Ag and said, "I need to use a bathroom. All the excitement has left my body in distress."

Ag nodded. "No problem."

Faye gave him her most charming tone of voice. "Let's find a store if that's okay with you. I'd like to get some water too."

Ag continued on for a few minutes until he came to a small, locally run convenience store in East Austin. "The security cameras in here should be low tech. It's our best bet, but take this cap and cover your face, and be quick. I'll wait here in case we need to get rolling fast."

Faye snugged the maroon Texas A&M ballcap onto her head. "Thanks. I'll be in and out."

Faye climbed out of the truck and went into the store. A small bell rang to alert the clerk behind the counter. A large wall of plexiglass protected the employee from robbers and abusive shoppers who might have had too much to drink.

Faye smiled at the clerk and followed a sign to the back of the store to a small bathroom that doubled as a storage room. It smelled of urine and Pine-Sol. She took care of her business quickly and searched through her pockets for cash. She only had about forty dollars, but that was enough for her purposes. She considered stealing, but if the clerk caught her, Ag would know what she was up to. When she went back out through the store, she grabbed two bottles of chilled water from the cold case and a burner phone from the end of the candy and chip aisle.

The clerk rang up the purchases. "Will that be it?"

"Yes, thanks."

"Need a bag?"

Faye gave her another of her charming smiles along with the money. "No, but could you open that phone for me? The plastic is really tough for me to handle with my arthritis."

The clerk cut the outer plastic from the phone with a box cutter and pushed the burner through the opening in the plexiglass. "Here you go."

"Thanks." Faye put the change in her pocket, pushed the phone into her waistband, and snugged her shirt down over it. She left the plastic packaging on the counter and went out to the truck where Ag waited to drive her to the warehouse.

65

The attorneys, newly freed McDonalds, and Ag reconnoitered at the St. Elmo film studio. Lucy sat close to her mother with Merit at the rough-hewn table. Merit used the laptop Ag had brought to access the internet and research travel opportunities. Ag dragged over a folding chair and sat down beside her while Jerry paced.

Ag offered his advice. "Flying would be fastest, but the airports have higher security and would require IDs for all three of us as passengers."

Merit agreed. "Fake IDs are out, as it would take days or weeks to procure them."

Faye looked at them. "I can drive. We'd have to sleep at rest stops or parking lots, but we could make it."

Merit looked at her. "Driving would require purchasing a car and making sure the title and license plates are properly registered."

Ag scratched his chin. "I'm afraid there might also be roadblocks or CCTV tracking. If you're stopped, there would be no easy escape."

Merit and Ag continued their search and landed on the Amtrak website. After checking the security policies, they all settled on the train as the best way to go. ID wasn't required to purchase all the tickets. It was only required for each passenger at the seat where the ticket was used, and the train would be long out of the station before the ticket taker came around to check.

They found that there were five hundred destinations to choose from as the trains went everywhere from Austin, except South Dakota and Wyoming. First, they considered Atlanta, but the train ride was over four days long with layovers and transfers.

After further research, the Texas Eagle to Chicago seemed a good bet. The city was multicultural and large enough to get lost in. Although the trip would take about two days, there was no reason to believe the stations beyond Austin would be watched. Also, Lucy and Faye could depart at any number of cities on the way if they felt they had been detected. The Sunset Limited intersected with the Texas Eagle in several of those cities. It went to Los Angeles from Dallas and other points north, so they had a backup plan in case the McDonalds felt they had been compromised and had to abandon Plan A.

Ag looked at the train schedule and route and determined that he should get them to Dallas and then return to Austin while they made their way to Chicago.

While Jerry watched, Lucy and Faye went online and loaded another nine thousand dollars on the Cedar Bank money card.

Jerry looked impressed. "This is enough cash to get you settled in Chicago, then you can access the rest of the money if you need it, providing the FBI hasn't snatched it. When you check the balance, be sure and do it from a public place as far away from where you're living as you can safely travel in a day or so."

Lucy nodded.

"Get a burner phone as soon as you arrive and text us that you're okay. Then, we'll continue the process here."

Faye was deadly quiet, watching and listening like a hawk.

Lucy looked worried. "What if something happens in Chicago?"

Jerry considered this question for a moment. "You can text me anytime, but the less contact you make, the better. I'll keep the one burner phone with the number you have until we can make another arrangement. Whatever you do, don't come back to Texas."

That's as far as the plan went, it was the best they could do in the time they had. All of them hoped it was enough.

Merit took Lucy and Faye into the wardrobe room of the studio, and the three sorted through the costumes hanging on the racks. Faye went for the jeans and T-shirts first. "I guess that wouldn't be much of a disguise."

Merit shook her head. "The FBI will be watching all the travel facilities. We need to get you past security and out of town. Once you're safe, Jerry and I can try to sort this out and you can leave Chicago if you want. You'll have to stay within the U.S., so you don't need a passport."

Lucy pulled a few ugly shirts and wrinkled her nose.

Merit laughed. "They're not supposed to be pretty. It's costuming for shooting in different time periods. We just need to find something that works for our purposes."

All three sorted through different options and rejected

them for various reasons. Merit pulled costumes from a rack of clothes that looked like they came from the Middle East. "No one would think to look for you as Muslims."

Lucy smiled. "I was thinking the same thing."

Merit took a black sack dress off the rack and a hijab, the scarf used to hide a woman's hair but not her face.

Faye tried on the outfit, and she looked very foreign except for her skin color.

"We'll get some olive-toned makeup and you should be set."

Faye grimaced as she looked at herself in the mirror.

When it was Lucy's turn, Merit considered her small frame and undeveloped female body. "I say we make you look like a boy."

Lucy giggled.

Merit pulled a thawb from the rack and pulled it over Lucy's head. The garment was a long pale blue shirt that hit below Lucy's knees. To complete the outfit, Merit gave her a pair of plain black pants. When Lucy was buttoned up, she looked like a Muslim boy except for one thing.

"Can we cut your hair? I don't see how we can hide it under a hat with this outfit."

Lucy looked at Faye, who nodded.

"I guess it'll grow back."

"Can you handle that, Faye? You can use the men's room or the shower room."

Faye picked up a pair of sewing shears, and she and Lucy went out.

Merit stood in the doorway behind them and motioned to Ag. "Your turn."

Ag joined her in the wardrobe room and froze as he looked at the volume of clothing.

Merit pulled a three-piece business suit, starched shirt, and tie from a rack. "You shouldn't be seen traveling with the

McDonalds, but you'll be able to blend in and keep an eye on them. I think you're better off looking like a respectable American in case something happens."

"I agree." Ag tried on the jacket for size. "This will do." They went to the shoe wall and found a pair of men's oxfords and a slightly worn briefcase to complete the look. Merit also selected two small well-worn carry-on bags for Lucy and Faye to use.

Merit turned to Ag. "I hate to have you leave town right now, but our best bet is that the FBI won't be looking for you. Jerry and I are too recognizable, and I'm afraid to let Faye and Lucy go alone. Jerry and I will stay here and try to leverage Duke with the affidavit and video from Lucy."

Ag took off the jacket, picked up the shoes, and looked at Merit. "I've got this. Do what you have to do."

Faye and Lucy went into the shower room because there was more light and a bigger mirror than in the men's room. Lucy stood in front of the mirror and looked at herself. "Bye bye, hair."

Faye picked up a long brunette lock of Lucy's hair, very similar in color to her own, and snipped off about ten inches.

Lucy laughed. "Ouch." She was so happy to be with her mother again.

Faye continued to cut and shape until Lucy had a boy's shaggy haircut. Then, she smoothed it out with water and her hands until it came under control. "You do look like a boy."

Lucy stared at herself in the mirror.

Faye turned her daughter around to look at her. "Lucy, this is our chance at a fresh start, but I have to do a few things first."

"What do you mean?"

"I need to make a phone call, and I don't want you to tell them I have a phone."

"Why? These people have been good to us. They've helped us."

"Yes, they have. But they don't know us. They just think they do. Where will they be when we get to Dallas? We'll be on our own again. We have to make some plans for our safety."

"But ..."

"Promise me you will not tell them about the phone."

"Yes, ma'am." All the laughter and giggles went out of Lucy's eyes.

"Watch the door." Faye stepped into the shower in the farthest corner of the room and dialed a number that had been in her memory for over ten years.

66

Merit left Jerry doing research on the laptop at the film studio. She drove Ag, Lucy, and Faye, in their designated costumes, to the Walgreens pharmacy on South Lamar. Merit drove past the front door of Walgreens and parked next door behind Maria's Taco Xpress. Ag walked back across the parking lot to the drugstore, keeping his head down around the CCTV cameras. He didn't think he was being sought by the FBI, but he didn't want to take any chances.

There was news that travelers were advised to wear masks because a new virus had been discovered in China and was spreading in New York. It prompted him to buy an additional item to complete their disguises. Ag located olive-colored liquid foundation in the makeup department, and the blue masks with elastic earpieces in the section near the pharmacy. He bought half a dozen masks, as well as the make-up, and checked out.

When Ag returned to the car, he gave Faye and Lucy each a mask along with the foundation. He put two masks in his jacket pocket and gave the last two to Merit just in case she wound up needing them. No one had reported the virus spreading to the south, especially Texas, but it was better to be prepared than not.

Merit continued driving on Lamar across Lady Bird Lake to the Amtrak station at the cross street of Cesar Chavez. She drove past the entrance and parked behind the YMCA next door. Ag, Lucy, and Faye gathered their backpack and bags. All three climbed out of the car, waved at Merit, and walked toward the entrance to the Amtrak station to face their possible capture, or worse. Merit stayed hidden in the Mercedes feeling helpless, useless, and hopeful that Ag could get them safely out of Austin.

Ag, looking respectable in his business suit, bought three tickets on the Texas Eagle to Chicago via Dallas. He bought one ticket in his real name, Albert Malone, and two in fake names for Lucy and Faye. He had to show ID, hence the use of his actual name, but he was betting that the FBI was not monitoring ticket sales for him. Although all travelers were required to have ID, they were betting that the tickets would be enough once Lucy and Faye were established on the train as paying passengers. Ag was to ride with them to Dallas, then catch a train back to Austin if nothing happened in the interim.

It was obvious that the station was being watched by law enforcement. Two FBI agents stood around, drinking coffee and reading magazines, looking like cliches from a thriller movie. The two women hid in the ladies' room until the last possible moment.

When the three walked toward the departure area, the FBI agents looked at the women in their Muslim garb and then at Ag walking about ten feet behind them, all wearing medical face masks, as were several other passengers. No red flags seemed to go up, and the three departed Austin, feeling as if there were large stones in the pits of their stomachs but without incident.

Merit watched the station doors and outdoor tracks from her hiding spot in the car and saw the Texas Eagle depart the station. When no one came out in handcuffs, she breathed a sigh of relief and returned to the St. Elmo studio to help Jerry.

Lucy and Faye established themselves in their coach, and Ag went to the dining car so that they would not appear to be traveling together. Once the train left the station and settled down to business as usual, he took several bottles of water, bags of chips, and sandwiches in plastic boxes back to the compartment. Luckily, no one was riding with them, and they were able to speak freely and share the food.

Nothing like a Muslim to get distance in Texas.

When the official came by to check their tickets, none of them offered ID and he didn't ask. Just checked their tickets, nodded, and proceeded on with his menial tasks.

It didn't take long for the three to reach Dallas. As they entered Eddie Bernice Johnson Union Station, all three looked up at the Reunion Tower, also known as the golf ball, anchoring the downtown Dallas skyline. A feeling of freedom seemed to sweep over Faye, and she smiled.

Ag turned to the two. "It looks as though we made it. I'll get off here. If I see anything hinky, I'll come back and continue on with you. If it looks all clear, I'll head back to Austin. Good luck, ladies. Be sure and stay in your costumes until the ticket takers change shifts."

Lucy looked at him. "Thank you so much, Ag."

Faye smiled with her lips in a thin line. "Yes, thank you."

Once Ag left the train in Dallas, he did not return, indicating that all was well in the station.

The two women looked at each other and almost celebrated.

Lucy and Faye travelled to Fort Worth, just one stop and about half an hour away. There, they exited the train, entered the first women's room they saw, and changed their clothes into jeans and T-shirts from their carry-on bags.

Faye tossed her costume in the trash. "Me, a Muslim. Right."

Lucy looked fearfully at her mother, but followed her instructions to get rid of the costume and put on her Spurs cap. They walked through the lobby and proceeded to the front door of Fort Worth Central Station. As soon as they stepped onto the sidewalk, they were greeted by two members of the Texas Gunrunners, who clapped Faye on the back and grabbed the bags. Lucy gave up her suitcase but hugged her backpack to her chest and looked like she might cry.

The men led the way out to a monstrous black Chevy Silverado Crew Cab with oversized tires and a swastika trailer hitch. Faye climbed in the front passenger seat of the double cab and started barking questions at her troops.

"When does the next gun shipment arrive?"

The driver sneered. "Tomorrow night. Coming in through the Houston ship channel, then up by truck to Snyder."

Faye nodded. "Good job."

Lucy sat in the back seat with the other man. When Faye turned around to look at Lucy, she looked at her mother with pleading eyes.

"They killed your father. We're not going to let that go."

Lucy's fate was sealed, as she saw it. FBI capture or domestic terrorists, not much of a choice. She wished she'd never told her mother about the bank account or the money card. She wished she had lovely parents from a middle-class neighborhood who ate dinner together every night and played board games and watched baseball.

67

Back in Austin, Merit and Jerry sat at the rough-hewn table at the St. Elmo studio warehouse. The burner phone sat on the table between them.

"Is Ag ever going to text? They should have been in Dallas half an hour ago."

"If they made it."

"If."

Merit opened the laptop. "Let's check the news online and see if there have been any new developments."

"Good idea."

A brief survey of NNN and several other news sources showed that reporters were occasionally rehashing McDonald's suicide and the bombing in general, but breaking news was no longer focused on Texas. A virus was invading New York and Northern California, making people sick in unprecedented numbers and driving hospitals to search for PPE and ventilators.

Merit looked at Jerry. "Good grief. Ag gave me these masks. I thought it was superfluous."

"Shocking."

A text from Ag popped on the screen. "Package delivered. On the train back."

Merit let out a sigh of relief. "Now what do we do?"

Jerry drummed his fingers on the table. "Now that they're safe, we have to come up with a way out of this. We can't hide forever."

Merit nodded. "We need to think of something incredibly brilliant."

"Like what?"

"I have no idea."

"If we let Duke know we have the flash drive and affidavit, we might be able to get him to cooperate, but we'd be looking over our shoulders for the rest of our lives."

"We could try for another decent FBI agent through Ag and Chaplain."

"Look how well that turned out last time."

"They're not all crooks. We just have to get around Duke."

At the end of the warehouse, the loading dock door started to go up. Merit and Jerry both stood and looked around for a place to hide, but it was too late. Duke was standing in the opening on the dock, as the metal rolled up above his head. A Glock was in his right hand down by his side.

Merit and Jerry froze when they saw the gun.

"How did you find us?"

"Two plus two does finally equal four. It took us a few days, but you left a trail here and there. Sanderson's house, Sanderson's car. It wasn't that hard."

Jerry started to walk around the table. "Look, Duke, we have something you want and you have our freedom. We can make a deal."

"Where are Faye and Lucy?"

"Not here."

Duke sneered. "Then you have nothing I want."

"We have an affidavit, bank records, and a video proving that you were running Bobby McDonald. It's stored in the Cloud, with instructions to very trustworthy friends. If anything happens to us, your little secret will be all over the news."

"Nice try. I don't believe you."

Merit tried again. "It's true. Lucy took a video of you and McDonald at one of your meetings in San Antonio. She was in the car waiting on her father. She also got copies of the bank records showing the fund transfers from the FBI to McDonald's secret account."

"You can't prove that came from the FBI."

"Maybe not, but circumstantial evidence will be enough to put your career in the toilet."

Duke motioned with the gun. "Along with both your careers."

Merit moved to join Jerry at the end of the table. "It doesn't have to be that way."

Duke raised the Glock and pointed it at Jerry. "Did you think you were going to just waltz through this and out the door?"

Merit looked at him in defiance. "Did you think you were going to break the law, murder anyone you wanted, and get away with it, all to cover up your secret games?"

Duke pointed the gun at Merit. "I don't see anyone around here to stop me."

Jerry stepped in front of Merit. "I'm the one you want. Let her go and the whole thing ends here."

Duke laughed. "Of course, you'd never tell anyone, would you Ms. Bridges? You think I'm going to let this country go soft and liberal while I still have a breath in my body?"

"How did you get so full of hate?"

"Just lucky, I guess."

Merit moved beside Jerry. "I expect you to keep the oath you took as an agent. To protect and defend this country and its Constitution until your last breath."

"What do you think I'm doing? The Constitution is exactly what I'm protecting."

"What about all those people in the San Antonio Market? What about the children in the cooking class? What about the babies in the strollers? Mothers? Fathers?"

"Half those people were illegals and the rest, well, there's collateral damage in any war."

Merit squared her shoulders. "What war? The only war is in your own mind, your prejudice, your hatefulness."

Jerry looked around the room for a means of escape or self-defense.

Duke saw Jerry's eyes shifting. "There's no one here to save you. Turn around and walk to the back of the warehouse."

Merit and Jerry walked toward the interior of the huge warehouse space. Merit looked at the novelty boxes, rough-hewn table, and shelving. Nothing gave them options for weapons or cover. Merit's Ruger was in the kitchen on the counter. She admonished herself, and they walked slowly, thinking, both searching with their eyes.

Duke closed the distance between his position and their backs. "All the way to the wall."

Merit looked over to the men's room hallway and wondered how many shots Duke could get off before she could dive in there. That would leave Jerry to take a hit unless he could bolt as well. Jerry's eyes met hers and he nodded.

Merit mouthed a countdown. One, two ...

A thud sounded behind them, and they turned around to see Ag, having tackled Duke, sprawled on top of him like a shell on a turtle. The impact had caused Duke to drop his gun and send it spinning about five feet away from him. Duke, on his belly, was crawling and elbowing his huge bulk toward the gun with Ag still on his back.

Jerry was closest to the pistol. He ran over and grabbed it just before Duke could grasp it. The agent rolled on his side, throwing Ag off his back.

Jerry stood up and pointed the gun at Duke. "Hold it right there."

Merit went over to help Ag. "You okay?"

"Yeah. Looks like I got here just in time for the party."

Merit looked down at his holstered gun. "Didn't feel like shooting anyone today?"

"Forgot my boy scout training. Wasn't prepared."

Merit smiled as she saw a sudden movement to the right. Duke ran straight toward Jerry who still had the gun in his hand.

Jerry, surprised, lost his focus and Duke closed the gap between them. Jerry could not bring his arm up in time to fire. Duke tried to take the gun, but Jerry held on. The two men struggled for the weapon, but Jerry was no match for Duke and his superior size and strength.

Ag turned, drew his weapon, and yelled, "Duke, stop. I'll shoot."

Duke ignored the warning and turned the gun into Jerry's chest, struggling to get his finger on the trigger.

Merit ran over to Duke and jumped on his back. Duke shrugged her off and she flew across the room, landed against the wall, and slid down into a heap. Blood poured from a cut, above her eye, on the left side of her head. She didn't move.

Ag watched Duke gain control over Jerry and the gun. Just

as Duke fired, Ag pulled the trigger on his Glock and shot Duke squarely in the head. Duke dropped the gun and fell to the floor. Jerry looked down at his thigh, saw blood coming through his jeans, and slumped to the floor.

Ag kicked the gun away from Duke and felt for a pulse on the dead man's neck. Assured the threat was eliminated, Ag ran over to Merit.

Jerry got his bearings and was able to stand. He found a soiled towel on one of the work benches and pressed it to his thigh. When the blood loss slowed, he joined Ag at Merit's side.

Ag inspected her wound, propped her up against the wall, and gently tried to revive her by patting her hand. "Merit, can you hear me?"

Her eyes fluttered open.

Both men knelt beside her and waited for her to get reoriented. She was shaking. "Duke?"

Ag looked over at Duke's body. "It's okay. He's dead."

Relief swept over Merit, and she began to sob. "Help me up."

Jerry looked at Ag. "I've got her."

Ag looked at Merit. "No, I've got her."

Merit circled her arms around Ag's neck as he lifted her up and carried her to a chair.

Ag called Chaplain and asked him to come to the scene and bring EMS. "Please keep it off the airwaves. We need to talk to you before the FBI gets here."

Both Merit and Jerry were lucky as their wounds were treated by EMS. Although they were advised to go to the hospital, they both declined and asked for pain relievers.

"If you won't go to the emergency room, we advise you to

see your doctors to make sure there's no infection or concussion."

"We will."

"First thing."

Chaplain took their statements about the shooting and turned to Ag. "Do you want to fill me in on what caused all this in the first place?"

68

Jerry and Merit went to her office, while Ag dealt with the last of the police questions at the warehouse. Chaplain had bent the rules to allow them to leave but told them both to remain available.

Merit, followed by Jerry, went into the breakroom and threw out the now warm ice pack she'd received from EMS. She dispensed fresh ice from the refrigerator into two plastic bags and wrapped them in paper towels. She handed one bag to Jerry and touched her wound gently with the other. The bandage the EMS had placed on her head seemed to be holding.

She looked at Jerry who sat at the breakroom table. "Chaplain will have notified the FBI about Duke by now. There will be more questions. We need to get our story straight."

Jerry placed the ice bag on his thigh. "If we try being open with the FBI again, we'll never get the story out. They'll bury it, even if we find one of the good guys. They'll clean up after Duke and deny it all."

Merit flinched as she pressed the ice harder. "Probably.

Who are they going to protect? Us, or their own people? Duke is already dead, so they have no reason to do anything except cover it up and hope no one finds out."

Jerry nodded. "We'll never stop looking over our shoulders. I don't know about you, but I'm not hiding and I'm not living like that."

Merit nodded. "Not to mention our careers. We still have the flash drive with the bank deposits and video proving McDonald was working with Duke, but how do we explain how we got it without revealing that we breached the Chinese Wall, and risking our law licenses?"

Merit threw the ice pack in the sink and pulled a bottle of ibuprofen from the medicine chest. "We have to trust someone, and we have to protect Ag, but we owe it to the public to get this out."

Jerry pointed to the pain relievers. "Give me a couple of those. Let's call the FBI guy again and hope Chaplain is right about him."

Merit handed the bottle to Jerry and downed two pills with a glass of water. "Agreed."

The two went down the hall to Merit's office where she dialed the number and asked for Agent Johnson. The person answering the phone promised to relay the message. "It's urgent." Merit made the receptionist write down Chaplain's name, as well as hers and Jerry's, before she hung up. "Fingers crossed."

Although there were plenty of places to sit, they both stood. Two minutes later, the office land line rang, and Merit looked at it, then at the clock on her credenza.

"That was fast. I don't think he could have gotten the

message yet."

She let it ring over half a dozen times before she carefully picked it up.

"Hello."

Rachel Ward was on the other end of the line. Merit put the call on speaker.

"We know you called Agent Johnson."

Merit tried to interject.

Rachel persisted. "Just hear me out."

"Why should we? You worked for Duke."

"I work for the FBI. We're not all like Duke. We were just starting to catch onto him."

Jerry interrupted. "Do you have agents on the way here?"

"Yes, but if we wanted to grab you or hurt you, I wouldn't have called first."

Merit and Jerry looked at the door and considered their options.

Merit spoke toward the phone on the desk. "You have three minutes."

"We didn't know how far Duke had gone. He was a rogue agent. We don't know exactly when he went off the deep end, but we're sorry for what he did to McDonald and tried to do to you two, Lucy, and Faye."

Jerry looked knowingly at Merit. "So, Duke did kill McDonald."

"That's off the record."

Merit frowned. "Everything about you guys is off the record. I've seen your secret documents, remember?"

"Yes, and you can't reveal them unless you want to lose your license and go to prison," Rachel said.

Jerry was angered. "So you can keep your thumb on us for the rest of our lives? No way. If we go down, you go down too."

Jerry looked at Merit who nodded her assent. "We have a

flash drive from Lucy with a video of McDonald and Duke, and evidence of bank deposits from the FBI to his account."

Rachel went silent, then her voice came over the speaker. "We have a proposal. If you give us the flash drive and whatever other evidence you have and let us clean this up quietly, we'll verify that Duke had gone rogue and that Ag killed him to protect you both. Nothing can come out about McDonald's death or the funds paid to him by Duke that financed the bombing. It will be Duke, McDonald, and Walsh and the small cell that was wiped out. No one left to investigate."

Merit looked at Jerry. "What about Faye and Lucy? Will you leave them alone? They're harmless."

"They'll be easy to find. You know that. We'll monitor them for a while to make sure they keep quiet. Who would believe them anyway?"

Merit and Jerry looked at the flash drive sitting on her desk.

"I'll take your silence as a yes."

"Just a minute." Merit pushed the speaker to mute.

"Let's try our hand with Johnson."

"Agreed."

Merit pushed the speaker button again. "We'd like to speak to Agent Johnson."

Jerry said into the speaker. "He can witness the deal between us. We still don't trust you."

Rachel didn't answer for a few seconds. "Okay. I'll have him there in twenty minutes."

Agent Johnson and Rachel tapped on the glass door to Merit's office. Merit turned the key at the bottom of the door and released the lock. "At least you didn't shoot your way in."

Rachel managed a weak smile. The four stood in the reception area but didn't sit.

"I'm Agent Edward Johnson."

Jerry looked at him. "Show me your credentials."

Johnson took his badge and ID out of his pocket and showed them to Jerry and then Merit.

"As you probably guessed, I'm Merit Bridges and this is Jerry Webb. We understand from our friend Chaplain that you can be trusted."

"Chaplain's a good guy. I've known him for years. Yes, you can trust me. Your prior message to me was intercepted and given to Duke. That obviously won't happen again." Johnson looked knowingly at Rachel who averted her eyes.

Jerry looked at Johnson as if to size him up. "We assume you've been briefed."

"Yes, and we've figured out a few more things through the documentation in Duke's office. We were already getting a whiff of his stinky business but hadn't put it all together until you two."

Merit shifted from foot to foot. "How was he running McDonald without your knowledge?"

"McDonald was arrested in L.A. when Duke was working international terrorism. Duke turned him and kept it quiet from the rest of the FBI. We allow that, to a point, for the protection of all involved, but Duke went too far."

Rachel filled in some detail. "McDonald was arrested as part of a cell in Bakersfield and bought his way out of a conviction by working for Duke. McDonald was brought in to be faux recruited by the Waco terrorist cell. Once he infiltrated the group, he was to report to Duke."

Jerry grunted. "How did the FBI miss the clues to the bombing?"

Rachel looked embarrassed. "Duke was watering down the

intel about the American Freedom Militia. We had no idea how much of a bigot he was."

Johnson looked at Rachel. "He was not a patriot. We didn't have redundancy in place as we should have."

Merit looked angry. "It was right under your noses and all those people died."

"Yes. I know this looks like the entire FBI is corrupt, but we're not. We're asking you not to tie our hands in the war on terrorism. I'm asking you to give me the flash drive and work with us."

Merit looked at Johnson. "We have a counteroffer. We'll give you the flash drive and you can lie that Duke was mistaken about McDonald. You can put it out there that McDonald was working as Duke's CI but was also a double agent for the American Freedom Militia. You don't have to reveal that Duke went rogue and gave McDonald the money for the bombing, just that he was stupid and deceived."

Johnson answered for her. "You can work with me. Rachel will follow my orders."

Rachel was pensive. "So, we say that Duke was duped by McDonald, he was running him as a confidential informant, but McDonald was feeding information to the militia. We conceal the money exchange and Lucy's documentation of the arrangement."

Jerry nodded. "Right. The FBI will take full responsibility for Duke's actions and let Lucy and Faye keep the rest of the money. They have no reason to tell what they know. You let them have a normal life."

Merit explained further. "If they ever talk, which they won't, it would just be seen as the rantings of a grieving family."

Jerry nodded. "Right. No one would believe them."

"We want to go back to our law firms."

Johnson nodded. "In the process of sniffing out what Duke

was up to, we traced him to Alistair at your firm. He helped him setup Riley and come after you with the car accident."

Jerry looked as though he would cry or kill someone. "What about Helen Sharp? Was she in on it?"

Johnson thought for a moment. "Not that we know of. If Alistair hasn't already fled the jurisdiction, we can work out a plea bargain with him. What choice does he have? Hide or plead. We'll keep him quiet either way, and away from you."

Merit picked up the thread. "You make public that Duke was killed in some way that protects Ag. You don't tell the court or anyone else that Jerry and I were working together before the trial ended and Duke came after us."

Johnson rubbed his chin. "So, you save your law licenses, Ag is a hero, and the FBI has egg on their face for a while."

Merit nodded. "That's about the size of it."

Johnson held out his hand. "I can live with that. Where's the flash drive?"

Merit and Jerry looked at each other. Neither of them wanted the agreement in writing, so they had to trust Johnson. Merit went to her office and got the flash drive from her desk. She came back to the reception area and handed it to Rachel. "Here. Take it."

69

EPILOGUE

Merit and Betty sat on the sofa in Merit's condo looking out over downtown Austin with Pepper, snoring lightly, sitting at their feet. Merit enjoyed a nice pricy Bodega Catena Zapata Malbec. It had been breathing for about an hour and was perfect. Betty had her usual Crown Royal on one big-ass cube of ice. The coffee table was strewn with bride's magazines and fabric swatches.

Betty raised her glass. "Cheers. How's your head?"

Merit clinked her glass with Betty's. "I'm fine. Stop fussing."

Merit's head and Jerry's thigh had been checked and rechecked by their private doctors, at Betty's insistence, and both had received a clean bill of health. Merit had closed the law firm for a week to get ready for Betty's wedding and heal her forehead. It was the least she could do, after neglecting her bridesmaid's duties for so long.

On the TV in the corner, NNN with Ernest Anguish, was recapping the last of the news about the San Antonio bombing and trial. Unbeknownst to Anguish, he reported the story just as Merit, Jerry, and the FBI had agreed, showing Duke as a rogue agent who was running McDonald as a CI. McDonald purportedly killed himself in order to save face with his fellow militia members and prevent the authorities from putting him to death. In the end, the kidnapping of Mayor Clover Thibodeaux of Austin and killing of Mayor Javier Sincero of San Antonio were connected to the American Freedom Militia that was completely wiped out in the Waco encampment raid. Nice and tidy.

Judge Ginsberg was quoted as saying, "It was a great American tragedy that was never prosecuted. I hope the outcome will give the families closure, even without a trial."

Betty took a long pull on her whiskey. "I'll drink to that."

After Tank heard the news that Merit, Ag, and Jerry had taken out Duke, he organized his men. Tank, Six-pack, and Cupcake pulled a stolen SUV loaded with guns, ammo, and supplies into the old farmhouse property near Bastrop registered in Duke's uncle's name. They pulled on gloves and worked quickly, checking every building. Tank found the staged body in the freezer after prying off the lock, re-closed the lid, and turned off the generator. Duke wouldn't be needing it anymore.

When Tank opened the old barn doors, he discovered the RV, motorcycle, canoe, and all the valuable assets Duke had hidden inside. Six-pack and Cupcake removed their supplies from the SUV and loaded them into Duke's RV. Cupcake backed the camper out of the barn. Six-pack pulled the emptied SUV into its place, wiped down the vehicle, and re-secured the barn doors.

The three departed the property on the back roads to the

Texas/Mexico border drinking Duke's beer with Tank humming "Happy Trails to You."

A few weeks later, a bombing occurred in Tulsa, Oklahoma, that was attributed to a splinter group of the American Freedom Militia, called Texas Gunrunners. Faye McDonald's body was found in the debris, and she was reported to have set the bomb.

After finding out that her mother was dead, Lucy left the camp house kept by the militia, by sliding down the drainpipe outside her window. She was never heard from again. She had library books and the Cedar Bank money card in her backpack.

On a beautiful Texas night, Betty walked out of the guest house at John and Ariana Sanderson's and along the pool toward the deep end. She wore a lavender tea length dress with three-quarter length sleeves and died-to-match sensible shoes. A matching pillbox hat with lavender lace sat atop her helmet hair. She looked lovingly at her husband to be, Bob Tom Jakes, standing under twinkling lights beside the waterfall in his tuxedo jacket, jeans, and cowboy boots.

Merit, as matron of honor, and Bobby, Bob Tom's son, as best man, stood next to the groom and the minister, waiting for Betty to join them.

Ag, Val, Clover and Kim Wan, Red Thallon, Chaplain, family and friends all sat in white folding chairs around the edge of the pool. John and Ariana Sanderson stood in the back. Beside the main house, a champagne fountain and four-tier wedding cake with lavender butter cream frosting roses awaited the guests. Floating in the pool were hundreds of tiny tea lights flickering in the slight breeze. It was idyllic and romantic, just as Betty deserved.

Betty joined hands with Bob Tom and smiled at Merit. The minister began, "Dearly beloved ..."

MANNING WOLFE

MERIT BRIDGES LEGAL THRILLER #1

DOLLAR SIGNS

TEXAS LADY LAWYER VS BOOTS KING

1

The smiling head of Greg Lee Wood burst into flames. Each animal surrounding him caught fire and burned. Two dogs, three cats, a sheep, and two goats all went in a giant ball of fire. Neither the director of PETA nor the animals made a sound, but the giant billboard buckled and groaned as the metal twisted and broke from the scaffolding holding it to the creosote columns erected into the sky. Falling pieces of wood broke windshields and car windows forty-five feet below. Three cars were crushed. Their gasoline tanks leaked fluid and exploded in the dark Austin night.

Tarantella 'Tireman' Estevez dangled from a metal halogen light, which was tearing away from the catwalk of the twisted scaffolding. As the metal ripped rivet by rivet, he dropped closer and closer to the flaming mayhem below. The sharp edge of the fixture cut into his skin as he looked down into the mess he had made. From this height, the cars below looked like flaming Hot Wheels.

His eyes searched South Congress Avenue, but did not find anyone walking about in the middle of the night. While he wanted help, he hoped he could free himself without being seen. If he called for assistance, there would be a witness to his act. He'd never intended to burn the cars, just the billboard. But here he was hanging and hoping and regretting.

He dropped another foot toward the ground as he heard voices yelling and coming closer. *Would he break his bones if he fell? Would he die?* His blood mixed with his sweat and lubricated his grip. He slipped to the end of the metal.

"Last chance."

Tireman flung his body as far as he could away from the heat. He let go, dropped, and fell across the top of a flaming Ford. He slid to the ground, rolled across the flames on his back, and crawled on all fours away from the heat. Hot glass mashed into his palms and knees. Voices and shrieks grew closer as he hid behind a stack of tires at the edge of the body shop. He tried to catch his breath and make sense of what he'd done.

It wasn't vandalism. The auto shop where the billboard resided belonged to him and his brother, but their lawyer had told them that the sign was not theirs. It sat in front of their business like a wart on the land reminding Tireman that someone could take from him all that he'd worked for.

Tireman was caught between his desire to be good and his demand for justice. He'd come to America for the dream, and his dream was now tarnished. He'd acted out of anger and frustration. He had no thought of long-term consequences. Nor did he realize he had just become the murderer of the homeless man passed out in the back seat of the flaming blue Chrysler, not five feet away from him.

2

B oots King was fired up and back in action. He got the call at 5:11 a.m., pulled on his signature snakeskin boots, jumped into his black diesel 4x4 and drove north to Austin from San Antonio. He'd worked for Nixon Outdoor Advertising for almost three years, and he was on call twenty-four seven. He arrived on South Congress about an hour later as the sun came up, hid his truck a few blocks away behind Weird Pizza, and walked toward the smoke. The yard at Estevez Tire and Auto Shop was a smoldering hot mess. The billboard was gone except for remnants of metal halogen lights and nubs of creosote poles. Several car carcasses were steaming and dripping water. A fire truck stood guard in case of flare up, and a uniformed Estevez employee helped firefighters hold people back from the sidewalk.

Boots chuckled to himself and whistled out loud as he looked at what was left of the giant billboard. "How in the hell did someone burn that down?" Boots asked. This was Boots' favorite part, the chaotic aftermath, second only to the rush he got when he conned the innocent and unsuspecting into signing the leases in the first place. In his years working for Nixon Outdoor Advertising, he'd caused more chaos and distress among small business operators and naive landowners than ten other ex-cons combined. This was a new one, even for Boots. No one had ever gone so far as to burn down one of the billboards.

Prior to working for Nixon's sign company, Boots had been a landman in West Texas conning small-town folks into executing oil and gas leases for a fraction of their worth. He had a knack. If he couldn't get the men to agree, he'd work on their wives. Women were his specialty. His old man had taught him to go for the women and they'd work on their men. It was sage advice from the best con man in the business, until Boots had surpassed even his father's expertise. He took pride in his ability to soften 'em up, sign 'em up, and watch 'em squirm trying to extricate themselves from the bad deals they'd struck with him and the people he worked for. He was a master.

King wasn't his real name of course. He'd gone through so many since the old man died he'd forgotten half of them. King was his favorite, and Boots just stuck from years of identification with the footwear.

After each sales job, Boots could no longer be contacted. He'd used aliases on most documents, and he changed phone numbers often. Nixon Outdoor Advertising would tell anyone who called that no one named King worked there.

"Could we be of service?" the receptionist would say.

Nixon wanted Boots to stay in the shadows just as he was today, watching and listening, but not showing his rugged face, his noticeable footwear, or transportation.

Boots eavesdropped on the conversation in the crowd and tried to get close enough to the fire truck to pick up on the official buzz.

A redheaded reporter in a short skirt with KNEW-9 on the

microphone interviewed several onlookers. As soon as she was off camera, she threw on a blanket to insulate her scantily clad body against the winter chill.

A policeman interviewed neighboring business owners as they arrived for work and unlocked their doors. Boots saw a cop leave the Congress Bake Shop, two doors down from Estevez Tire and Auto Shop. Boots strolled in and smiled at the pretty woman behind the counter who was putting on a tie-dyed apron.

"I'll take a cup of coffee when you get one brewed," he said, pushing his sunglasses up onto his wavy hair and giving her the full benefit of his sparkling blue peepers.

"Comin' right up." The shopkeeper blushed and avoided eye contact, focusing on the coffee preparations.

"What happened over there?" Boots asked.

"Cop said someone burned down the sign during the night. Don't know who yet. Wanted to know if we'd seen anything," she said as she measured the coffee and switched on the urn.

"Why would anyone burn down a sign?" he asked.

Boots picked up a pair of tongs and served himself a fried pie.

"They've been fighting over that billboard for a year," she said. "It's huge. Was huge, that is. Trashes up the place, and from what I hear, they tricked the Estevez brothers into signing the lease in the first place."

"Really?"

"I don't know. If it had been me, I'd have burned it too. Don't know if they did it though. Innocent until proven guilty, and all that." She handed him the steaming coffee and wiped her hands on her apron.

He laid a ten spot on the counter.

She rang up the sale, gave him his change, and said, "Stay as long as you like, I've got to set up the rest."

He dropped the change into the tip cup and gestured at her with the pastry. "Thanks."

Outside, he took one bite of the pie and tossed the rest into the grass by the building. He lit a cigarette and took a deep drag and a scalding swallow of coffee. He speed dialed a number on his smartphone.

"Hey, it's Boots King. I need to talk to Old Man Nixon."

He listened.

"I'm on South Congress. It's Estevez. Cops can't prove it yet, but they did it. I'm sure of it. If we didn't have the case made already, this insures it." He laughed, taking a drag on the cig and slapping the phone against his thigh.

3

"Here comes another one," Merit Bridges groaned. She reached over John's naked body and grabbed her cell phone off the charger. The clock behind it glowed indigo: 4:11 a.m. Her brain switched on, and she thanked God that it was not her son's Jimmy Vaughan guitar riff ringtone.

She tried to register the number as she cleared last night's wine fog, pushed the talk button, and spoke into the speaker, "This better be important."

"Merit, it's Manuel Estevez, my brother did something really bad. We need your help."

"Manny, hold on," Merit said. She climbed out of bed, hit the mute button, and took the phone into the bathroom. She pulled up her Longhorn t-shirt, sat down on the toilet, willed herself awake, and re-activated the call. "Ok, what is it?"

"Tireman burned down the sign at the South Congress shop and a bunch of cars blew up under it. The police and fire department are here and they're asking questions."

"Was anyone hurt?"

"No."

"Do they know he did it?"

"Not yet."

"Is he there with you?"

"Yes."

"Did anyone see him do it?"

"I don't think so."

"Have they interviewed him yet?"

"No."

"I need to talk with him before the police do."

"I'll send him to the junkyard office on Airport."

"I'll meet him there in twenty minutes. You stay and deal with the police. Don't tell them anything yet, but don't lie to them. Meet us at the junkyard when you get the situation under control."

"Okay."

"And, most of all, don't talk to the press."

Merit went into the closet and wiggled into a pair of faded jeans and a Rice Owl sweatshirt. She spoke over her shoulder to John. "I've got to go help a client with a problem. I'll call you later."

Merit rooted around for shoes in the closet. She could not see John take a surreptitious peek at her last call number.

"Want me to go with you? I don't have to be at the station until later."

"Yeah, right, let me take my twenty-eight-year-old boyfriend along at six in the morning," Merit said as she slid her thirty-eightyear-old perfectly manicured feet into a pair of leather flats.

"Okay, good point. Later."

John appeared to be asleep before Merit was out the door and in the garage. Even if it was in vogue to do the cougar thing, it wasn't good for business for a woman to be seen dating a younger man. Demi Moore might get away with it, but Merit was no movie star.

Merit could see her breath in the cold garage. She slid into her SUV, hit the garage door opener and waited for the panel to rise. As she pushed the button to start the BMW, she organized her thoughts.

Merit had been the business attorney for the Estevez brothers for more than ten years. Her practice was rooted in real estate with a twist. She handled all things related to land, on or under; real estate, development, buildings, oil and gas, and civil litigation where contracts were involved. Manny Estevez had been referred to her when he purchased his first business in Austin.

Manuel and Tarantella Estevez had emigrated from Mexico, speaking Spanish thanks to their father and Italian thanks to their mother; but no English, thanks to both of them. Manny had arrived first and set up one shop, then another and another. He established a junkyard on Old Airport Boulevard where wrecked cars were stockpiled for use as parts supply. Tireman moved to Austin five years later and acquired his nickname because no one could pronounce Tarantella, and because he sold more tires than any other shop in town. He shared his brother's work ethic, but never quite attained Manny's command of the language and business savvy. He made up for that with his knowledge of cars. He could tell just by the sound what was wrong with an engine, and usually had it fixed in less time than most repair shops. Manny bought expensive diagnostic equipment, but used it mostly to prove that Tireman was right.

Merit had been trying to work out a peaceful solution to the sign problem for months. Why would anyone sign a contract without a lawyer? After the issue with Nixon on the sign, she'd put the Estevez brothers on retainer. She didn't want them to have any excuse not to call her regardless of how small an issue might seem. If Manny had just consulted her before he'd executed Nixon's billboard lease, none of this would have happened, and she wouldn't be driving across town at this hour to fix what should never have been broken.

Continue reading DOLLAR SIGNS
www.manningwolfe.com/books

ABOUT THE AUTHOR

Manning Wolfe, an award-winning author and attorney residing in Austin, Texas, writes cinematic-style, fast-paced crime fiction. Her legal thriller series features Austin Lawyer Merit Bridges. Manning is co-author of the popular Bullet Books Speed Reads, a series of crime fiction books for readers on the go. As a graduate of Rice University and the University of Texas School of Law, Manning's experience has given her a voyeur's peek into some shady characters' lives and a front row seat to watch the good people who stand against them.

www.manningwolfe.com

Printed in the USA
CPSIA information can be obtained
at www.ICGtesting.com
LVHW091302080424
776759LV00007B/34